reSet

Cape Breton is the Thought-Control Centre of Canada
RAY SMITH

A Night at the Opera
RAY SMITH

Going Down Slow
JOHN METCALF

Century
RAY SMITH

Quickening
TERRY GRIGGS

Moody Food
RAY ROBERTSON

Alphabet
KATHY PAGE

Lunar Attractions
CLARK BLAISE

Lord Nelson Tavern
RAY SMITH

The Iconoclast's Journal
TERRY GRIGGS

Heroes
RAY ROBERTSON

An Aesthetic Underground
JOHN METCALF

A History of Forgetting
CAROLINE ADDERSON

The Camera Always Lies
HUGH HOOD

Canada Made Me
NORMAN LEVINE

Vital Signs (a reSet Original)
JOHN METCALF

A Good Baby
LEON ROOKE

First Things First (a reSet Original)
DIANE SCHOEMPERLEN

I Don't Want to Know Anyone Too Well (a reSet Original)
NORMAN LEVINE

The Stand-In
DAVID HELWIG

Light Shining Out of Darkness (a reSet Original)
HUGH HOOD

Bad Imaginings
CAROLINE ADDERSON

FINDING AGAIN THE WORLD

Finding Again the World

JOHN METCALF

SELECTED STORIES

FOREWORD BY KEATH FRASER

BIBLIOASIS
WINDSOR, ONTARIO

FIRST EDITION

Library and Archives Canada Cataloguing in Publication

Metcalf, John, 1938–
[Short stories. Selections]
Finding again the world : selected stories / John Metcalf.

Issued in print and electronic formats.

ISBN 978-1-77196-252-0 (softcover).—ISBN 978-1-77196-253-7 (ebook)

I. Title.

PS8576.E83A6 2018 C813'.54 C2018-901737-6
C2018-901738-4

Readied for the Press by Daniel Wells
Copy-edited by Emily Donaldson
Cover and text design by Gordon Robertson

The goofy but charming hare on the cover, surveying its world for possible beagles, is after an early British Delft tile that sits on my desk as a coaster.

Canada Council for the Arts
Conseil des Arts du Canada
Canada
ONTARIO ARTS COUNCIL
CONSEIL DES ARTS DE L'ONTARIO
an Ontario government agency
un organisme du gouvernement de l'Ontario
Ontario
Ontario Media Development Corporation

Published with the generous assistance of the Canada Council for the Arts, which last year invested $153 million to bring the arts to Canadians throughout the country, and the financial support of the Government of Canada. Biblioasis also acknowledges the support of the Ontario Arts Council (OAC), an agency of the Government of Ontario, which last year funded 1,709 individual artists and 1,078 organizations in 204 communities across Ontario, for a total of $52.1 million, and the contribution of the Government of Ontario through the Ontario Book Publishing Tax Credit and the Ontario Media Development Corporation.

PRINTED AND BOUND IN CANADA

FSC
www.fsc.org
MIX
Paper from responsible sources
FSC® C004071

This book is for Daniel Wells
Visionary friend and fount of inspiration

O swallows, swallows, poems are not
The point. Finding again the world,
That is the point...

— *The Blue Swallows*. Howard Nemerov.

...I've come close to matching the feeling of the night in 1944 in music, when I first heard Diz and Bird, but I've never quite got there. I've gotten close, but not all the way there. I'm always looking for it, listening and feeling for it...

— *Miles: The Autobiography*

CONTENTS

Foreword *by Keath Fraser* 1
The Children Green and Golden 15
Keys and Watercress 33
The Estuary 45
Robert, standing 61
Single Gents Only 73
The Eastmill Reception Centre 93
Gentle as Flowers Make the Stones 121
Dandelions 145
The Years in Exile 153
The Nipples of Venus 175
Ceazer Salad 201
The Museum at the End of the World 225

FOREWORD

YOU might be forgiven if the first thing you notice about his fiction isn't the fiction. Instead, a sensibility. "How I hug these words to myself, savouring them." He's the frail novelist in exile, imbiber of digitalis and glycerine capsules, recollecting a bucolic English childhood of luminous wonder. Another story begins: "I sometimes think my tiredness is different from other people's. A different *kind* of thing." Already weary at twenty, this narrator too experiences a luminous flashback once the right words arise to talk about it. Or a wheezy Boer War vet, instructing a baffled child: "Waterford glass—brilliant. Can you see the colours? The green of the cress and the drops of water like diamonds? Brilliant. A question of the lead-content, you see. You *do* see, don't you. You do understand what I'm telling you" (even an *antagonist* discriminates, passionately). "Always be attentive. Always accumulate *facts*." John Metcalf, *arbiter elegantiae* at thirty, seemed uncommon from the start. You get the picture in these early stories—the old novelist with his "images that haunt my nights and days"—of a fervent curator in full command of his art and more than willing to share its secrets. What is authentic? How is it done?

John once urged his stories on young readers as "things to be lived through and experienced"—as autobiographical in the reading, he hoped, as they were in the writing. But he cautioned against reading them *as* autobiography—not that autobiography, like fiction, wasn't also invented to refurbish its subject. Art, not life, determined reality. What really mattered was whether selected events *felt* alive, not whether or not they happened to the author.

You do wonder how they could *not* have happened to him, when he hugged words to himself (as he does in these stories) like "facts":

> If I wrote CAT, he would stare at the word with a troubled frown. When I sounded out C-A-T, he would say indignantly: Well, it's *cat*, innit? We had a cat, old tom-cat. Furry knackers, he had, and if you stroked 'em . . .

When you read a Metcalf story you never forget who's writing it, the language charged with the purpose of its being. *His* being. "And it is to language that I have given my heart." (An early essay reminds us that the author had not given it to themes and induced plots.) This metaphor comes from someone who inherited as much a condition of the heart from his cleric-father as he did a devotion to the word—though not necessarily the one in Genesis:

> C-O-W evoked his Auntie Fran—right old scrubber *she* was, having it away for the price of a pint . . .

—segueing into a vivid if less than elegant culture:

> Such remarks would spill over into general debate on the ethics of white women having it off with spades and Pakis, they was heathen, wasn't they? Said their prayers to gods and that, didn't they. *Didn't* they? Well, there you

are then. *And* their houses stank of curry and that. You couldn't deny it. Not if you knew what you was talking about.

In the beginning, then, the word.

Followed inevitably by linguistic theatre of a very entertaining order.

Among his early productions, this one in "The Eastmill Reception Centre," of the young narrator teaching language to delinquents, moves on to a second act where the older man, now a middle-age writer in Canada, laments the "desolating emptiness" of his civilized life compared to what he remembers of the intense lives of those semi-literate charges. "Words!" *His*, it seems, are paltry and mere "blathering!" he calls them, no consolation for his having missed out ever since on the pyrotechnic lives of unreconstructed juveniles.

Is this coda convincing? Possibly not if the writer has already seduced us into thinking his words, gloriously deployed in recounting his time teaching words, are every bit as vivid as the menacing tattoos he now insists will never be his. After such empathy, bathos? But this brings up something characteristic of John's endings. They're often elegiac, because the perspective of time and its attenuation obsesses him. No other Canadian writer embodies as he does Eliot's dissociation of sensibility, the notion of present time fallen from a time when metaphysical poets such as Donne had felt their thought as intimately as the odour of a rose. "A thought to Donne was an experience," wrote Eliot, "it modified his sensibility." Metcalf's allegiance to metaphor over exposition has long been his way of expressing sensuous thought. "All else is tricks of the trade or inexpressible," comments his old novelist in "The Years in Exile"—not, incidentally, a fan of Wordsworth's "abstractions." "My mind is full of pictures."

When I hinted earlier that John's voice seemed worldly before his time, weary even, it's as though his understanding of a less than whole (or complete) life was with him since he started writing these stories. A worry for characters, a warning to himself. His passion for language has long fueled a desire to rekindle through it the feeling that the material world is indeed radiant if it isn't over-thought, mislaid, or replaced with the ersatz.

Which is Howard Nemerov's exhortation in "The Blue Swallows," the poem from which he has here chosen his title. The poet, divided between intellect and imagination, rediscovers through words the rapture of the world. "Seeing," as the poem goes, "the swallows' tails as nibs / Dipped in invisible ink, writing . . ." In John's stories the world of nature is always an important means of educating sensibility. "It is only the natural world", he wrote in that essay for schoolchildren, "which *makes sense*." In an essay of his own, Nemerov has written that "Poetry is getting something right in language . . ." And so does Metcalf's fiction: "The caterpillar humped its body and started to flow over the edge of the cigarette-packet. Its body creased into a row of folds like a tiny concertina." Such a pastoral vision, as he called it, "occurs again and again in my stories." Indeed the vision of swallows is a happy, final one for his recurrent character David in this story "The Children Green and Golden".

Finding Again the World includes stories from the 1960s through the writer's middle period in the 1980s. It also contains two Robert Forde stories from some years later, after returning to this fictional alter-ego whom he'd first imagined in "Travelling Northward" as a protagonist of curatorial heft and dazzling comic intelligence. Not included here are any of the non-Forde novellas he published during his middle years, which, as remarkable as those are, don't supplant the briefer, early stories, which stand on their own as overlooked contributions to Canadian writing. They are often sterling examples of the genre to which Metcalf has long devoted himself as a writer and editor. (Critic, too, the brilliance of whose insight into the qualitative differences between Hemingway's stories and Morley Callaghan's, say, only reinforcing his credentials for having made such discriminations down the decades.)

When he came to Canada in 1962, his credentials for becoming a published author were modest but probably worth, in today's pennies, a pretty MFA. In other words, very little. At twenty-something he'd read Dylan Thomas (having reveled in similar seascapes as a child), responded deeply enough to Katherine Mansfield's stories, and in Spain shaken in admiration Ernest Hemingway's hand. He possessed a degree in literature and some sort of teaching certificate qualifying him to teach in an English detention centre followed by time in a remedial secondary called Bluebell Modern. Over the stultifying turmoil of those places, he opted for emigration. By comparison he found his new high school in Montreal resembled a rest home.

"The students were polite," he recounts in the memoir *An Aesthetic Underground*, "tolerant of the idea of learning, and mostly able to read. No one threatened me with a knife. It was refreshing." Desolate, he means, if once again comic. Cultural absurdity would prove an irresistible theme when he began writing, a key means of italicizing through the vivid, assimilated language of lodestone characters like David Hendricks and the later Robert Forde, an ardent tradition he longed to conserve, commemorate, collect against an attenuated present. This reaches its fullest articulation in Forde, visiting say the Archeological Museum in Odessa: "And the highlight of all for Forde was a hoard of Scythian silver tetradrachmas." Kneeling for a better view of these coins heaped theatrically on black velvet, "He was gripped by the iconography, fascinated by the way the style had perfected itself. . . . 'Sheila!' he called. 'Come and see how *alive* these horses are.'"

Reconstituting literacy among students in schools also meant, if he hoped to write fiction, teaching himself to discard, distrust, and deepen his own language. He read the stories of

Richard Yates, the early Alice Munro, and contemporaries like Hugh Hood and Clark Blaise with whom he formed in the early 1970s an alliance of fiction writers in Montreal Storytellers. He began to publish in little magazines and to be broadcast on CBC. Theatrical fiction, the way its parts and characters performed, such as in Waugh and Wodehouse, was already in his genetic juice; but in his early stories it is the painter's hand we notice first, the impeccable eye, accompanied by an unusually flawless ear that could nail an image, balance a periodic sentence, or carry a scene by counterpoint.

Magic tossed off, as if by shorthand:

> Blasts on its whistle, the train slowing through a small country station.
>
> Nether Hindlop.
>
> On the platform, rolls of fencing wire, wicker crates of racing pigeons, holding a ginger cat in his arms, a porter.
>
> "Single Gents Only"

Or, in a later story, movement achieved by an arresting predicate:

> A tug, its bridge blazing with lights, its sides armoured with tires like a row of shields, thrashed past them out to sea.
>
> "The Museum at the End of the World"

Or even, by way of careful technique, a climax slowed down:

> He felt a mounting excitement.
> *All, all, dear ladies, a question of balance.*
> And he'd found it.
> His balancing pole, as it were, commas.
> COMMAS
> No risk of falling now; no staggering run up the incline of a sagging rope.

Earth COMMA *lie lightly on her* COMMA *who* COMMA
who COMMA
Living COMMA *scarcely burdened you.*
"Gentle as Flowers Make the Stones"

Here a Montreal poet is mentally translating a lyric from the Latin poet Martial, about a pet slave girl's death, while being seduced by a groupie. With much rehearsing he manages to deliver his lines in a kind of risky, linguistic climax, both elegiac and comic. Long before the on-going selfies of Norwegian novelists, John was struggling with the comforts afforded by his profession and finding them endlessly *un*comfortable—working through, as Jim Haine does in this story, technical innovation, constant revisions, low sales. (Wasn't it another Latin poet, adapting Hippocrates, who observed *ars longa, vita brevis*?) John's perspective has always been gleefully, movingly, paradoxical. The title of his character's *un*reviewed book of poems is (what else?) *The Distance Travelled.*

If anything his fiction has become *more* autobiographical over the last half century. His Forde stories, now part of the Canadian canon, are idiosyncratic as no other contemporary writing is (Forde *is* Metcalf); but so are the early stories idiosyncratic, a sensibility at work under the John Metcalf brand, his style chronically determined in every line to be neither generic nor received, perforce catawampus and thereby eccentric, deceptively at odds with whatever traditional models his distillations might resemble.

Bicarbonato di soda?
... polenta, rigatoni, tortellini ...
Praaaaaaaaap ...
Scooters on the Via Sistina.
Praaaaaaaaap ...
Helen passing gas.
"The Nipples of Venus"

Those traditional models began at home. "I studied my father. He was, unknowingly, teaching me what is now my craft." "The Teeth of My Father" is dedicated to Alice Munro and seems to nod at childhood's influence on the early stories of both writers. But there was more to it. This story, and one of hers dedicated to him (as he tells us in the essay "Picking Winners"), "arose in part out of our discussions of theoretical problems." She and he "were toying with certain 'postmodern' problems as early as 1971. We were both writing stories which commented on themselves or which quoted other texts...."

In the beginning was the word—but in "The Teeth of My Father" whose word? The chicken-and-egg question of genesis is buried not so deep here as the Canadian narrator looks back on stories he wrote about his alter ego David growing up in southern England. It's structured as a compendium of earlier fragments and stories this author has chosen to gather within the shell-memoir of his eccentric father (and mother), a kind of "loose box" of bizarre dental kits and cobbling lasts, family idiosyncrasies of which there are many. Such particulars drive the story, as they always do in Metcalf, dauntingly. "After the bleeding stopped, pyorrhea set in followed by general pyemia, and he was confined to bed for nearly three weeks in high fever. I can remember the stench in the bedroom and looking at the blobs of pus that gathered at the corners of his sleeping mouth."

I find unexpectedly moving the final scene at the rail station between a now weakened father, driving his old Morris, and David just back from term at university. It's rendered in the shy, affectionate language of emotional avoidance, very understated, as though in elegiac contrast to the charged speech we recall as the seminal influence on David's nascent craft. "Inside my head, I practised the voices and inflections of his rhetoric, the rise and fall, the timing of the pause, the silence, the understated gesture, the rhetorical series of questions and their thundering denial. As early as ten, I could predict the emotional flow of the sermon, sense its pattern."

This autobiographical mode, currently on offer in Karl Ove Knausgaard's novels, will resonate among readers weary of old-hat fiction. But Metcalf's mode is perhaps more intolerant of quotidian life's longueurs. He wants metaphorical movement more than he wants and-then/and-then narrative. For him, life requires ceremonial attention—as much to knee scabs and dandelions as to humdrum coach tours and sipping beer in a piazza—if he's to reconfigure such commonalities in fiction. Their style is in the display of what the old novelist calls "particular life." (Is there any other writer, by the way, who wrings more theatre from a restaurant meal than John? I'm thinking here of the ritual in his novellas like "The Girl in Gingham" and "Polly Ongle"; but also of shipboard dining in "The Museum at the End of the World".) It isn't solipsism driving his work but a kind of self-curatorship, collecting words he will live by, into sentences resembling little picture galleries, his paragraphs sometimes self-effacing exhibitions in order to interweave past and present. The effect can be disorienting.

> Afterwards, the younger people had strolled back through deep lanes to the family house for the reception. I'd walked with a girl called Susan who turned out to be the sister of one of the bridesmaids. She'd picked a buttercup and lodged it behind her ear. She'd said:
>
> *Do you know what this means in Tahiti?*
>
> Late in the evening they'd been wandering about the house calling to us to come and eat strawberries, calling out that I had to make another speech.
>
> *Jack?*
>
> *We know you're there!*
>
> *Susan?*
>
> *Jack and Su-san!*
>
> The larger drawing-room was warm and quick with candlelight. In the centre of the dark polished refectory

table stood a gleaming silver épergne piled with tiny wild strawberries. By the side of it stood octagonal silver sugar casters. The candelabra on the table glossed the wood's dark grain. Reflected in the épergne's curves and facets, points of flame quivered.

You will pay attention to your right . . .

Traffic was thickening.

Fisher!

The bus was slowing.

Susan Fisher!

. . . above the piazza. The Villa is still owned by the Aldobrandini family. You will notice the central avenue of box trees. The park is noted for its grottos and Baroque fountains.

"Doubtless by Bernini," I said.

"Is that a *palm* tree?" said Helen.

"The Nipples of Venus"

Several years ago in a review of Lydia Davis's collected stories, the *TLS* included a sentence I think applicable to Metcalf's stories: "What suspense there is, is often external to the story, in the sense that Davis's formal experiments become craft-conscious performances, the pleasure of following them a combination of following the wit and humour within, while also wondering if Davis can successfully pull off the framing experiment."

John's fiction is curiously underappreciated, perhaps even among those who admire it. Is this the usual case of readers fondling and forgetting books, what happens to many writers who flash and burn (in Canada, more like spark and smolder)—or in *his* case, might it be a subtle question of our not bothering to read it carefully enough after concluding it's derivative? A case even of our *resenting* it, as the familiar English stuff we've long read, seen on screen, had our fill of with types and tropes and textures ever since England was invented to swamp the colonies with acerbic novels and class-conscious dramas?

For someone so indebted to the legacy of English prose, Metcalf is agnostic and iconoclastic. His method is pawky, astonishingly precise, a little dangerous. He is always performing himself, drolly, often jazzily, and in endless rehearsal whether in letters, essays, or fiction. His are riffs tempered by an infinite capacity to get right what he's listening for. Languid, he is no heartthrob, yet I sometimes think of Sinatra. The unexpected phrasings, the way he inhabits a line or delivers a lyric. The balladeer with an impish ear for the ring-a-ding-ding and yet a simultaneous immersion in craft (here, grammar) making him sound like no other writer (his character is pondering a misspelled poster in the window of a "holistic" pharmacy, WHERE HAS ALL THE GOOD BACTERIA GONE?):

> ... He wondered who would be rash enough to swallow something called Slippery Elm on the advice of people unable to distinguish singular from plural. He thought of going in and trying to make this point to the girl behind the counter, but the ochre hair and the cluster of stainless-steel surgical clamps climbing the cartilage of her right ear dissuaded him.

His reifications of youth, woo-able women, staring regretfully into the abyss at three a.m.

> The desk clerk gave him a key. As he opened the door a man who was sitting in an armchair watching television turned an astonished head. He was naked except for a dove-grey Stetson and mauve ankle socks.

Or championing—as Sinatra did, the long-play album in the forties—the short story collection in the sixties, and ever since, as an interpretive showcase for the shorter single. One imagines Sinatra's hit ballad *All or Nothing at All* as an umbrella title for the collected Metcalf memoirs. Mainly, though, it's hard to forget after hearing it, the voice. No slurrings. Captivating and clear as a Waterford tumbler of single-malt. A writer who can hold his liquor, aware of the challenge in committing to a line and then delivering unwaveringly:

> "In Alberta," he said, "there is nothing old. The buildings are brutal. The streets merely numbered. Bottle-openers are screwed to the headboards of hotel beds."

Here in "Ceazer Salad," a bravura state-of-the-nation story, the itinerant voice renders in rueful rant and elegiac awareness a sensibility uncommon in Canada. On Parliament Hill, "Forde stood behind the cannon's cascabel, running his fingertip over the Broad Arrow cut into the metal. He patted the sun-warmed bronze and walked around the cannon, looking at the touchhole, trunnions, quoins, and tompion, reveling in this antique terminology...."

> The cannon with its Broad Arrow, the statues of Louis-Philippe Hébert, the Gothic Revival buildings behind him, all spoke the same cultural language, all belonged to the same world, a world for which his education had groomed him, a world now as relevant as potsherds and shell-middens.

Equally curatorial, "The Museum at the End of the World" re-travels this recurrent passion of Robert Forde's to be made whole again by associating himself with history, art, language. A blending of cultural reference and natural worlds (he really is a crooner, this writer, at the ship's bar with his *Famous Grouse* Scotch), taking precise note of the mysterious, white enchantment blooming alongside their hull in the Black Sea:

"The rise and fall was like a stately carousel, a slow-motion firework display, an underwater Swan Lake of jellyfish." Even when fusions of art and life disappoint Forde—as when touring Chekov's house he finds it gives up "nothing" of the "heroic energy" or tubercular pain through which the playwright once wrote—Metcalf will compose his own sentence to bring *inside* this museum the "particular life" long favoured by his fading writer in exile. (Gatekeepers need not apply, only a writer forges conjunctions like these: "Forde prowled the house on his own, photographing the rooms hoping for some emanation of the spirit who'd written *Uncle Vanya*, who'd delighted in catching crayfish and picking mushrooms and wild berries, who'd loved a pet mongoose called Sod, which roamed the house at night extracting corks from bottles.")

Among immigrant writers who have influenced our literature by their style (Leacock, Wilson, Lowry, Ondaatje) Metcalf must be included. As he must among our best native-born writers of the short story, Mavis Gallant and Alice Munro. Of a fellow story writer, among dozens he has championed, he wrote in *Shut Up He Explained*, "There is in every thing she writes clarity and lucidity. I have over thirty-five years of reading typescripts come to realize that these qualities are rare indeed. Her very clarity is a form of passion." *Finding Again the World* serves to remind us this passionate clarity is what he has long revered in his own stories. "Writers' first books often recreate the intensity with which children experience and apprehend the world. Those remembered worlds, worlds outside time, live in luminous and holy detail."

I think of the parablist simplicity yet intricate technique of "The Children Green and Golden." Of its plain prose collecting the story's cards and caterpillars, along with its high-summer experiences foreshadowing a poetic tradition for the young character David. When the poet is ideally suited to his work, according to Eliot, he is perpetually melding into metaphor, from experiences as disparate as the noise of a typewriter and the smell of cooking, new ways of seeing. This is why John's old novelist in exile, beset by "the insistence of . . . pictures," is unable to sleep in the summer heat. He's too old to write any more, but these pictures are the legacy he is to go on living by, after he is no longer going on.

This picture, for instance, remembered from his childhood, the gamekeeper's gibbet strung with the corpses of stoats and weasels . . .

> Over the bodies in a gauze of sound crawled the iridescent flies.
>
> In the beginning, yes, the word.
> *Gauze!*

Keath Fraser
2018

THE CHILDREN GREEN AND GOLDEN

DAVID waited outside the gate while Pete went up the steps to the front door. They didn't like going to Rory's house because his mother was funny. She always said things like, "So you are Rory's little friends," and she never seemed to get dressed. She was always wearing a nightdress and her toenails were bright red. Rory's father had gone away. Rory used to steal money from her purse and one day he had watched her through the keyhole when she was having a bath.

"Good morning, Mrs. Callaghan. Can Rory come out, please?"

"Rory! Rory, darling! Your friends are here for you."

They walked slowly along the hot pavement, towels under their arms and hands in pockets, towards the path that led down to the Promenade. The sun was already melting the tar between the paving-stones and forcing it up into shining bubbles. In the gardens, the sweet-chestnut trees with their mounds of cool leaves were quite still in the morning heat. Pete was rattling a careless stick along the slats of the fences. Turning to the others he said, "Who's got any money on them?"

"I've got a couple of bob," said Rory.

"Let's get ten *Weights*."

"No. *Park Drive*. They're stronger."

David stopped stamping on the tar-bubbles and said, "And three banana ices at Rossi's."

"Whose money *is* it?" said Rory.

"All right. All right," said David. "She give it to you?"

"No, I nicked it. So what? *You* got any money?"

"Yes. It just so happens that I have."

"Show us then."

David slipped back behind Rory and Pete, pretending to grope in his pocket, and flicked his towel at the back of Rory's head. As David ran out into the road Rory shouted, "You wait, sodguts," and they chased each other back and forth across the road fighting with their towels. Suddenly Pete shouted, "Squirrel!" and the three of them searched the gutter for stones and pebbles.

When they neared the cliff-path Pete said, "Let's go along the top and through the park."

"What about going across the golf-course? See if we can find some balls."

"Yes, but if we go through the park we can have a deck at the ponds, can't we?"

They strolled along the cliff-top path leading to the park, stopping every now and then to throw stones at the grey squirrels or to hurl their pen-knives into the tree trunks. The morning was heavy with the smell of pine trees and the sun came in brilliant yellow patches through their shade. David stabbed at the top of a fence post but the blade of his knife closed and cut his little finger.

They stopped at the wooden kiosk by the park gates and Rory said to the old man, "Can I have ten *Park Drive*, please?"

"I can't sell cigarettes to minors, son. You can see the notice for yourself."

"Oh, they're not for me. They're for my Dad. He's waiting down on the beach."

"Well, if you're sure they're not for you. . . ."

Rory called to David, "Did he say he wanted matches?"

"No. He's got his lighter, hasn't he?"

"Yes. That's all, thank you."

And they strolled on into the park. The park-benches were grouped around two oblong fish-ponds which were covered with water-lilies. The ponds were teeming with orange and silver goldfish, huge lazy fish lying near the surface under the lily-pads. The park-keeper in his brown suit walked round and round.

"You could get them with a spear," said Pete. "One of those with three prongs like they use for dabfish."

"Or nightlines," said David.

"Bombs would be best," said Rory. "You could climb in at night and dynamite them."

They stood staring at the fish. Suddenly Rory said, "Come on. Let's get going. The parkie's coming and we don't want to be recognized."

They left the park and wandered down the path towards the dunes.

"Shall we go to the cliff?" said Pete.

"Hey, yes. Perhaps those swifts are nesting again."

"They're not swifts," said Pete. "They're swallows."

"Swifts. You can tell by the shape of the tail."

"Swallows. They're swallows, I tell you. Didn't you see the blue on their backs?"

"It'd be difficult to get up there," said Rory. "You'd need ropes and climbing irons. Or you could lower someone on a rope from the top."

They were still arguing as the path petered out into the loose sand of the dunes. The coarse silver-green dune grass cut against their bare legs. Suddenly Rory checked them with an outstretched hand. He pointed over to the right where, half-hidden behind a rise, a man and woman lay in the sun. He gestured Pete to the right and David to the left and they crouched low and worked their way towards the dune. When they were getting close, all three sank flat into the sand and wormed their way nearer.

They peered over the edge into the hollow. The man was lying beside the woman, one arm around her. The straps of her bathing costume were undone and the man was rubbing suntan oil on her back. They stared at the white bulge of her breasts which the loosened costume revealed. When she rolled over completely onto her stomach Rory gestured them back. They slid carefully down the bank. He raised his eyebrows in question and Pete and David nodded. Pete was biting on his fingers to keep from laughing. Rory nodded and they sprang up in sight of the couple and he shouted, "Give her a big belly!"

And then they were running. Running with their mouths open and their hearts pounding, running and stumbling for dear life through the heavy sand of the dunes. They did not look back, but ran and ran until the blood pounded in their temples and their throats were dry and aching and they could run no more. Eventually, with shaking legs, they collapsed into the dunes near their favourite cliff.

David was fighting for breath and crying tears of laughter at the same time. Pete shouted, in a voice trembling with laughter, "Give her a big belly!" and hurled himself upon Rory. They wrestled backwards and forwards until Pete threw Rory and sat on his chest, pinning his arms to the ground. He said, "Did you see them coming after us, Dave?"

"I didn't look. I was going too fast."

"Hey, get off, Pete, you silly bugger. You're hurting."

"Did you see him, Rory?"

Rory sprang to his feet, and shook the sand out of his hair. "No. I didn't happen to be watching."

"He was coming fast. I think we just made it. Hey, what if he'd caught us?"

"There's three of us. We could have got him down."

"We'd have beat him up."

"We'd have given him a rabbit punch."

"Hit him right in the neck with a rabbit punch."

They settled back, using their towels as pillows, and stared up into the blue of the sky. Gulls dipped and floated lazily over the edge of the cliff towards the sea. David took off his shoes and socks and dug his feet into the sand, letting it trickle between his toes. He unbuttoned his shirt to let the heat sink into his chest and stomach and wriggled his shoulders in the loose sand until he was comfortable. It was so quiet they could hear the whisper of the dune grass. High up against the sandstone cliff the black shapes of the swallows flickered like the blink of an eyelash. The heat seemed to roll in waves.

Pete said, "Are you going in today, Dave?" David only grunted.

"Are you?"

"Dunno."

"Got your cozzie?"

"Mmmm. Got it on."

Rory was lying on his stomach looking over the edge of the low cliff. Below, there was a level stretch of beach, an arc contained in the curve of the cliffs.

"Hey! Come and look at this," called Rory.

"What?"

"Come and look."

Near the tide-line a few small children were playing with buckets and spades, but nearer to the foot of the cliff a man and woman were putting up a sort of flag or banner which drooped between two poles. The boys could not read what it said because it faced out towards the beach. Near the banner were two boxes, like huge suitcases.

"What do you think they're doing?" said Rory.

"Dunno. Can't see from here."

"Let's go down and look."

"Shall we?"

"Yes, come on. We can look at the swallow nests later."

With their towels round their necks, they scrambled down the fault where the cliff had crumbled into large boulders and heaps of rubble, and ran the final few yards onto the beach.

* * *

Uncle Michael held up his handkerchief. "On your marks!" The boys and girls forced their toes into the sand. "Get set!" A boy with ginger hair called Brian made a false start.

"Get set!"

"Go!"

They sprinted towards the woman called Auntie Mary who was standing holding another handkerchief to mark the finishing line. Pete finished first and Uncle Michael shouted, "Oh, well done! Well done. Peter, isn't it? A beautiful race!"

He trotted up to the group of boys and girls who were standing around Auntie Mary. "Who came second and third?" he asked.

"These two were tied for second place," said Auntie Mary. "John and. . . ."

"David."

"Oh, yes. David."

"Well, I think an effort like that deserves a prize," said Uncle Michael. "So I'm going to give Peter here two cards and John and David one each. That'll make a grand start for your album."

He gave the cards to the winners and Rory said to Pete, "What did you get?" They looked at the coloured pictures and read the titles. One was *Christ Cleanses the Temple of the Money-Changers,* and the other was *Christ Baptized of John the Baptist.*

Uncle Michael, clapping his hands for attention, said, "Now then, everybody. You're not too tired, are you? Let's play a quick game of Leap-Frog. Yes, *and* you smaller ones. It's great fun. Come along, now. Let's make a long line."

Rory said to Pete, "Bloody hot, isn't it?"

Bending down, hands braced on knees, Uncle Michael shouted, "I'll be Frog."

They played energetically for a few minutes until one of the bigger boys banged his knee against a small boy's head. The game quickly collapsed. While Auntie Mary held the boy and stroked his hair, the others drifted away into small groups. A few chased each other throwing sand until Uncle Michael called, "I say, steady on there. We don't want anyone to get sand in their eyes, do we?" Four of the boys were holding a competition to see who could do the most push-ups. A girl called Mary kept slapping her young sister and saying, "Just wait till I get you home." A small boy in a blue bathing costume was quietly burying a small girl.

David said to Brian, the boy with ginger hair, "What school do you go to?"

"Brentwood Junior."

"Pete and Rory and me go to Parkview Junior."

"You in the scholarship class?"

"Yes, you?"

Uncle Michael came and interrupted their conversation. "Would you chaps like to gather everyone together for me," he said. "We're going to have a story next."

Auntie Mary said to the little boy, "Big boys don't cry, do they?"

"No," said the little boy.

"And you don't want to be a cry-baby, do you?"

"No," snuffed the little boy.

"And if you're brave, perhaps we'll give you a present. Would you like that?"

"Yes."

"A nice present for your book?"

The boy smiled watery through the big tears.

"There you are," she said. "Shall we go and join the others now?"

Holding his hand she walked towards the semi-circle sitting around Uncle Michael. He was wearing grey flannels and a white shirt, open at the neck, with a paisley choker. Behind him hung the drooping banner which read SUFFER THE CHILDREN CAMPAIGN.

Rory whispered to Pete, "See that kid. She gave him a card."

"That's not fair, is it?"

"Well, I mean he didn't win it, did he?"

"Come along, now!" said Uncle Michael. "We can't have everyone talking at once, can we?" He smiled at Pete and Rory. "Now. If we're all listening. I'm going to tell you a story.

"Once there was a little boy, just like some of you, and his name was Jack. But he wasn't *quite* like you because, you see, nobody loved him. His father used to drink and when he was drunk he would sometimes beat Jack for no reason at all. You see, he wasn't *in control of himself.* And that's what drinking can do for you." Uncle Michael stopped, and looked seriously and slowly around the group.

"And what about Jack's mother? Well, Jack's mother had nine other children to look after and she was too tired to pay a lot of attention to poor Jack. So what do you think poor Jack decided to do? He felt *so* unhappy that one night, after his father and mother had gone to bed, he packed up the few clothes he had and put them in his suitcase and he. . . . Well, what do you think he was going to do?"

One of the small boys put up his hand and said, "My name is Andrew and I think he was going to run away."

"Yes. That's right. Jack was *so* unhappy he was going to run away! He was going to run away to LONDON. But poor Jack hadn't any money so he had to try and get a lift in a car or on a lorry. So he stood by the side of the road for hours and hours but nobody stopped and he was getting colder and colder. And then a very strange thing happened! A car stopped and who do you think was driving it?"

Andrew said, "His father."

"No. No, you'll never guess. It was the minister of the church that Jack attended! And so the minister said, 'Hello, Jack, my lad. Where are you off to at this time of night?' And Jack told him his story."

"Silly bastard," whispered Rory.

"'Cheer up, Jack,' said the minister, when he'd finished. 'Someone loves you very much.' Jack stared at the minister but he couldn't think who it might be. . . . Can any of you think who it was who loved Jack so much?"

Uncle Michael smiled at the silent group in front of him, the sunlight glinting on his spectacles.

"No? Can't anybody guess? Well, Jack couldn't either. So the minister said, 'There's someone who loves each and every one of us, Jack, and that someone is God. Why, He must have sent me to you tonight when you were so unhappy.' And the minister told Jack how God really does love us all, and especially boys and girls. And the minister took Jack home with him and gave him a cup of hot chocolate before he phoned his father."

"Told you," whispered Rory.

"And after that, whenever Jack felt unhappy he always prayed to God as the minister had taught him and he always felt at peace.

"And now I want everyone to close their eyes and we're going to say the prayer that Jack said."

Led by Uncle Michael they recited the Lord's Prayer. As soon as the prayer was finished he nodded to Auntie Mary who sat down at the harmonium and started to play.

"No, it isn't a piano. It's a sort of organ," he explained as they all gathered round. "And how would you like to sing a few songs? I think we could persuade Auntie Mary to play for us." He smiled across at her, his eyes twinkling. "And I've even got some papers here with the words on."

Pete looked across at Rory and said, "I'm afraid we'll have to be going now. We have to be back for tea."

"That's fine, boys," smiled Uncle Michael. "But you'll come again tomorrow, won't you? Remember the badges are for attending three days in a row."

"Oh, yes," said David. "We'll see you tomorrow. Bye."

"See you," said Brian.

As they walked away and started to climb the cliff the singing started. At first it was thin and ragged but it soon gathered strength drowning the shush of the sea and the cries of the gulls.

A sunbeam, a sunbeam,
Jesus wants me for a sunbeam,
A sunbeam, a sunbeam,
I'll be a sunbeam for him.

David, Pete, and Rory received the badges on their third day. The badges were blue with the letters SCC in gilt. Each badge was in a tiny box, and wrapped in tissue-paper.

For each day they received a picture-card. Each album had fifty spaces and after attending for five days the empty slots seemed endless. "It'd take us years," said Pete. "Yes, but you can win 'em," David said.

Rory had ten cards but he'd given one of the small boys two piggy-backs in return for an *Agony in the Garden* and a *Do This in Remembrance of Me.*

The morning was already hot as they turned into the park on the cliff-top. They did not linger by the fishponds as they used to do, but followed the path that led out onto the dunes. Near the park-gates Pete stopped and bent over a poplar-sapling, turning the silver underside of the leaves.

"What are you doing?"

"Looking for hawkmoth caterpillars. Poplar Hawks. Jim said he'd got some near here last Saturday."

"Oh, come on, Pete. We haven't got time now."

"All right, all right. What's so important?"

"You know he likes us there early," said David.

"Oh, piss," said Pete. "You go on and I'll catch you up."

When they neared the sandstone cliff they could hear the sounds of the children playing and the voice of Auntie Mary. She was playing tag with four little girls and the small boy called Andrew. The little girls ran after her squealing with delight and Auntie Mary kept shouting, "You can't catch *me*! You can't catch *me*!"

Uncle Michael was striding along the beach with his head bent. As they scrambled down the last few yards and approached him he was saying "... nineteen, twenty, twenty-one, twenty-two . . ." They followed him. He stopped at "twenty-five" and ground his heel into the sand.

"Good morning, boys. Isn't Peter with you today?"

"Yes, he's just coming. What are you doing?"

"Marking out a pitch. Would you like to help me before the others get here?"

"Okay. What do you want us to do?"

"Get a stick and draw lines from the four marks I've made. It's for a game of touch football."

As they edged the first line they saw Pete climbing down the cliff. A voice behind them said, "It's no use whining. You're here and you're going to stay here." Mary and her little sister. Rory called to her, "Hey! You've got a big spot on your back!" She turned and blushed. "I'm not going to speak to you so you needn't think that I am," she said. "So there."

Pete sauntered up to them holding a *Craven A* packet in his hand.

"Where you been?"

"Up the top."

"You'd better put those fags away," said David.

Peter grinned. "I haven't got any fags."

"What is it?"

"What you got, Pete?"

They dropped the sticks and looked at the packet as Pete eased it open. Inside was a Poplar-Hawk caterpillar. It was about two inches long and beautifully coloured. The back was a soft dove-grey and the underside a pale lime-green. Along its sides were rows of scarlet dots like eyes.

"Isn't it a beauty?" said Pete.

"Are there any more?"

"Hey, come on. Let's go."

"I didn't *see* any more."

"Come on, you chaps," a voice shouted. "Let's get that marking finished."

"Oh, shutup!" said Rory quietly.

"I'm going to keep it until it turns into a moth," said Pete.

"Isn't it *big!*" said David.

They watched the caterpillar in fascination as it reared its head and lifted the front part of its body off the ground, weaving from side to side as though seeing dimly with the scarlet eyes of its markings.

"Come on, you three!" shouted Uncle Michael.

"All right!" shouted Rory.

While they had been talking most of the others had arrived. Uncle Michael shepherded the crowd over towards the pitch and explained the rules of the game. Auntie Mary had taken the small children and was playing "Black Pudding" with them.

"Now remember!" shouted Uncle Michael. "All passes must be *forward* passes. Brian! Let's have you over here as captain of Red Team." He put his hand round Brian's shoulder and looked at the group in front of him. "And... Rory...you're Blue Team, here." He took a sixpence from his pocket and spun it into the air. "Call! Heads it is. Brian, you have first pick."

The teams were quickly sorted out. Rory, as he chose last, was left with the thin boy with thick glasses who ran with his arms held at a funny angle. Punctuated by silver blasts on Uncle Michael's whistle, the game got under way. There were seven players on each side and the ball was fumbled and hasselled from end to end of the pitch. Every few minutes Uncle

Michael would shout, "Oh, well done! A beautiful pass! Play *up,* Blue Team!"

Red Team was four goals ahead and most of the players were crowded down around Rory's goal when Peter suddenly caught the ball which Rory had flicked out from the centre of the struggling mob. Rory and he started to run up the nearly empty pitch towards Brian's goal. Three players sprinted towards Peter to intercept him. "Pete!" yelled Rory. "Over here! Pass over here. *Pass,* you silly bastard!"

The silver whistle cut the game short. Uncle Michael trotted out into the centre of the pitch. "Rory?" he called. "That isn't the sort of language we use, is it? Is it, Rory?"

"No."

"Now, I must insist that you apologize to Peter and be a good sportsman about it."

Rory stared at him incredulously. Then turning towards Peter, he said, "I'm sorry I called you a. . . ."

"Rory!"

"I'm sorry I was rude to you."

"Now, I don't want to cut your game short," said Uncle Michael, "but Auntie Mary and I have prepared a surprise for you, so if we all sit down for a few minutes to catch our breath I can tell you about it after the story."

The group of boys and girls trailed over towards the harmonium where Auntie Mary already had the small children sitting quietly. David and Pete sat at one end of the semi-circle so that they were partially hidden by the harmonium. Uncle Michael and Auntie Mary came along the line handing out the picture-cards. Pete already had the cigarette-packet open on the sand by his side. He put his card into his shirt-pocket and uncovered the cigarette-packet again. David's card was *The Soldiers Dice for Jesus's Robe.*

"Hey Pete."

"What?"

"Do you want to swap me?"

"Swap what?"

"My card for the caterpillar."

"You've got a hope!" laughed Peter.

Uncle Michael clapped his hands sharply to silence the chatter and said, smiling, "Now, when we're all ready, I'm going to tell you a story. It's not a new story. Actually, it's a very old one, one that Jesus Himself told. It's called the *Parable of the Sower.* Who knows what a parable is? Anybody? Yes? Charles, isn't it?"

The thin boy with thick glasses said, "Well, it's sort of a story . . . and it isn't really . . . well, I mean. . . ." He picked nervously at the cluster of white spots near his lip. ". . . well, it isn't about what it's about."

"Good!" said Uncle Michael. "That's right. It's a story that has two meanings. And now here's the story just as Our Lord told it.

"Once upon a time, a man was sowing wheat in his field and as he threw each handful some of the seeds fell in different places.

"Some of the seed fell onto the path that ran along the side of his field and it was crushed underfoot as the people walked along or it was eaten by the crows and sparrows.

"And some of the seeds fell onto places where there were lots of stones and rocks and . . ."

"Why do you think it's got that little horn on top of its head?" whispered David.

"It's to make it look fierce," said Pete, "so birds won't peck at it."

"Does it just eat poplar leaves?"

"Yes, but it should be nearly ready to turn into a cocoon now."

"And some of the seeds fell into good ground and grew up into strong plants that gave a hundred seeds from the *one* they had grown from."

He paused, and there was silence. "Now what is the story *really* about?" There was no reply. Suddenly in the silence Rory said, "I don't know."

Uncle Michael's face tightened slightly and then he smiled again as he said, "Is there anybody who *does* know?"

Rory flicked sand at Mary's back, hoping that she would turn around, but she took no notice. The voice went on and on. Rory watched the slow swoop of a gull as it dipped down over the cliff. At the edge of the shore where the waves ran up and frothed upon the sand, he could just see the white, scurrying shapes of sand-pipers.

"And the rocky ground stands for the sort of people who are very enthusiastic at first but give way as soon as temptation comes along. I expect that all of you . . . "

The caterpillar humped its body and started to flow over the edge of the cigarette-packet. Its body creased into a row of folds like a tiny concertina. Pete headed it off with a match stick.

". . . close our eyes and pray to our Lord Jesus that we may be like the *good* ground.

"Oh God, Our Holy Father, look down on these Thy little ones, and grant that they, in Thy infinite Mercy, may find Salvation and that eternal peace which Thou hast promised. Lead them, guide them, shelter them under Thy wings of Love; take away from them the burden of their Sin, that they may, at the last, enter Thy Kingdom, perfect in Thy Holy Love. . . . Amen."

After a slight pause, Uncle Michael raised his head and said in a bright voice, "And now boys and girls, Auntie Mary is going to tell us about the surprise she has for us."

Auntie Mary moved across to stand by Uncle Michael's side. She clasped her hands in front of her and stirred the sand with the toe of her gym-shoe.

"Well, children," she started.

"Children!" whispered Pete.

"We're going to have a treasure hunt!"

The smaller children started to squirm about in the sand and even Mary unbent to say to her little sister, "A treasure hunt! *Isn't* that nice?"

"And," continued Auntie Mary, "we're going to give you all the first clue on a slip of paper, then you must find the others. When you find the first hiding place you come to me for the second clue. And so on."

The first clue said, "Under a red **** near the cliff. (What Jesus called Peter.)"

Everyone split up into small groups and wandered aimlessly about the beach.

"What's it *mean?*" said Pete.

"I dunno. Where's Rory?"

"He's walking around with that girl."

"Do you reckon there's any more?"

"What?"

"Caterpillars."

"Yes, I should think there *probably* are."

Uncle Michael was standing near the fallen rubble at the base of the cliff. When people came near him he would cry, "That's the spirit. Warm. Warmer. Oh, *very* warm! No. No. Cold, I'm afraid. Completely cold."

Most of the smaller children were playing at their own concerns, building castles, digging holes, or just sitting and patting the smooth sand happily.

David and Peter, tiring of the search, sat down to play with the caterpillar. Uncle Michael called to them, "That's not a warm place at all. Come on, fellows, you'd be very warm *indeed* over here!"

They were just getting to their feet when Rory passed them and beckoned with a turn of his head. As they caught up with him they said, "What's up?"

"Come on. We're going."

"Why? What's wrong?"

"Nothing. Let's get going."

Rory's face was set with a contained and infectious delight.

"What is it, Rory?"

Rory hurried on, the current of his excitement drawing them after him. They started to scramble their way up the cliff-path, Rory setting the pace.

"Hey, you three!" shouted Uncle Michael. "You're *very* cold up there."

They paused for a moment and looked down on him, then struggled on towards the lip of the cliff and the dunes beyond.

They hurried to the hidden hollow in the dunes, almost running, caught by Rory's excitement.

"What did you do?"

"What is it, Rory?"

Rory unbuttoned his shirt and groped inside. He brought out a fountain pen. It was blue with a gold arrow for a clip.

"Nicked it out of his jacket," explained Rory.

They examined it carefully. "Hey, it's one of those good ones," said Pete.

"It's a Parker 51," said David. "They're worth a lot of money."

"Let's sell it," said Pete.

"Yeah, we could sell it at school," said David.

"No," said Rory. His tone of voice made them look at him. "I nicked it; so I'm deciding what to do with it."

"What *are* you going to do, then?"

Rory stood considering. Then he stuck the pen into the sand. "I'm going to throw rocks at it," he said. Pete and David hung back while Rory threw a stone. He missed and, almost frantically, started to hunt for stones and pebbles.

Pete and David watched him. Their silence seemed to drive him on. He tore and grubbed for stones at the roots of the tough dune grass as though he were possessed. Standing twenty paces off, he threw the stones from his pile as fast as he could bend to pick them up, and as he threw he began to laugh.

He became more and more incapable as his laughter consumed him and Pete and David started to pick up the wild-thrown stones. Soon the stones were raining down around the pen and the echoes of their laughter filled the air.

"Got it!" shouted Pete.

David ran to set it up again.

"And again!" shouted Rory. "Bombs away!"

With a lucky shot David smashed the top part of the pen away.

"It's mine!" shouted Rory. "Leave it alone!" And picking up a heavy rock he held it directly above the stump of the pen and let it go. The rock hit the pen at an angle and smashed the casing. Ink spurted out onto the sand and Rory stamped on the broken pieces driving them out of sight. His eyes were shining with excitement. He stamped on the fragments until his foot had worn a small crater in the sand. Then suddenly, without warning, he rushed at Pete and grabbed him in a wrestling hold.

"Give in?"

Pete grunted and squirmed and bucked, trying to throw him off.

"You wait, bloody Callaghan."

Rory worked his knees into Pete's arms.

"Give in?"

"Come on, Rory. Get off. You're hurting."

Rory rolled off into the warm sand and pillowed his head on his hands. David propped himself up and lighted a cigarette. The heat seemed to roll in waves. High up against the sandstone cliff the black shapes of the swallows flickered like the blink of an eyelash. With a sigh of contentment, David unbuttoned his shirt and settled down to let the warmth soak through him. Swimming in the darkness behind his closed eyes were gentle globes of light, red and glowing.

Pete said, "We could try for those swallow nests this afternoon."

"Swifts," murmured David.

"Swallows."

"Mmmm," sighed David happily.

KEYS AND WATERCRESS

DAVID, with great concentration, worked the tip of his thumbnail under the fat scab on his knee. He carefully lifted the edges of the scab enjoying the tingling sensation as it tore free. His rod was propped against his other leg and he could just see the red blur of his float from the corner of his eye. He started to probe the centre of the crust.

"Had any luck?" a voice behind him said suddenly.

Startled, his thumbnail jumped, ripping the scab away. A bright bead of blood welled into the pit. The sun, breaking from behind the clouds, swept the meadow into a brighter green and made the bead of blood glisten like the bezel of a ring.

"Had any luck?" the old man said again. David twisted round to look at him. He wasn't in uniform and he wasn't wearing a badge and anyway he was far too old to be a bailiff. Unless he was a Club Member—and they could report you, too. And break your fishing rod.

David glanced down the river towards the bridge and the forbidding white sign. "I'm only fishing for eels," he said "With a seahook."

"Slippery fellows, eels," said the old man. "Difficult to catch."

"I haven't caught any yet," said David, hoping the old man wouldn't notice the grey eel-slime on the bank and the smeared fishing-bag.

The old man started to sit down. Wheezing harshly with the effort, he lowered himself until he was kneeling, and then, supporting himself on his hands, laboriously stretched out each leg like a dying insect in a jam jar. His anguished breathing eased slowly away into a throaty mutter. David felt more confident because he knew he could run nearly to the bridge by the time the old man had struggled to his feet.

Taking a blue silk handkerchief from the top pocket of his linen jacket, the old man dabbed at his forehead. "My word, yes!" he said. "Extremely slippery fellows." He took off his straw hat and rubbed his bald head with the blue handkerchief.

"They're a nuisance," said David. "The Club Members don't like catching them."

"And why is that?"

"Because they swallow the hook right down and you can't get it out," said David.

"You've hurt your knee," said the old man. The bead of blood had grown too large and toppled over, trickling down his knee to run into the top of his stocking.

"Oh, that's nothing," said David. "Only a scab."

"Yes," said the old man reflectively, "it's a pleasant day. A beautiful sky—beautiful afternoon clouds."

They sat silently staring across the flow of the river. Near the far bank in the shallows under the elderberry bushes the huge roach and chub basked in the sunshine, rising every now and then to nose soft circles in the water.

"Do you know the name of clouds like those?" asked the old man suddenly. "The *proper* name, I mean."

"No," said David.

"Well, the correct name is cumulus. Cumulus. You say it yourself."

"Cumulus," said David.

"Good! You won't forget, will you? Promise me you won't forget." There was a silence while the old man put on his spectacles from a tin case. Then, taking a fountain pen and a small black book from his inside pocket, he said, "But boys forget things. It's no use denying it—boys forget. So I'm going to write it down." He tore a page from the notebook and printed on it: Cumulus (clouds).

As David tucked the paper into his shirt-pocket, he looked across at the old man who was staring into the water, a vague and absent look in his eyes. David watched him for a moment and then turned back to his float, watching the current break and flow past it in a constant flurry. He tried to follow the invisible nylon line down into the depths where it ended in a ledger-weight and a turning, twisting worm.

"Every evening," said the old man, speaking slowly and more to himself than David, "when the light begins to fail, the cattle come down here to drink. Just as the night closes in."

"They've trampled the bank down further up-stream," said David.

"And I watch them coming across the fields," said the old man as though he hadn't heard. "I see them from my window."

The old man's voice died away into silence but suddenly, without warning, he belched loudly—long, rumbling, unforced belches of which he seemed quite unaware. David looked away. To cover his embarrassment, he started reeling in his line to check the bait and the clack of the ratchet seemed to arouse the old man. He groped inside his jacket and pulled out a large flat watch. With a click the lid sprang open. "Have you ever seen such a watch before?" he asked. "Such a beautiful watch?" He held it out on the palm of his hand.

"Do you know what watches like these are called?"

"No," said David. "I've never seen one before."

"They're called Hunters. And numbers like these are called roman numerals."

As the old man counted off the numbers on the watch-face, David stared at the old man's hand. The mottled flesh was puffy and gorged with fat blue veins which stood beneath the skin. He tried to take the watch without touching the hand which held it.

"What time does the watch say?" asked the old man.

"Half-past four," said David.

"Well, then, it's time we had our tea," said the old man. "And you shall come and have tea with me."

"Thank you," said David, "but I've got to go home."

"But tea's prepared," said the old man, and as he spoke he started to struggle to his feet. "Tea's prepared. In the house across the bridge—in the house with the big garden."

"But I really have to go," said David. "My mother'll be angry if I'm late."

"Nonsense!" said the old man loudly. "Quite untrue."

"Really. I do have to. . . ."

"We won't be long," said the old man. "You like my watch, don't you? You *do* like my watch."

"Oh, yes."

"Well, there you are then. What more proof do you need? *And*," said the old man, "I have many treasures in my house." He stared at David angrily. "You would be a rude boy to refuse."

"Well . . ." said David. "I really mustn't be long."

"Do you go to school?" the old man asked suddenly.

"Parkview Junior," said David.

"Yes," said the old man, "I went to school when I was a boy."

As David was sliding the rod-sections into the cloth case, the old man gripped his arm and said, "You may keep the watch in your pocket until we reach the bridge. Or you could hold it in your hand. Whichever you like." Then stopping David again he said, "And such a watch is called a. . . ?"

"A Hunter," said David.

The old man relaxed his hold on David's arm and said, "Excellent! Quite excellent! Always be attentive. Always accumulate *facts.*" He seemed very pleased and as they walked slowly along the river-path towards the bridge made little chuckling sounds inside his throat.

His breath labouring again after the incline from the bridge, the old man rested for a few moments with his hand on the garden gate. Then, pushing the gate open, he said, "Come along, boy. Come along. Raspberry canes everywhere, just as I told you."

David followed the old man along the path and into the cool hall. His eyes were bewildered at first after the strong sunlight, and he stumbled against the dark shape of the hall-stand.

"Just leave your things here," said the old man, "and we'll go straight in to tea."

David dropped his fishing-bag behind the door and stood his rod in the umbrella-stand. The old man went ahead down the passage and ushered him into the sitting room.

The room was long and, in spite of the French windows at the far end, rather dark. It was stuffy and smelled like his grandma.

In the centre of the room stood a table covered with green baize, but tea was laid out on a small cardtable at the far end of the room in front of the French windows.

Bookshelves lined the walls and books ran from ceiling to floor. The floor, too, was covered with piles of books and papers; old books with leather covers, musty and smelling of damp and dust, and perilous stacks of yellow *National Geographic* magazines.

A vast mirror, the biggest he'd ever seen, bigger even than the one in the barber's, stood above the fireplace, carved and golden with golden statues on each side.

David stared and stared about him, but his eyes kept returning to the lion which stood in front of the fireplace.

"Do you like it?" asked the old man. "It's stuffed."

"Oh, yes!" exclaimed David. "Can I touch it?"

"I've often wondered," said the old man, "if it's in good taste."

"Where did it come from?"

"Oh, Africa. Undoubtedly Africa. They all do, you know."

"I think it's terrific," said David.

"You may stay here, then, and I will go and put the kettle on," said the old man. As soon as the door had closed, David went and stuck his hand into the lion's snarling mouth and stroked the dusty orbs of its eyes with his fingertips. When he heard the old man's footsteps shuffling back down the passage, he moved away from the lion and pretended to be looking at a book.

"Do you take sugar?" asked the old man as they sat down at the cardtable in front of the French windows.

"No thank you," said David. "Just milk."

"No? Most interesting! *Most* interesting. In my experience, boys like sweet things. A deplorable taste, of course. Youth and inexperience."

He passed the teacup across the table and said sternly, "The palate must be educated." David didn't know what to say and because the old man was staring at him looked away and moved the teaspoon in his saucer. Putting down the silver teapot, the old man wrote in his notebook: *The love of sweetness is an uneducated love.* Handing the note across the table he said, "Facts, eh? *Facts.*" He chuckled again inside his throat.

"And now," he continued—but then broke off again as he saw David staring out of the window into the orchard. "If you're quite ready? We have brown bread. Wholemeal. Thin-cut. And with Cornish butter." He ticked off each point on his fingers. "To be eaten with fresh watercress. Do you think that will please you?"

"Very nice, thank you," said David politely.

"But it's not simply a matter of *taste,* you see," said the old man fixing David with his eye. He shook his head slowly.

"Not simple at all."

"What isn't?" asked David.

"Not at all simple. Taste, yes, I grant you," said the old man, "but what about texture? Umm? Umm? What about vision?"

"What isn't simple?" David asked again.

The old man clicked his tongue in annoyance and said, "Come along, boy!" He glared across the table. "Your attention is lax. Always be attentive." He leaned across the cardtable and held up his finger. "Observe!" he said. "Observe the tablecloth. Cotton? Dear me, no! Irish linen. And *this*." His fingertips rubbed slowly over the facets of the bowl. "Waterford glass—brilliant. Can you see the colours? The green of the cress and the drops of water like diamonds? Brilliant. A question of the lead-content, you see. You *do* see, don't you. You do understand what I'm telling you."

"Well . . . please," said David, "what's a texture?"

And once again the old man took out his notebook and his fountain pen.

When tea was finished, the old man wiped his lips with a linen napkin and said eagerly, "Well? Do you think you're ready? Shall you see them?"

"Please," said David, "I'd like to very much."

The old man pulled on the thick, tasselled rope which hung by the side of the window and slowly closed the red velvet curtains. "We don't want to be overlooked," he whispered.

"But there's no one there," said David. The old man was excitedly brushing the green baize and didn't seem to hear. With the red curtains closed, the room smelled even more stuffy, hot and stifling, as if the air itself were thick and red. And in the warm gloom the lion lost its colour and turned into a dark shape, a pinpoint of light glinting off its dusty eye. As David crossed over to the table he saw himself moving in the mysterious depths of the mirror.

"Come along, boy!" said the old man impatiently. "We'll start with the yellow box. There. Under the table."

The old man lifted the lid of the box and took out three small leather sacks. They were like the pictures in pirate books and as he laid them on the baize they chinked and jangled. Slowly, while David watched, very slowly, the old fingers trembled at the knots, and then suddenly the old man tipped the first sack spreading keys across the tabletop.

There were hundreds of keys; long rusted keys, flat keys, keys with little round numbers tied to them, keys bunched together on rings, here and there sparkling new Yale keys, keys to fit clocks, and keys for clockwork toys. The old man's fingers played greedily among them, spreading them, separating large and small.

"Well?" he said, looking up suddenly.

"I've never seen so many," said David.

"Few people have," said the old man. "Few people have." His eyes turned back to the table, and he moved one or two of the keys as though they were not in their proper place. And then, as if remembering his manners, he said, "You may touch them. I don't mind if you do."

David picked up a few keys and looked at them. His hands became red with rust, and he dropped the keys back on the table, stirring them about idly with his fingertip.

"Not like that!" snapped the old man suddenly. "Do it properly! You have to heap them up and scatter them. If you're going to do it do it properly."

He pulled at the strings on the other bag and cascaded a stream of keys onto the table. The air swam with red rust. David sneezed loudly and the old man said, "Pay attention!"

He raked the keys together into a large heap and burrowed his hands deep into them. When they were quite buried, he stopped, his eyes gleaming with a tense excitement. His breathing was loud and shallow. He looked up at David, and his eyes widened. "Now!" he shouted, and heaved his hands into the air.

Keys rained and rattled about the room, clicking against the mirror, breaking a cup on the cardtable, slapping against the leather-covered books, and falling loudly on the floorboards. A small key hit David on the forehead. The old man remained bent across the table as if the excitement had exhausted him. The silence deepened.

Suddenly, a key which had landed on the edge of the mantelpiece overbalanced and fell, rattling loudly on the tiles of the hearth. Still the old man did not move. David shifted his weight restlessly and said into the silence, "I think I'll have to be getting home now. My mother's expecting me."

The old man gave no sign that he had heard. David said again, "I'll have to be going now." His voice sounded flat and awkward in the silent room.

The old man pushed himself up from the table. Deep lines of irritation scored the side of his mouth. David began to blush under the fierceness of the old man's eyes. "I can't quite make up my mind about you," the old man said slowly. He did not take his eyes from David's face.

"Sometimes I think you're a polite boy and sometimes I think you're a rude boy." He paused. "It's unsettling." David looked down and fiddled with one of the buttons on his shirt. "Lift up another box of keys," said the old man suddenly.

"But I have to go home," said David.

"Quite untrue," said the old man.

"Really I do."

"A lie!" shouted the old man. "You are lying. You are telling lies!" He pounded on the table with his fist so that the keys jumped. "I will not tolerate the telling of lies!"

"Please," said David, "can I open the curtains?"

"I'm beginning to suspect," said the old man slowly, "that you don't really like my keys. I'm beginning to think that I was mistaken in you. "

"Please. Honest. I have to," said David, his voice high and tight with fear of the old man's anger.

"Very well," said the old man curtly. "But you are a rude boy with very little appreciation. I want you to know that." Reaching inside his jacket, leaving brown rust marks on the lapel, he took out his notebook and wrote in it. He passed the piece of paper across the table. David read: *You have very little appreciation.*

The old man turned away, presenting his silent and offended back. David didn't know what to do. Hesitantly he said, "I do like the keys. Really I do. And the lion. And thank you for the tea."

"So you're going now, are you?" asked the old man without turning around.

"Well, I have to," said David .

"It's a great pity because I don't show it to many people," said the old man.

"Show what?"

"It would only take a moment," said the old man turning round, "but you're in too much of a hurry."

"What is it?"

"Can you really spare me two minutes? Could you bear to stay with me that long?" Suddenly he chuckled. "Of *course* you want to," he said. "Go and sit on the settee over there and I'll bring it to you."

"Can I open the curtains now?" asked David. "I don't . . . I mean, it's hot with them closed."

"Don't touch them! No. You mustn't!" said the old man. He was struggling to take something from one of the bookshelves. He came and stood over David and then stooped so that David could see the black leather case in his hands. It was so stuffy in the room that it was difficult to breathe properly, and when the old man was so close to him David became aware of a strong smell of urine. He tried to move away.

Almost reverently, the old man opened the leather case. Lying on the red silk lining was a small grey ball. They looked at it in silence.

"There!" breathed the old man. "Do you know what it is?"

"No," said David.

"Go on! Go on!" urged the old man.

"I don't know," said David.

"Try."

"A marble?"

"A marble!" shouted the old man. "Why would I keep a marble in a leather case! Of course it isn't a marble! That's one of the most stupid remarks I've ever heard."

"I'm sorry," said David, frightened again by the anger in the old man's glaring face.

"You're an extremely silly boy. A brainless boy. A stupid boy." He slammed shut the leather case. "Stupid! Silly!" shouted the old man.

"I want to go home now," said David, beginning to get up from the settee. The old man pushed him back. "A marble!" he muttered.

"Please . . ." said David.

"It's a bullet!" shouted the old man. "A rifle bullet."

"I didn't know," said David. He tried to get up again, but he was hemmed in by an occasional table and the crowding presence of the old man. The dim light in the room seemed to be failing into darkness. David's throat was dry and aching.

"This bullet," said the old man, "was cut out of my leg in 1899. December 1899. Next I suppose you'll tell me that you've never heard of the Boer War!"

David said nothing, and the old man's black shape loomed over him.

"*Have* you heard of the Boer War?"

David began to cry.

"*Have* you?"

"I want to go home," said David in a small and uncertain voice.

"Quite untrue," said the old man. "I will not tolerate liars. You told me you went to school, and yet you claim not to have heard of the Boer War." He gripped David by the shoulder. "Why? Why are you lying to me?"

"Please," said David. "I'm not telling lies. Please let me go."

"Oh, very well," said the old man. "Maybe you aren't. But stop crying. It irritates me. Here. You may touch the bullet." He opened and held out the leather case.

"There's no need to cry."

"I want to go home," snuffled David.

"I know!" said the old man. "I know what you'd like. I'll show you my leg. The bullet smashed the bone, you know. You *would* like that, wouldn't you?"

"No," said David.

"Of course you would."

The old man moved even nearer to the settee, and leaning forward over David, lifting with his hands, slowly raised his leg until his foot was resting on the cushion. The harsh wheezing of his breath seemed to fill the silent room. The smell of stale urine was strong on the still air. Slowly he began to tug at his trouser-leg, inching it upwards. The calf of his leg was white and hairless. The flesh sank deep, seamed and puckered, shiny, livid white and purple, towards a central pit.

"If you press hard," said the old man, "it sinks right in."

David shrank further away from the white leg. The old man reached down and grasped David's hand. "Give me your finger," he said.

David tore his hand free and, kicking over the coffee table, rolled off the settee. At first, in his panic, he wrenched the doorknob the wrong way. As he ran out of the darkened room, he heard the old man saying, "I've tried to teach you. I've tried to teach you. But you have *no appreciation*."

THE ESTUARY

I SOMETIMES think my tiredness is different from other people's. A different *kind* of thing. Once, I think it was in *Reader's Digest,* I saw the words "depth fatigue" and I'm pretty sure that's what I've got. Take the way I feel when I wake up in the morning. Apart from the specific things—dull headache, sore throat, inflamed eyelids, and nausea—I feel chronically tired all over. It's as if all the cartilage has melted from between the bones and pads of tiredness have filled the spaces. And every morning these aching pads stiffen my back and legs and make it difficult for me to get out of bed.

The pain is in no way imaginary, I can assure you, although I *know* it's psychosomatic. The doctor I was using last year left me in no doubt about *that.* (Marvellous it was. I must have had about three weeks of working days off in trips to the hospital—allergy, lungs, heart, diabetes, ears, nose and throat—they tested everything before they threw me out.)

And so I took his pills—purple for go and blue for stop—until he refused to renew the prescription. He got rather moral towards the end and told me sternly that I ought to take myself in hand. And perhaps it was a good thing really because the purple ones only made me feel tired at a more active level.

I *know* it's psychosomatic but knowing *why* you're ill doesn't cure you. The important thing is to remove the cause. *As* I told him and which he didn't appreciate. (But I wasn't too bothered about that because he'd stopped giving me time off work anyway.) No, you've got to remove the cause and in my case that'd necessitate a pension—which creates certain problems when you're only twenty. I could present a case to the Ministry of Pensions that seems to me logically watertight—I'm tired because I'm bored and I'm bored because I hate working—but unfortunately they're not the most compassionate of institutions.

I'm sure my boredom's partly seasonal. Like tides. I offered that idea, which I consider quite original, to Dr. Cottle when I had to go and see him the other day but he's not a man who's attuned to the philosophic outlook. Oh, he's kind and well meaning but he's difficult to talk with. Though I'd rather one hour with him every two weeks than have done the thirty days.

His main fault is that he's obsessive. Every visit we get back to the same thing. *Why were you crying? Why were you shouting? What did the words mean?* But I always deny any knowledge; tell him I was too upset to remember.

Then he says, "You can't hold out for ever. You *need* to tell me." He is, of course, very wrong but I keep on going because—well, lots of reasons. The probation officer from the court checks up. Mrs. Grice the welfare lady, who told me she prays for me. *And* the appointments are always on Thursdays when I'm low on cigarettes and he keeps on offering me *Players No. 3* which are a welcome change from tipped *Woodbines*.

Dr. Cottle interests me. The first few times I went he managed to control himself—he was using a Carl Rogers technique then—but the periods of silence seemed to eat his nerves raw. After a couple of visits I got a library book on Rogers and the non-directive method which gave me the whiphand. Since then, I've managed to bring him out quite a lot.

I think I disturb him. I chat away about my mother and father, my brother and sister, infancy and adolescence, work and relaxations, uncle tom cobbley and all. I offer him ideas and theories and I smoke his cigarettes.

And we sit there in his office. Two big leather armchairs. A small and expensively simple mahogany coffee-table. A Persian rug. Two Georgian sherry decanters. (One filled with Harvey's Bristol Cream and the other with Tio Pepe.) Vast glass ashtrays which slowly fill with butts. And on the just off-white wall a large, and in my opinion, rather pretentious, hard edge abstract.

And he always says—he's got one of those lazy, chocolate brown voices—"You can trust me, David. You know that, don't you?" And always at some point or other, "I'm not an officer of the court, you know." And whenever he says that I can always picture over by the door the small, discreet filing-cabinet (pastel; oyster grey, *of course)* and I say in *my* intense voice, "I know that, Doctor." He tries not to show it but it irritates him when I call him that.

And just before I go he always says, "Do you think you're feeling happier *in yourself!*" And I always reply, "I'm always happy *in myself.*" Then he usually smiles his roguish smile, which must have wreaked transference on Christ knows how many ladies, and says, "No more notions of doing anything silly?" (He's far too delicate to come right out with it. If he said the word "suicide" it'd embarrass him.)

And that's what I mean when I say he's difficult to talk with. I told him the very first time that I saw him that I hadn't been trying to commit suicide but there was no shaking him. He must have got a really strong line from the police and the two fishermen so I've given up arguing now.

I suppose the fishermen and the other man—I never did find out whether he was a local or a visitor—I suppose they felt they had a stake in me after getting soaked to the armpits and hauling me ashore and nothing I could say was going to do them out of their moment of glory. So as far as Dr. Maximillian Cottle is concerned it was a desperate bid at self-destruction. The whole matter's basically too simple for him to understand though he's cottoned onto the fact that I'm hiding something. So every visit we get back to *Why were you crying? Why were you shouting? What did the words mean?*

The last time I went he abandoned all pretence of finesse. He was using his no nonsense, all cards on the table voice.

"When you were carried back to the beach," he said, having a quick refresher from my dossier, "you were crying in an hysterical manner."

PAUSE. Looks at me. Waits hopefully.

"The fishermen reported that when they first reached you, you were shouting, 'Don't go! Don't GO. Please don't go!'"

PAUSE. Looks up enquiringly and irritably scratches the back of his hand.

"On the beach you cried and said over and over again, and I quote, 'You can't leave me. You can't just go away.'"

The silence slowly builds.

And then I gave a little half shake of my head (I didn't want to overdo it because he watches me like a hawk) and I did my half embarrassed and half exasperated laugh and said, "I *really* can't remember. I really can't. I'm as mystified as you are."

Then he said, "I feel, David, that until you admit to yourself that you *were* shouting; until you explain your words; until you *acknowledge* them as yours you won't be able to enter into a period of adjustment."

So we sat there in the black armchairs, silently, and I tried to look as if I was struggling to remember. Every now and then, I breathed heavily through my nose. I frowned slightly. I pinched at my lower lip.

He lay stretched out in his chair staring at me and pressing his fingertips into a steeple; making his fingertips march up and down. Then after he'd played all the finger games he could think of he said, *very* reluctantly, "Perhaps you'd care to talk about something else...?"

And so I told him again about being bored.

I told him about the No. 93 bus. About catching it every morning at 8:15 at the Canning Road terminus. About the people in the bus queue. A schoolboy with ginger hair. The woman who works as a char at the United Hospital and who doesn't sleep at night because of the pain in her legs. The girl who works in Josiah's Beauty Salon on Papermill Road whose hands are always raw from peroxide. A labourer, his boots white with cement dust. A small man, stooped in a shabby raincoat, carrying a cheap cardboard attaché case, who stands rigidly staring across the road at nothing. And every morning the same bus-conductor. An old man with white hair who has to stop half-way up the stairs to the top deck to catch his breath; who wears gloves with the fingers cut off. An old man whose fingers are so stiff and clumsy that they slip on the keys of his ticket machine.

Dr. Cottle seemed a bit restive so I said, "That's most important. Important to *me*, Dr. Cottle."

He said, "You feel the bus-conductor to be important?"

"Yes," I said. "I do."

He always regresses to an uninspired and dreary Rogers sort of response when he doesn't think he's getting anywhere. But I didn't give him a chance to try anything else. I bore on relentlessly. I told him all about the library again.

I told him about Miss Nevins. How her slip always shows at the back of her dress. A dress which ends only six or seven inches above the ankle. And how the slip is always mauve trimmed with mauve lace. And how she always has a hankie, trimmed with mauve lace, tucked into the sleeve of her cardigan. And how she always moves in a cloud of lavender like something put away in a winter drawer.

He crossed his legs carefully, making sure he didn't crush the crease in his trousers, and said, "I've heard this before,

David. Do you think it's possible you're telling me this to avoid telling me something else?"

"Oh, no," I said. "This is more important than anything else."

And then I told him about explaining that with two tickets you could take out *one* Fiction and *one* Non-Fiction but not *two* Fiction or *two* Non-Fiction; that Fiction means a story book that isn't true and Non-Fiction means for example a book about history or science; and, no madam, biography is Non-Fiction although yes it *is* a story—the story of somebody's life—but the difference is that it's a true story and not an untrue story. Which *is* a funny way of dividing things up but no not even this once and the book must be replaced because the library has strict rules.

He'd been getting more and more restless as I'd been talking. He'd even done a few of his isometric exercises. And suddenly he said, "Really, David! You're indulging yourself again—enjoying your self-pity. I thought we'd got past all that. I'd really thought you were beginning to move into a more *constructive* phase."

I sneaked a flash at my watch—only twenty more minutes to fill in—and said, "Well, you see, Doctor, I'm trying to fill in the way I *felt*—you know—*why* I went to Wales. I thought it might be helpful."

And I hurried on and told him about waking up in the morning with the tiredness where the cartilage used to be. And the impossible search for excuses. Colds. Influenza. Diarrhoea. Migraine. The repeated deaths of close relatives. Sprained ankles. Buses breaking down; the mechanical failure of my alarm clock. Ringing up with balls of paper in my mouth pretending to be my landlord. A sullen gathering of boredom which ripened every few weeks screaming for the lancet.

He broke in again and said, "David! David, I want you to stop and *think* about what you've just told me. You see that you're repeating a depressive pattern, don't you? I think it's obvious even to you. But I still feel that you're not quite prepared to break that pattern yet—to accept that your world is *necessarily* as it is. Umm? Do you think that's fair?"

"I do see what you mean, Doctor," I said.

He smiled his wise smile and said, "You have to want to adjust, David. You have to *commit* yourself. What you've just been telling me is obviously impossible as a way of life, isn't it?"

"Yes. I realize that now," I said.

"And," he said, "you have the future to think about."

I *didn't* tell him to what extent the future *did* possess me; how it shadowed each passing day; because that was precisely what he didn't want to hear. I didn't tell him how I feared the future which is only my present repeated CLICK click CLICK repeated. I didn't tell him that if I rolled round the strips of rubber on the date-stamp I would age with them. In November, January, April, or May, this year, next year, each and every year the library floor would still gleam with polish; Miss Nevins' slip would still be peeping from beneath her withered dress; the electric clock would still be humming through the endless afternoon and my life would be slowly stamped away CLICK click CLICK of the date-stamp CLICK click CLICK stamping my life away two weeks from now two weeks from then two weeks from *then*. And fines for being late.

"Yes," I said. "Of course, you're right."

He smiled encouragingly and, pulling back inches of snowy cuff, looked at his watch. "We've about fifteen minutes left to us today. Shall we have another try at the events in Wales?" But he almost sighed as he said that.

He reached over for the folder which contained the notes on my case and as he picked it up some of the papers slipped out. I ducked to pick them up for him because I'd been wanting to get a glance at them for weeks. But he took them too quickly.

"Now then," he said. "On the day in question you'd overslept and were late for work. You were often late and as a result your relationship with Mr."—he checked the typescript—"with Mr. Prippet was not a happy one. And so, deciding that you might as well be hanged, as it were, for a sheep as a lamb, you took the whole day off. You went first to a café where you ate breakfast and then you sat in a park. Is that right? Am I leaving anything out?"

(There'd been an old man in the park muffled up against the cold. A huddled figure on a municipal bench staring over the neat gravel path and the trim lawn at the central bed of municipal flowers. And near his feet a grey sea of pigeons heaving and fluttering over a paper bag. The pigeons had horrid red feet—not pretty pink like coral—raw, red like sores. Like the hands of the girl in the bus queue.)

"No," I said. "That's what happened."

"And then you left the park and wandered around the streets for an hour or so. Quite by chance, you found yourself in front of the railway station and you went in, on impulse, and boarded the North Wales train without a ticket."

I nodded.

"Why North Wales? Had you been there before?"

"No," I said. "I don't really know why. There was an attractive poster outside. Mountains. A stream. I don't really know why."

"But didn't you think at all of the consequences of not being able to pay for the ticket?"

"No," I said. "I don't think it really crossed my mind."

"And it didn't cross your mind about what you were going to do when you got there? About paying for a hotel room and food?"

"No," I said. "I just wanted to go away."

"Was it, perhaps, because you knew before you went that there wasn't likely to *be* a reckoning? That your mind was filled with some rather silly notions. . . ?"

He leaned forward eagerly but I just shrugged and looked down at the patterns in the rug.

I'd enjoyed the journey on the train. Travelling always induces a wonderfully soothing state in me rather like a trance—a trance that seems to mingle past and present, merging pictures from the passing landscape and images from memory. Thoughts without thinking.

The carriage had been empty most of the way and the click of the wheels and the clack-clacking of the knob of the window cord against the glass, irregular, sometimes fast, sometimes slow, shuffling with a blur and rattle over points, had echoed in my mind the sound of my father's painful typing as he hammered out the Sunday sermon in his study. And I'd remembered—a flood of pictures—but strangely and insistently the summer-house at the bottom of the garden where I'd lock myself on summer evenings and light my stubs of candles. Sacks tacked over the windows. And the smell of jute and wood and oiled tools.

And moving aside my father's implements, forks, spades, dibbers, balls of twine, bundles of canes and pea-sticks, seed packets, trays of little plant pots, rags, paint cans, and stiffened brushes, I'd take out my hidden bottles and range them on the broken cardtable. Bottles I'd found in the spinney near my house—Gin and Whiskey, Port, Sherry, Rum and Brandy. And I'd filled them all with lemonade made from Robinson's Lemonade Crystals. And in the warm light, sitting in an uncomfortable deckchair, I read Conan Doyle and Edgar Rice Burroughs and drank from each bottle pretending to be drunk.

Picture after picture—the past transfiguring the dingy carriage as the landscape changed and climbed towards Wales.

"The stop was an unscheduled stop," he said.

"Pardon?" I said.

"The stop—where you got off the train—it wasn't a regular station."

"No. That's right."

"You still remember these details?"

"Oh, yes," I said.

"Why did you choose to get out where you did?"

"Well, the train stopped near a red signal—I think there was a tunnel ahead—and it seemed to wait there a long time and I could see the lights of a village below so—well, I just got out."

"How did you feel? Resigned? Depressed?"

"I don't think I felt anything particularly," I said.

(It had been extremely cold after the warmth of the carriage and while I was standing by the side of the train as it started to move on into the tunnel a jet of white steam had burst from beneath one of the carriages to hang for a few moments in the blackness. By the time it had crumbled and whisped away into the night the train was only a distant rumble and the darkness had completely closed me in.

And I'd stood looking down at the spark and shine of the village lights and the soft movements of the moon on the sea. And I'd wanted to laugh out loud but didn't because of the silence.)

He checked his notes again and then said, "When you reached the village you went to the pub and asked the landlord—a Mr. Davies—for a room and dinner. We've no need to bother about *that* aspect of things. That's a legal matter—nothing to do with me—and was dealt with by the court." He smiled at me and said, "I merely render unto Caesar, as it were." I smiled back at him.

"But," he said, "what does concern us is this: you said a minute ago that when you got off the train you weren't feeling 'anything in particular.' You weren't unhappy. You weren't depressed. You've told me before that you went to bed immediately after you'd eaten and were soon sound asleep. You woke up fairly early and went for a walk along the beach. Yet the next thing we know is that you're being rescued from the sea. You're weeping and shouting hysterically. It doesn't make sense, does it, David?"

I made a selection of agreeing and being bewildered faces and inwardly cursed myself that I hadn't handled the matter in a more intelligent fashion. Right from the start I should have admitted to severe depression, attempted suicide, religious ecstasy, and a vision of Jesus in a white gown appearing over the bay to carry me off in His arms. Then, gradually, he could have cured me of that and everyone would have been quite happy. But now I'd landed myself with amnesia or some sort of mental block and I couldn't see any end to this series of Happy Hours.

"We have to find out," he said, "or admit, what happened to make you feel desperate enough to—to become so disturbed. And when we do *that*, David, then . . ."

"I can remember . . ." I said.

"Yes," he said.

"I can remember waking up and how quiet it was. And I can remember getting dressed and going out across the road to the beach and walking along the beach. . . ."

"Did you meet anyone?" he asked.

"No. Definitely. The street was deserted and I could see along the shore for miles."

"Go on."

"Well, all I can remember is standing on some rocks."

"Yes."

"That's all."

"Nothing else at all?"

"No. Nothing."

"You were depressed," he said.

"I don't know. I just can't remember. There's nothing there."

"And that's all?"

"Well, I remember being soaked and standing on the beach and a lot of people talking and shouting—but that must have been afterwards."

"You don't know why you were crying?" he said. "Or what you were shouting? 'Don't go! Don't GO. You can't just leave me.' This doesn't mean anything to you?"

I stared at him with my honest and troubled gaze and said, "I'm sorry, Doctor, I *know* how important it is but . . . well—there's just nothing *there.*"

Another long silence.

I sighed.

But behind my frank and honest eyes, quite safe from Dr. Maximillian Cottle, I treasured the gleaming sweep of the estuary; and louder than his questions the sound of gulls.

And as near as the sound of gulls would allow I'd told him the truth. I *had* gone to bed early that night and it was certainly true that I *was* soon asleep. But I hadn't told him of the thick linen sheets and the engraving of General Picton at Waterloo which hung over the fireplace. Nor, just as I was falling asleep, of the sound of boots echoing along the road, each footstep caught and ringing for a second against the rock face of the mountain which towered sheer behind the houses.

And I'd kept from him, too, the beauty of the early morning. The estuary, gleaming like a sheet of old pewter, cradled by the humpy Welsh mountains, purple and grey, which disappeared into more distant ranges indistinguishable from cloud.

And the morning had been alive with sound. The soft slap of water against the sea-wall. The low tinkle and murmur of the ebb tide running, leaving the air sharp with the smell of mud and seaweed. And raucous crows and jackdaws circling the bare tree tops, squabbling and squawking as they wheeled and fluttered. And every few minutes a crow flaking away on black wings from the cliff face and drifting down over the street, wavering on the air like a walker on an invisible tightrope, to suddenly swoop, and strut along the ebbing tide line.

As I'd stood gazing out over the estuary the sun had begun to glint on the water and tinge the grey rain clouds yellow like a fading bruise. A sandbank was slowly growing out of the water as the tide scoured out through the central channel and the moored yachts and dinghies turned and yawed at their ropes, creaking as the water rippled past them. And I watched the incredibly white gulls riding the tide and sitting on the boats as though they owned them.

Nearer to me, gulls were sitting stolidly on the posts of a ruined jetty which ran out towards the deeper water. I clapped my hands to see if they'd fly away but they wouldn't even turn their heads. Then I threw a pebble into the water near them to see if they'd swoop down but they were far too wise for such poor tourist tricks. And so I started to hunt along the beach for something that they'd eat.

I found a cabbage stalk and a piece of bread and it was when I straightened up and looked out towards the jetty again that I first saw them. Two black patches moving slowly through the water. At first, they looked like the dorsal fins of a big fish. I ran down to the edge of the water but whatever it was had moved under the piles of the jetty. Then I saw one of the black patches again just below one of the slimy posts. As I watched, the patch of blackness in the water grew larger and larger and I saw a creature's back like the swirl of a rolling black barrel. Then nothing. Nothing but grey water.

I continued staring at the spot where it had disappeared but suddenly, further up the beach, one of the things arched out of the water to vanish again with a loud splash. I hurried after it, scanning the surface of the estuary as I ran. And then, only yards from where I was standing, the water broke again and a porpoise curved into the air in a shower of spray.

Its bulk, black and shining, its glistening curve of a back, blotted out the sea and mountains. And in that second cold drops of water from its spray flicked my face. Then just before the water closed over it, I heard the warm huff and snort of its breath.

The pulse of my heart was knocking in my throat and I stood staring at the smooth water unable to move. I could feel the spray drops trickling down my cheek, following the curve of my lip, and I opened my mouth to taste the salt gift.

Then suddenly, further out, they both burst from the water, one of them jumping in a series of sleek curves, until the sea threshed around them. Leaping over each other, sliding, rolling, driving in towards the beach then gliding, after a sharp turn, towards the deeper water.

I followed their play as they forged up the estuary. I had to run to keep up with them. Sometimes they didn't surface for minutes on end and it was just as I was becoming anxious that I'd see the roll and swirl of their backs far away beyond the central channel on the other side of the estuary. Then, as my eyes were straining the distance, they'd suddenly reappear on my side—sudden black explosions—shooting out of the water as though they were playing a game—enjoying the fierce struggle of crossing and recrossing the scour of the tide-race. But even when they were far away from me, the sound of their snorting, the great blow of their breath, carried clearly across the water.

When they were close to me the sound seemed to change—though I probably imagined it—and it seemed more like a whistle; a signal, as though they were calling to each other across the still air.

As I ran after them, seeking over the surface of the water, I remember falling heavily on some rocks. I ripped my shirt across the ribs but it was only later that the cut started to hurt me and it was only later that I realized the palm of my hand was grazed raw and bleeding. And it was while I was standing on these rocks that the porpoises turned and started travelling down the estuary again towards the open sea.

They came in close to the shore only once more. I'd followed them back down the beach until I reached the old jetty again. The tide was much further out and most of the boats were lying keeled over rocking gently in about two feet of water.

They swerved in towards the more distant of the moored boats and seemed to be diving underneath them. And suddenly I knew something. It sounds silly but I knew that although I couldn't see them they were diving close under the boats for the pleasure of scratching their backs. I could hear the slap of little waves and the quiet huff of their breath. And I *knew* what they were doing.

Then, appearing from underneath the nearest boat, they glided into the shallow water. It seemed that they'd deliberately come close to me.

They lay, rolling slightly, as if resting. Only fifteen feet or so separated us. I stepped into the water. The stones and pebbles underfoot were slippery with slime and seawrack. I placed my feet at each step, not wanting to stumble and frighten them. I was breathing through my open mouth. There was a tin-can, I remember, shining, and its label washed almost free trailing with the motion of the tide.

I was within six feet of them when they turned and planed down into deeper water. Slowly; not at all frightened. I stood still, the water round my waist. The larger one surfaced about twenty yards ahead of me and I saw the swirling gleam of his back and heard his whistle.

I moved deeper searching over the empty water, waiting, but the grey surface was quite undisturbed. The only movement was the turbulence of the central tide-water, brief riffling whirlpools, topped with foam, spinning and spinning until they flattened into the water's flow.

The sandbank, as I watched and waited, was dotted with scurrying terns and oyster-catchers but nothing rose to break the water round its edge.

I waited, straining to hear the familiar call, but the only sounds were the slap of tiny waves against the hulls of the yachts and the wheeling gulls screaming in the air.

There came no whistle, no warm huff of breath. Nothing rose to shine above the water. Only the grey surface curving in towards the sandbar at the estuary mouth—a sandbar marked by a distant line of white, troubled water and, beyond, the vastness of the open sea.

And vaguely, yet more insistent than the screaming gulls, I could hear somewhere behind me, distantly, people shouting and a car-horn honking. And then I felt hands grasping my arms and voices talking. Voices talking. Gentling voices. Voices that talk to a frightened horse. And the voices said,

"There we are. You're all right now."

"You'll be all right, boy."

"Steady now."

I felt cold water slop against my shirt as I stumbled.

"Have you got him?" said a voice. And then another voice said, "Nothing to worry about, boy. We've got you safe."

And the hands, the hands and the voices, guided me back to the beach.

ROBERT, STANDING

THE HOT-WATER bottle bulgy in his lap, Robert pushed himself down the passage and into the bathroom. The wheels of his chair rippled over the uneven woodblock floor and squawked as he made the turn. A strong push with his right hand brought the chair round to face the washbasin. Gripping the edge of the basin with his right hand, he pulled the chair closer.

Tipping the chair forward, he reached up and over the basin to open the bathroom cabinet. He took down the bottle of Dettol and stood it between the taps. Holding the hot-water bottle pressed against his chest with his left arm he unscrewed the stopper and then poured the urine down the sink.

He ran the water for a few moments and then flopped the mouth of the hot-water bottle under the tap. When it was half full he held it pressed against the edge of the basin with his left hand while he poured in some Dettol so that it wouldn't smell.

He pushed against the basin and moved himself over to the bath. Leaning out from the chair, he turned on both taps. The bath was an old fashioned one his brother had bought from a demolition company, legs and claw feet, its enamel chipped away in spots leaving blue-black roughnesses. The original bath had been too low for him to get into without help.

He took off his pyjama jacket and draped it over the back of his chair. He lifted himself with his good arm and worked the pyjama bottoms from under him, pushing them down his legs to wrinkle round his ankles. He sat naked in the canvas chair as the bathroom filled with steam.

From his broad shoulders hung the single, paunchy mound of his chest and stomach. His left arm was stick thin, the wrist and hand twisted, fingers splayed. Below, both legs were thin and useless, the kneecaps rising like huge swellings. At the end of the wasted legs his feet sat like big boots on a rag puppet.

He freed his feet from the folds of the pyjamas and then, jamming the wheelchair against the tub, worked himself forward to the edge of the blue canvas seat. Holding the pressure against the bath to try and stop the chair from being pushed away, he heaved up his bulk on the strength of his right arm. The chair tipping, sliding, he lurched sideways, straining upwards to lodge one buttock on the white enamel. The breath soughing in and out of him, he rested there for a moment, and then worked himself higher until he was sitting on the edge of the tub.

Using both arms, he lifted up his right leg, hoisted it over the rim, and dumped it into the water. Then the left leg. He sat resting again, facing the wall.

The skin of his back and buttocks was pitted with the scars of boils and sores, wounds which erupted again and again from the same chafed sites leaving scar tissue like soft scale.

He shuffled himself along the edge of the bath to the curved end. His legs dragged out behind him. Then, getting a good grip with his hand, he allowed his buttocks to slide down. His quivering arm held for a moment and then his bulk fell, water slopping out onto the floor. The shock of the hot water stopped his breath. He lay motionless as the water surged up and down.

When his breathing returned, he levered himself into a sitting position and hauled at his legs to straighten them out.

Sweat was standing out on his forehead. A vein, a muscle, something in his neck was jerking. He lay back in the rising steam, his eyes closed, waiting for the pounding of his heart to slow. He could feel the water still lapping at the island of his stomach. He opened his eyes and stared up at the tiled wall. It was furred with gathering beads of moisture.

Grey cement lines between the white spaces climbing, zigzags, verticals, building block lines, near the top edge a band of blue tiles, a single drop hung. Already impossibly heavy. Still on his desk. The weekly folder of playscripts from the CBC still lay on his desk. They'd have to be mailed off today or he'd have to pay for special delivery. But if he could finish reading the last play and write the four reports by eleven and then get the last three chapters of the novel read for the *Gazette* review—say twelve, twelve-thirty—he could get the carriage out and go to the drive-in on Decarie for lunch. The drop of water pulled others tributary and hung swelling. It broke suddenly into a meandering run. It was three days now since he'd been out. But if he went a bit later she wouldn't be so busy. One-thirty. One-thirty might be better, when the cars had thinned out.

As it checked, and paused, and changed direction to run again, it was leaving a clear trail shining down the tiles. One-thirty might be better. The soap slipped from his hand and he groped for it under his wasted thighs.

Bringing his tray, the edge of the peasant blouse decorated with blue and pink stitched flowers. Leaning into the carriage, the blouse falling away, a tiny gold crucifix on a gold chain deep between her breasts. The drop of water gathered again and then streaked down below the edge of the tub and out of sight.

"Are you going to be long, Bob?" yelled his brother.

"Nearly finished," he called back.

He could hear Jim in the kitchen now; the tap running, a pan on the gas-stove. He pushed himself higher and twisted round to reach the two towels on the chair behind him. He spread the first on the seat of his wheelchair so that he wouldn't have to sit on wet canvas for hours. He draped the other down the inside curve of the bath and splashed water on it. He heaved himself up again on his right arm and grunted his way up the towel's roughness until he was lodged on the rim of the bath.

Jim rapped on the bathroom door and rushed in. He was wearing a dark suit and carrying a briefcase. "Sorry, Bob," he said. "It's half-past eight." He wrenched on the cold tap and splashed water on his face.

"Didn't you sleep again?" he said.

"Fair. I just woke up early."

Jim squeezed tooth paste onto his brush and leaned over the basin. When he had wiped his mouth, Robert said, "You've still got toothpaste on your moustache."

"Okay. See you tonight then. There's some coffee for you in the kitchen." He peered into the mirror again. "Nothing you want?"

"No, I don't think so, thanks." Then he called after him, "Jim! Are you going to be late tonight?"

"No. Usual."

"Shall I make supper?"

"Okay. Bye."

The front door slammed shut. Robert sat on the edge of the bath.

He struggled back into his chair and started to dry himself. When he touched his legs the flesh dented into white fingerprints which slowly faded up again to red.

He wheeled himself over to the basin and waited for the water to run hot. He propped the small hand-mirror between the taps and reached down his razor and the can of foam. As he peered into the mirror his fingertips explored a nest of spots under the angle of his jaw.

He put his hand into the water to test the heat and sat staring down into the basin. No scrubbing ever cleaned his calloused palm and fingers which were grimy with an ingrained dirt from the rubber wheels. He sat in the silence, staring. His hand looked disembodied, yellowish, like some strange creature in an aquarium.

Before going back to his room, he dusted his buttocks and groin with Johnson's Baby Powder.

Sitting tailor fashion on his bed, he worked the socks onto his feet. Then pulling his legs apart, he stuffed his feet into his underpants. He got the pants up round his knees and then rolled onto his back to pull them up. He repeated the manoeuvre to get his trousers on. As he had decided on going out, he put on his new turtle-neck sweater. Then he rolled back into his chair again and wheeled himself over to face his desk.

The empty apartment was shifting, settling into silence. He moved the folder of plays to one side and taking a large manila envelope from the middle drawer wrote:

The Script Department,
CBC,
P.O. Box 500,
Toronto.

He found his mind drifting into the clock's rhythm, speeding up and slowing down, emphasizing now this beat, now that. He could hear the faint twinge of cooling metal from the gas-stove in the kitchen. Outside on the street he could hear the rattle of tricycles, the faint shouts of children. If he looked up he would see the side wall of the next duplex and in the top left corner of the window part of a branch. The desk top was a sheen of light.

The room behind him was familiar country, his own unchanging landscape. On top of the chest of drawers stood the photographs of his mother and father, ebony and silver frames. Beside them stood the small silver cup won long ago in his school days. On the end wall were the two rows of Hogarth prints—a complete set of *The Rake's Progress* and three odd prints from *Marriage a la Mode.* By the fake fireplace and the green armchair were his record-player, tape-recorder, and the FM radio. And the rank and order of his books memorized, the colours of their bindings.

Facing him on the desk were three shoeboxes. They were packed with file cards—the bones of his abandoned thesis for the University of Montreal. He was always intending to move the boxes and put them away but he never seemed to get round to it.

The wild yapping of the upstairs dog aroused him. His eyes focused and he found that his pen had covered the envelope with doodling lines and squiggles. He quickly wheeled himself out to the front door. The mailman was just walking up the concrete ramp.

"Hello!" said Robert. "How are you?"

"Oh, fine. Just fine."

He handed Robert two letters.

"Did you go away anywhere?" Robert asked.

"No, I took it easy, you know. Did a few jobs round the house."

He smiled and started to walk away down the slope.

"The man replacing you got everybody's mail mixed up all the time," called Robert.

"Oh, these temporaries, *they* don't care," he said.

"It must be hard getting back to it after a holiday," Robert called. The mailman paused on the pavement and shrugged. "Oh, it gets kind of boring round the house," he said. He hitched up his bag and walked on up the road. Robert sat in the open doorway and looked at the letters. One was a bill from Hydro-Quebec and the other contained a three cent voucher for New Luxol detergent.

He backed his chair and closed the door. He knew it must be at least nine-thirty. Perhaps more coffee would help. He was just about to wheel himself into the kitchen when the dog started its frantic barking again. He sat in the hall waiting. It had to be somebody for upstairs. But then the bell rang. He waited for a few moments and then moved up to open the door. Two young women stood looking at him.

"Good morning," said one.

"We're messengers of the Lord," said the other.

"Well, you'd better come in, then," said Robert.

He ushered them into his room. "Do sit down," he said, pointing to the armchair by the record-player. "I'll just. . . ." He started to drag over a wooden kitchen chair.

"Can I help you with that?" asked the younger one.

"No, no. I can manage, thank you."

He placed the chair and the two of them sat down. The older one smoothed her skirt carefully, pulling it down taut over her knees. Robert guessed she was in her late twenties. She had straight hair, cut short, and a pale, almost pasty face. She bent to take something from her briefcase.

The younger one was prettier except that her hair was rigidly permed. She was wearing white ankle socks, a tartan skirt, and a blue blazer with brass buttons.

"Well," said the older one, "we'd like to talk with you for a few minutes if you can spare us the time?"

"Sure," said Robert. "Certainly."

"We'd like to talk about the Lord Jesus?"

"Can I get you anything?" asked Robert. "Tea, coffee?"

"No, thank you."

He moved his wheelchair so that he could look at both of them at once.

"We're members of the Church of Jesus Christ of Latter-day Saints?" said the younger one.

"Commonly called 'Mormons,'" said the other, pointing to a blue, paperback book she had taken from her briefcase. On the bookcover, a man in gold robes was blowing a trumpet. "After this book, *The Book of Mormon.*"

"Yes," said Robert. "Would you like some lemonade, perhaps?"

"We should have introduced ourselves," said the older one. "This is Miss Adetti and I'm Miss Stevens."

"Hardwick," said Robert. "Robert Hardwick."

"Tell me, Mr. Hardwick, are you a member of a church?"

"No, I don't go to church," said Robert.

"Do you believe in the Lord Jesus Christ?" asked Miss Stevens.

"Not in any active way," said Robert.

"We'd like to present the Lord Jesus to you this morning, if you'll let us?" said Miss Stevens.

"By all means. . . ." said Robert.

She fixed him with her eyes. "Mr. Hardwick. Why did the Lord Jesus come into the world?"

"Allegedly to save it," said Robert.

"'And he cometh into the world that he may save all men if they harken unto his voice; for behold, he suffereth the pains of all men, yea, the pains of every living creature . . .'" said Miss Stevens.

"Second Book of Nephi. Chapter Nine. Verse twenty-one," said Miss Adetti.

"There are many misconceptions about the Mormon faith, Mr. Hardwick," said Miss Stevens.

"You mean wives and so on?" said Robert.

"Some people say we aren't even Christians and that *The Book of Mormon* is our Bible," said Miss Stevens.

"Which just isn't true," said Miss Adetti.

"*The Book of Mormon,*" said Miss Stevens, "*reinforces* the Bible. It *doesn't* replace it. It adds its witness to Christ's word."

"'Wherefore murmur ye,'" said Miss Adetti, "'because that ye shall receive more of my word?'"

"And again from Second Nephi," said Miss Stevens. "'And because my words shall hiss forth—many of the Gentiles shall say: A Bible! A Bible! We have got a Bible and there cannot be any more Bible.'"

She paused and then said, "And what was the Lord God's answer, Mr. Hardwick?"

"'O fools!'" said Miss Adetti.

"Well, that certainly seems a reasonable point," said Robert.

Miss Stevens bent into her briefcase again and came out with a long cylinder. She took the cap off and pulled out an assortment of metal rods. Robert hauled his feet further in on the footplate and shifted his buttocks on the hard canvas. Miss Stevens did not shave her legs and he stared at the matted hair under her nylons.

"*The Book of Mormon,*" she said—her fingers were building the rods into a sort of frame or easel—"was first given to the world in 1830. We'd like to tell you a little of the miraculous history of that book. I have here a visual aid. . . ." She stretched over and stood the easel thing on top of the record-player. Robert saw with sudden interest that her baggy blouse concealed absolutely enormous breasts.

"But you see," said Robert, "it's not history that concerns me. Before we bother about history we ought to answer other questions. How do we know that the Lord God even exists?"

"'And by the power of the Holy Ghost ye may know the truth of all things,'" said Miss Adetti. "Moroni 10:4-5," she added.

"But I don't know that the Holy Ghost exists," said Robert.

"I have known the Lord Jesus in my life, Mr. Hardwick," said Miss Stevens.

"But I haven't," said Robert.

"You must have faith," said Miss Adetti. "'For the natural man is an enemy to God and has been from the fall of Adam, and will be, forever and ever, unless he yields to the enticings of the Holy Spirit.' Mosiah 3:19-20."

"'He who wishes to become a saint must become as a child,'" said Miss Stevens. "'Submissive, meek, humble, patient, full of love, willing to submit to all things which the Lord seeth fit to inflict upon him, even. . . .'"

"But how," interrupted Robert, "can you have faith in something you don't believe in?"

"There's such a beautiful story in The Book of Alma," said Miss Adetti, "that answers that very question. May I tell it to you?" Miss Stevens nodded.

"'Korihor said to Alma: If thou wilt show me a sign that I may be convinced that there is a God'—you see—the very question you asked us. 'But Alma said unto him: Thou hast had signs enough; will ye tempt your God? Will ye say, Show unto me a sign, when ye have the testimony of all these thy brethren, and also all the holy prophets? The scriptures are laid before thee, yea, and all things denote there is a God; yea, even the earth, and all things that are upon the face of it, yea, and its motion, yea, and also all the planets which move in their regular form do witness that there is a Supreme Creator.'"

She finished and there was a silence. Her face was flushed. The silence deepened. Robert nodded slowly. He bent and pushed his left foot forward on the footplate. He straightened up and looked at them.

"Oh, Mr. Hardwick!" burst out Miss Stevens. "Let the Lord Jesus enter into your life!"

"Let us say a prayer!" said Miss Adetti.

He leaned back in his chair and watched them. They screwed up their eyes tight like children and lifted up their faces. They intoned their words antiphonally and his eyes followed from face to face.

"And let us," said Miss Stevens, "remind ourselves of that promise thou hast made to us in The Book of Moroni: 'If ye by the grace of God are perfect in Christ, and deny not his power, then are ye sanctified in Christ by the grace of God..."'

Miss Adetti's voice took up, "'... through the shedding of the blood of Christ, which is in the covenant of the Father..."'

Both voices rose in unison, "'... unto the remission of your sins, that ye become holy, without spot."'

They lowered their heads and sat for a few moments in silence.

"Thank you," said Robert quietly.

Miss Stevens glanced at Miss Adetti and then said, "Mr. Hardwick, we'd like to leave this book with you for a few days. We'd like to have you read it?" She stood up and picked up her briefcase. Miss Adetti got up and took the wooden chair back to the other side of the room. "And perhaps we could call back on you in a few days' time?"

"I shall look forward to it," said Robert. He wheeled himself ahead of them and opened the door. As they stood by the front door, Miss Adetti said, "Well, it's been just fine meeting you, Mr. Hardwick." She smiled warmly at him.

He backed his chair away and started to close the door. They were just turning out onto the pavement. Miss Stevens hitched her briefcase higher under her arm. Suddenly he pulled the door open again and rammed his chair forward, bucking the wheels over the fibre mat.

"Hey! You!"

Two startled faces turned to stare at him. His body bent forward from the chair.

"If I was standing up," he bellowed, "I'd be six foot three."

SINGLE GENTS ONLY

AFTER David had again wrested the heavy suitcase from his father's obstinately polite grip and after he'd bought the ticket and assured his mother he wouldn't lose it, the three of them stood in the echoing booking hall of the railway station. His mother was wearing a hat that looked like a pink felt Christmas pudding.

David knew that they appeared to others as obvious characters from a church-basement play. His father was trying to project affability or benevolence by moving his head in an almost imperceptible nodding motion while gazing with seeming approval at a Bovril advertisement.

The pink felt hat was secured by a hat-pin which ended in a huge turquoise knob.

Beyond his father's shoulder, looking over the paperbacks on the W H. Smith stall, was a woman in a sari. David kept under observation the vision of the bare midriff and the ponderous hand of the station clock while pretending to listen to the knit-one-purl-one of his mother's precepts.

His father eventually made throat-clearing noises and David promptly shook his hand. He stooped to kiss his mother's cheek. Her hat smelled of lavender, her cheek, or possibly neck, of lily-of-the-valley. He assured her that the ticket was safe, that he knew where it was; that he'd definitely remember to let her know in the letter for which she'd be waiting if the train had been crowded; if he'd managed to get a seat.

The loudspeakers blared into demented announcement flurrying the pigeons up into the echoing girders. The onslaught of this amplified gargle and ricochet coincided with his mother's peroration, which seemed to be, from the odd phrase he caught, a general reworking of the Polonius and Mr. Micawber material, warnings against profligacy, going to bed late, burning the candle at both ends, debt, promiscuity, not wearing undershirts, and drink.

She gripped his hand.

He watched her face working.

As the metal voice clicked silent, she was left shouting,

"THE SECRET OF A HAPPY LIFE IS..."

Mortified, David turned his back on the gawping porter.

She continued in a fierce whisper,

"... is to *apportion* your money."

He returned their wavings, watching them until they were safely down into the tiled tunnel which led to the car-park, and then lugged his case over to the nearest waste basket, into which he dropped the embarrassing paper bag of sandwiches.

With only minutes to go before his train's departure, the barmaid in the Great North-Western Bar and Buffet set before him a double Scotch, a half of best bitter, and a packet of Balkan Sobranie cigarettes. Flipping open his new wallet, he riffed the crisp notes with the ball of his thumb. The notes were parchment stiff, the wallet so new it creaked. Smiling, he dismissed the considerable change.

The Scotch made him shudder. The aroma of the Sobranie cigarettes as he broke the seal and raised the lid was dark, strange, and rich. He was aware of the shape and weight of the wallet in his jacket's inside pocket. Stamped in gold inside the wallet were words which gave him obscure pleasure: *Genuine Bombay Goat.* With a deft flick of his wrist, he extinguished the match and let it fall from a height into the ashtray; the cigarette was stronger than he could have imagined. He raised the half of bitter in surreptitious toast to his reflection behind the bar's bottles. Smoke curling from his nostrils, he eyed the Cypriot barmaid, whose upper front teeth were edged in gold.

* * *

He sat in a window seat of the empty carriage feeling special, feeling regal, an expansive feeling as physical and filling as indigestion. He crossed his legs, taking care not to blunt the immaculate crease in his trousers, admiring his shined shoes. A mountain of luggage clanked past, steam billowed up over the window, a whistle blew. And then the carriage door opened and a toddler was bundled in from the platform followed by a suitcase and parcels and carrier-bags and its mother. Who hauled in after her an awkward stroller.

Doors slamming down the length of the train.

"Ooh, isn't the gentleman kind!" said the woman to the toddler as David heaved the suitcase up onto the luggage rack.

"And these?" said David.

From one of the carrier-bags, a yellow crocodile made of wood fell onto his head.

The toddler started to struggle and whine as the train pulled out. It was given a banana. It was pasty-looking and on its face was a sort of crust. Old food, perhaps. Possibly a skin disease. It started to mush the banana in its hands.

Turning away, David gazed out over the backs of old jerry-built houses, cobbled streets, cemeteries, mouldering buildings housing strange companies found in the hidden parts of town visible only from trains: Victoria Sanitation and Brass, Global Furniture and Rattan, Allied Refuse. Clotheslines. The narrow garden strips behind the house looking as if receding waters had left there a tide-line of haphazard junk.

The train cleared the neat suburbs, the gardens, the playing fields for employees, picked up speed, vistas of distant pitheads, slag-heaps, towering chimneys and kilns spreading palls of ochre smoke, all giving way to fields and hedges, hedges and fields.

Inside his head, like an incantation, David repeated:

The train is thundering south.

Beside the shape of the wallet in his jacket's pocket was the letter from Mrs. Vivian Something, the University's Accommodations Officer. The tone of the letter brusque. He had not replied promptly as he had been instructed so to do and no vacancies now existed in the Men's Halls of Residence. Nor were rooms now available on the Preferred List. Only Alternative Accommodation remained.

274 Jubilee Street.

The morning sunshine strong, the train thundering south, the very address propitious, *Jubilee.*

As the train bore him on towards this future, he found himself rehearsing yet again the kind of person he'd become. What kind of person this was he wasn't really sure except that he'd known without having to think about it that it wasn't the kind of person who lived in Men's Halls of Residence.

Blasts on its whistle, the train slowing through a small country station.

Nether Hindlop.

On the platform, rolls of fencing wire, wicker crates of racing pigeons, holding a ginger cat in his arms, a porter.

But at the least, he thought, the kind of person who bestowed coins on *grateful* porters. He still blushed remembering how on his last expedition to London he'd tipped a taxi-driver a shilling and the man had said,

"Are you sure you can spare it?"

And later, even more mortifying, after a day in the Tate and National galleries, he had sat next to a table of very interesting people, obviously artistic, in a crowded cafe in Soho. He'd listened avidly as they chatted about Victor this and Victor that and he'd realized gradually that Victor must be Victor *Pasmore.* And as they were leaving, the man with the earring had paused by his table and said in a loud voice,

"So glad to have had you with us."

Even though he had been seared with shame and burned even now to think of it, he had in a way been grateful. He admired the rudeness and aggression and the ability to be rude and aggressive *in public;* the realm of books apart, he still considered it the most splendid thing that he had heard another person actually *say.*

But he found it easier to approach what he would become by defining what he was leaving behind. What he most definitely *wasn't*—hideous images came to mind: sachets of dried lavender, Post Office Savings Books, hyacinth bulbs in bowls, the *Radio Times* in a padded leather cover embossed with the words *Radio Times,* Sunday-best silver tongs for removing sugar-cubes from sugar-bowls, plump armchairs.

But *how,* he wondered, his thoughts churning deeper into the same old ruts, *how* did one change from David Hendricks, permanent resident of 37 Manor Way, ex-Library Prefect and winner of a State Scholarship, to something more . . . more raffish.

"Hold a woman by the waist and a bottle by the neck."

Yes.

Somerset Maugham, was it?

Not much of a point of etiquette in his own teetotal home, he thought with great bitterness, where wild festivities were celebrated in Tizer the Appetizer and where women were not held at all.

"Whoopsee!" cried the mother.

The toddler was launched towards him, was upon him. He looked down at his trousers. He tried to prise the clenched, slimy fingers from the bunched material.

"There," he said, "there's a good boy . . ."

"Not afraid of anything, *she* isn't!" said the woman proudly.

David blushed.

"Proper little tomboy, encha?"

David smiled.

And regarded his ruined knees.

* * *

The house stood on a corner; the front of the house faced onto Jubilee Street, the side of the house faced the cemetery on the other side of Kitchener Street. From the coping of the low wall which bounded the cemetery, rusted iron stumps stuck up, presumably the remains of an ornamental fence cut down for munitions during the Second World War. In an aisle of grass between two rows of tombstones, a small dog bunched, jerking tail, its eyes anguished.

There were no facing houses on the other side of Jubilee; there was a canal, tidal the driver had told him, connecting with the docks. The tide was out. Seagulls screeched over the glistening banks of mud. The smell came from the canal itself and from the massive redbrick brewery which stood on its far side.

Most of the tiny front garden was taken up by an old motorbike under a tarpaulin.

"*Not* Mr. Porteous?" she said.

"No," said David, "I'm afraid not."

She held the letter down at a distance, her lips moving. Wiry hairs grew on the upper lip. He suddenly blushed remembering that her house had been described as Alternative Accommodation and hoping that she wouldn't be embarrassed or hurt.

Her gross body was divided by the buried string of the grubby pinafore. Her hair was grey and mannish, short back and sides with a parting, the sort of haircut he'd noticed on mentally defective women in chartered buses. The torn tartan slippers revealed toes.

"They didn't mark that down," she said.

"Pardon?"

"About the back double."

"Double?"

"With the Oxford gentleman."

"Oh," said David. "You mean. . . ?"

"Yes," she said. "They should have marked that down."

He manoeuvred his suitcase round the hatstand and bicycle in the gloom of the narrow passage and followed her ponderous rump up the stairs. Reaching for the banister, grunting, she hauled herself onto the dark landing.

Even the air seemed brown.

"This is the bathroom," she said, "and the plumbing."

He sensed her so close behind him that he felt impelled to step inside. The room was narrow and was largely taken up by a claw-foot bathtub. Over the tub, the height of the room and braced to the wall, bulked the monstrous copper tank of an ancient geyser.

She was standing behind him, breathing.

He began to feel hysterical.

The lower part of the tank and the copper spout which swung out over the tub were green with crusty verdigris; water sweating down the copper had streaked the tub's enamel green and yellow. Wet, charred newspaper half blocked the gas-burners in the geyser's insides.

"If you wanted a bath, it's a shilling," she said, slippers shuffling ahead of him, "with one day's warning."

Following her into the bedroom, he stared at the vast plaster elephant.

Two single beds stood on the brown linoleum. The wallpaper was very pink. Pinned on the wall between the beds was a reproduction cut from a magazine of Annigoni's portrait of Queen Elizabeth.

"You can come and go as you please—the key's on a string in the letterbox—but we don't have visitors."

David nodded.

"I don't hold with young ladies in rooms."

"No, of course," said David. "Quite."

His gaze kept returning to the elephant on the mantelpiece. Inside the crenellated gold of the howdah sat a brown personage in a turquoise Nehru jacket sporting a turban decorated with a ruby.

"Well . . ." he said.

Staring at him, doughy face expressionless, she unscrewed a Vicks Nasal Inhaler and, pressing one nostril closed, stuck it up the other.

He politely pretended an interest in the view.

Below him, a staggering fence patched with warped plyboard and rusted lengths of tin enclosed a square of bare, packed earth.

There was a bright orange bit of carrot.

On one of the sheets of tin, it was still possible to make out an advertisement for Fry's Chocolate.

In the middle of this garden sat a disconsolate rabbit.

When the sounds seemed to have stopped, he turned back to face the room. He looked round nodding judiciously, aware even as he was doing it that it was the sort of thing his father did. He had, he realized, no idea of how to conclude these negotiations.

"And this other person? The man from Oxford?"

"Mr. Porteous."

"He's . . . ?"

"We had a telegram."

"Ah," said David, "yes. I see."

"Cooked breakfast and evening meal included," she said, "it's three pound ten."

"Well," said David, contemplating the elephant, "that sounds . . ."

"And I'll trouble you," she said, "in advance."

* * *

He shoved the empty suitcase under the bed.

The thin quilt, the sheets, the pillow, all felt cold and damp.

He thought of turning on the gas-fire but didn't have a shilling piece; he thought of putting a sweater on.

Jingled the change in his pocket for a bit, inspected the wallpaper more closely; the motif was lilac blossoms in pink edged with purple. It was five-thirty. He wondered at what time, and where, this evening meal was served, if "evening meal" meant tea in some form or dinner.

Voices.

Slap of slippers on lino.

He eased his door open a crack.

"*Evening Post.* Now that should serve her nicely, the *Evening Post.* Six pages of the *Post.* Read the newspaper, do you? Not much of a fellow for the reading. Scars, though! Now that's a different story entirely. Did I show you me scars?"

Through the banisters, an old man's head with hanging wings of white hair. Behind him, a stout boy in a brown dressing-gown.

The boy stood holding a sponge bag by its string; his calves were white and plump.

"Now there's a dreadful thing!" said the old man, who was scrabbling about on his hands and knees with the sheets of newspaper manufacturing a giant spill. "A dreadful thing! Two hundred homeless. Will you look at that! There, look, and there's a footballer. Follow the football, do you? Fill in the Pools? Never a drop of luck I've had. Spot the Ball? But a raffle, now! A raffle. I fancy the odds in a raffle. A raffle's a more reasonable creature than Spot the Ball."

He disappeared into the bathroom.

The front door slammed shaking the house.

Boots clumping.

Then the dreadful voice of Mrs. Heaney.

"PERCY?"

"WHAT?"

"PERCE!"

"Quick, now!" shouted the old man. "Quick! Holy Mother, she's in full flow!"

Matches shaking from the box, he secured one against his chest and then rasped it into flame. He set fire to the drooping spill.

"BACK, BOY! BACK!"

Body shielded by the door, face averted, he lunged blindly. The expanding sheet of light reminded David of war films. The old man's quavering cry and the explosion were nearly simultaneous.

Brown shoulders blocking the view.

Suddenly from below, at great volume, Paul Anka.

I'M JUST A LONELY BOY . . .

The old man was in the smoke stamping on the spill.

Ash, grey and tremulous, floated on the air.

* * *

In front of Mrs. Heaney's place at the head of the table stood a bottle of Cream Soda.

The kitchen was silent except for the budgerigar ringing its bell and stropping itself on the cuttlefish. The cooked evening meal was a fried egg, a wafer of cold ham, a quarter of a tomato, and three boiled potatoes.

The slice of ham had an iridescent quality, hints of green and mauve.

In the centre of the oilcloth stood Heinz Ketchup, Crosse and Blackwell's Salad Cream, HP Sauce, Branston Pickle, OK Sauce, Daddy's Favourite, Al Sauce, a bottle of Camp Coffee, and a punctured tin of Nestle's Evaporated Milk.

Sliced white bread was piled on a plate.

The old man bobbed and fidgeted darting glances.

The fat boy was called Asa Bregg and was from Manchester and had come to university to study mathematics. Ken, who had acne and a Slim Jim tie and lots of ballpoint pens, was an apprentice at Hawker-Siddeley. Percy, presumably Mrs. Heaney's son, glimpsed earlier in overalls, was resplendent in a black Teddy-boy suit, white ruffled shirt, and bootlace tie. What forehead he had was covered by a greasy elaborate wave. He was florid and had very small eyes. The old man was addressed as "Father" but David was unable to decide what this meant.

Cutlery clinked.

Percy belched against the back of his hand.

The old man, whose agitation had been building, suddenly burst out,

"Like ham, do you? A nice slice of ham? Tasty slice of ham? Have to go a long way to beat . . ."

"Father!" said Mrs. Heaney.

". . . a nice slice of ham."

"Do you want to go to the cellar!"

Cowed, the old man ducked his head, mumbling.

The budgerigar ejected seeds and detritus.

David studied the havildar or whatever he was on the label of the Camp Coffee bottle.

Mrs. Heaney rose heavily and opened four tins of Ambrosia Creamed Rice, slopping them into a saucepan.

Percy said,

"Hey, tosh."

"Pardon?" said David.

"Pass us the slide."

"Pardon? The what?"

Percy stared.

"Margarine," said Ken.

"Oh! Sorry!" said David.

Crouched on the draining-board, the cat was watching the Ambrosia Creamed Rice.

The old man, who'd been increasingly busy with the cruet, suddenly shouted,

"Like trains, do you? Interested in trains? Like the railway, do you? Fond of engines?"

"*Father!*"

Into the silence, Asa Bregg said,

"*I* am. I'm interested in trains. I collect train numbers."

The old man stared at him.

Even Percy half turned.

Ken's face lifted from his plate.

Asa Bregg turned bright red.

"I'm a member of the Train-Spotters Club."

* * *

Alone in the room that was his, David stared at the plaster elephant. He wondered how they'd got the sparkles in.

After the ham and Ambrosia Creamed Rice, he'd walked the neighbourhood—dark factories across the canal, bomb-sites, news agents, fish and chips, Primitive Methodist Church, barber, The Adora Grill, and had ended up in the Leighton Arms where in deepening depression he drank five pints of the stuff manufactured opposite his room an independent product called George's Glucose Stout.

The pub had been empty except for an old woman drinking Babycham and the publican's wife, who was knitting and listening to *The Archers.*

At the pub's off-licence, as a gesture of some kind, he'd bought a bottle of cognac.

He arranged on top of the chest of drawers the few books he'd been able to carry, the standard editions of Chaucer and Spenser serving as bookends, and settled himself on the bed with Cottle's *Anglo-Saxon Grammar and Reader.* Skipping over some tiresome introductory guff about anomalous auxiliary and preterite-present verbs and using the glossary, he attempted a line of the actual stuff but was defeated by the conglomeration of diphthongs, thorns, and wens; he had a presentiment that Anglo-Saxon was not going to be his cup of tea.

Heavy traffic up the stairs, voices, a strange jangle and clinking. Mrs. Heaney appeared in the doorway and behind her a tall man with blond hair.

"This is Mr. Porteous," she said, "from Oxford."

"David Hendricks."

"How do you do? Jeremy Porteous. If I could trouble you?" he said, handing the tightly furled umbrella to Mrs. Heaney. He dropped the canvas hold-all on the floor and, slipping off the coiled nylon rope and the jangling carabiner and pitons, tossed them and the duffle coat onto the bed.

He glanced round.

"Splendid," he said. "Splendid. Now, in the morning, Mrs. . . . ah . . . Heaney, isn't it? . . . I think, *tea.*"

"About the rent, Mr. Porteous."

"A matter for discussion, Mrs. Heaney, if you'd be so kind, following breakfast. I've had rather a gruesome day."

And somehow, seconds later, he was closing the door on her.

He smiled.

"There's a person downstairs," he said, "called 'Father.' Seemed to want to know, rather insistently, if I enjoyed travelling by bus."

David grinned.

Advancing on the gas fire and elephant Jeremy said, "There's a special name, isn't there, for this chocolate chap? The one on its neck?"

"Mahout," said David.

Seemingly absorbed, Jeremy moved back a pace the better to view the elephant. He had a slight limp, David noticed, and was favouring his right leg.

"Pardon?" said David.

"A plate,'" repeated Jeremy, "'of Spam.'"

David wondered how it was possible to wear a white shirt in combination with an anorak smeared with mud and at the same time look as suave as the men in the whisky advertisements.

"What are you going to . . ." David hesitated ". . . read at university?"

"Actually," said Jeremy, "I'm supposed to be involved in some research nonsense."

"Oh!" said David. "I'm terribly sorry. I just assumed . . . What did you do at Oxford?"

"I spent the better part of my time," said Jeremy still intent on the elephant, "amassing an extraordinarily large collection of photographs of naked eleven-year-old girls with their ankles bound."

David stared at the elegant back.

He could think of absolutely nothing to say.

The gas fire was making popping noises.

Desperate to break the silence, David said,

"Have you been climbing? Today, I mean?"

"Just toddling about on The Slabs at Llanberis. Are any of these free? I really must rest these shirts."

As he wrestled open a drawer in the chest, the mirrored door of the wardrobe silently opened, the flash of the glass startling him.

"Did you hurt your leg today?" said David, embarrassed still and feeling it necessary to ease the silence. "When you were climbing?"

"I hurt it," said Jeremy, dropping on his bed toothpaste, toothbrush, towel and a large green book, "not minutes ago, and quite exquisitely, in what is probably referred to as the hall. On a sodding *bicycle*."

He added to his toiletries a pair of flannel pyjamas decorated with blue battleships.

"Good God!" he said, pulling back the quilt, patting further and further down the bed. "This bed is positively *wet*."

"Mine feels damp, too," said David.

"*Yours* may be damp," said Jeremy. "*Mine* is *wet*."

He hurled the rope and the climbing hardware into a corner.

"Wet!" he shouted, striking the bed with his furled umbrella, "*Wet! Wet! Wet!*"

He seemed almost to vibrate with rage.

He pounded on the lino with the umbrella's ferrule.

"Can you hear me, Mrs. Heaney? Are you listening, you gravid sow?"

He stamped so hard the room shook and the wardrobe door swung open.

"WET!"

He glared about him.

He snatched at the string between the beds.

It broke.

With a loud *clung*, the gas-meter turned itself off.

He stood beside the bed with his eyes closed, one arm still rigid in the air holding the snapped string as though he were miming a straphanger in the underground. Light glinted on the gold and onyx cuff-link. Slowly, very slowly, he lowered the arm. Opening his fingers, he let the length of string fall to the floor. Eyes still closed, he let out his pent breath in a long sigh.

He limped over to the window. He swept aside the yellowed muslin curtains. He wrenched the window high. He limped to the mantel. He hurled the elephant into the night.

David realized that he, too, had been holding his breath.

The edges of the curtains trembled against the black square.

David cleared his throat.

"Would you," he said, reaching under the bed, "would you like a drink?"

"Ummm?" said Jeremy, turning, wiping his hands with a handkerchief.

"A drink?"

"Ah, brandy!" said Jeremy. "Good man! It might help in warding off what these beds will doubtless incubate. Sciatica, for a start."

"Lumbago," said David.

"Rheumatoid arthritis," said Jeremy.

"Mould," said David.

Jeremy laughed delightedly.

Digging into his hold-all, he came up with a black case that contained telescoping silver drinking cups which, with a twist, separated into small beakers. He caught David's expression and said,

"Yes, a foible, I'm afraid, but I've always been averse to the necks of bottles. Equal in the eyes of God and all that sort of thing, certainly, but would one share one's toothbrush? Well, bung-ho!"

Along the rim of the beaker, David saw the shapes of hallmarks.

"'Lumbago,'" said Jeremy. "Don't you find that certain words make you think of things they don't mean? 'Emolument,' for example. Makes me think of very naked, very fat, black women. Something I read as a stripling about an African king's wives who were kept in pens and fed starchy tubers—so fat they couldn't get up—just rolled around—and *oiled* all over, rather like . . ." his hands sketched a shape ". . . rather like immense *seals* . . . What was I starting to say?"

"Lumbago," said David.

"Yes," said Jeremy. "I wonder why?"

There was a silence.

"So!" said Jeremy.

David nodded.

Jeremy held out his cup.

"What are you going to do?" said David.

"In the morning," said Jeremy, "we shall fold our tents. What was that woman called?"

"Mrs. Heaney?"

"No. The lodgings woman."

"The Accommodations Officer?"

"*She's* the one. Cornbury? Crownbury? We shall proceed against her."

"But I thought—well, from her letter, that there *wasn't* anywhere else."

"Nonsense."

"Are you just *allowed* to leave a . . . ?"

"*Who*," demanded Jeremy, "who got us into this—this *Lazarhouse* in the first place? The responsibility is purely hers. We shall question her judgment with indignation and bitterness."

"But . . ."

"With *voluble* indignation and bitterness. We shall demand reparations. *Silver*," he said, "is so comforting to the touch, isn't it?"

David held up the brandy bottle.

"Well," said Jeremy, "*yes*."

"But you see . . ." said David.

"See what?"

"I paid her a week's rent."

"Always," said Jeremy, "try to *postpone* payment. On the other hand," he said judiciously, "never bilk."

"Well," said David, "now that you've . . . I mean, she's not likely to return my . . ."

"Life," said Jeremy, climbing into his pyjama bottoms, "is very much a *balancing*, a trading-off of this against that. It's a simple question, surely? The question is: Are you the sort of person who lives in a place like this? To which," he said, working a khaki sweater down over his pyjama top, "one hopes there can be but one reply."

He reassembled the bed and spread his duffle coat over the quilt and on the duffle coat spread two sweaters and his rope.

"I find sleep impossible," he said, "without *weight*."

Whistling "We Plough the Fields and Scatter," he went out with toothbrush and towel.

David sat on the bed enjoying the brandy, enjoying the weight and balance of the silver cup, savouring Jeremy's use of the word: *we*. Thinking about the amazing fluctuations of the long day, he decided that the flavour of events was exactly caught in the casual connective of biblical narrative: *And it came to pass . . .*

The wallpaper made him feel as if he were sitting inside a friendly pink cave.

He was, he realized, drunk.

Jeremy returned whistling the hymn about those in peril on the sea and started to work himself under the layer of bedding. He asked David to pass him the book, a large paper edition of *The Wind in the Willows* with illustrations by Ernest Shepard.

"I say," said Jeremy. "Would you . . . I mean, would it be a terrible imposition?"

"Would what?"

"Just to read a few paragraphs?"

"I haven't read this," said David, "since I was a child."

"Oh, but you should!" said Jeremy with great earnestness. "It never lets you down."

"From the beginning?"

"No," said Jeremy. "Let me think. Oh, this is *lovely!* There's the field mice singing carols to Ratty and Mole at 'Mole End'—that's always very nice. But . . . *I* know! Let's have the part where Ratty and Mole go to visit Toad. Remember? Where the motor-car wrecks Toad's caravan? Yes here it is."

He passed over the book.

He closed his eyes, composed his hands.

"Most kind of you."

David began.

The old grey horse, dreaming, as he plodded along, of his quiet paddock, in a new raw situation such as this simply abandoned himself to his natural emotions. Rearing, plunging, backing steadily, in spite of all the Mole's efforts at his head, and all the Mole's lively language directed at his better feelings, he drove the cart backwards towards the deep ditch at the side of the road. It wavered an instant—then there was a heart-rending crash—and the canary-coloured cart, their pride and joy, lay on its side in the ditch, an irredeemable wreck . . .

Toad sat straight down in the middle of the dusty road, his legs stretched out before him, and stared fixedly in the direction of the disappearing motor-car. He breathed short, his face wore a placid, satisfied expression, and at intervals he faintly murmured “Poop-poop!”

The Mole was busy trying to quiet the horse, which he succeeded in doing after a time. Then he went to look at the cart, on its side in the ditch. It was indeed a sorry sight . . .

The Rat came to help him, but their united efforts were not sufficient to right the cart. “Hi! Toad.’” they cried. “Come and bear a hand, can't you!”

David, turning the page, glanced over at Jeremy. His eyes were closed, his breathing deepening.

“Glorious, stirring sight!” murmured Toad, never offering to move. “The poetry of motion! The real *way to travel! The* only *way to travel! Here today—in next week tomorrow! Villages skipped, towns and cities jumped—always somebody else's horizon! O bliss! O poop-poop! O my! O my!”*

“O stop *being an ass, Toad!” cried the Mole despairingly.*

“And to think I never knew!” *went on the Toad in a dreamy monotone.*

David looked up.

With a long sigh, Jeremy had turned on his side.

His breathing deepened into a snore.

The coiled rope was balanced on the hump of his shoulder.

"All those wasted years," David continued, reading aloud in the pink bedroom, *"that lie behind me, I never knew, never even* dreamt! *But now—but now that I know, now that I fully realize! Oh what a flowery track lies spread before me, henceforth! What dust-clouds shall spring up behind me as I speed on my reckless way!"*

Jeremy's exhalations were a faint, breathy whistle.

David closed the book.

The edges of the curtains trembled against the black square of the open window.

He switched off the light.

He pulled the quilt up to his chin and lay in the darkness listening.

Somewhere far distant in the night, in the docks perhaps, perhaps slipping its moorings and preparing to move out down the river to the sea, a ship was sounding, sounding.

THE EASTMILL RECEPTION CENTRE

AFTER a year in the university's Department of Education, a year worn thin discussing the application of Plato to the secondary Modern School and enduring my tutor, a mad dirndl woman who placed her faith in Choral Speaking, this was to be my first taste of the real world.

While Uncle Arthur was assembling a ring of the necessary keys, I stood looking down from his office window into the asphalt quadrangle where the boys were lounging and smoking, strolling, dribbling a football about. They all wore grey denim overalls and black boots.

"The wife and I," said Uncle Arthur, "were not blessed with issue."

I turned and nodded slowly.

"So in a sense—well, the way *we* feel about it—every last one of these lads is *our* lad."

I nodded and smiled.

Uncle Arthur was short and tubby and was wearing grey flannels and a grey sleeveless pullover. Strands of fine blond hair were trained across his reddened pate. He looked jolly. In the centre of the strained pullover was a darn in wool of a darker grey. It drew attention like a wart.

"Here's your keys, then. They're all tagged. And use them at *all* times. Artful as a barrel-load of monkeys, they are, and absconders is the *last* thing we want. One whistle with lanyard. There's your timetable. And a word of advice, a word to the wise. If you get yourself into difficulties, just you come to me. I'm House Father and it's what I'm here for. Comprendo?"

"Thanks," I said. "I'll remember that."

"Right, then . . ." said Uncle Arthur.

I glanced at my timetable.

"Gardening?"

"Oh, everyone takes a hand at gardening," said Uncle Arthur. "Very keen on gardening, the Old Man is. Doesn't know you're here, does he? The Old Man? You didn't phone from the station?"

"No," I said. "Was I supposed to?"

"Probably wiser," said Uncle Arthur, "yes, to wait till morning."

I nodded.

"*Mid*-morning," he added.

I looked at him.

"A nod's as good as a wink," he said, "if you get my drift."

"Oh, right," I said. "Of course."

"That's the ticket!" said Uncle Arthur. "Well, you come along with me, then, do the evening rounds, get the hang of things."

I followed him along the disinfectant- and polish-smelling corridor, down the echoing steel stairs, out into the warmth of the summer evening.

Pallid faces, cropped hair, army boots. I was the centre of much obvious speculation. I kept close to Uncle Arthur and endeavoured to look bored. I nodded as casually as I could at the faces which stared most openly.

We mounted the steps of the North Building. Uncle Arthur blew one long blast on his whistle and all motion froze. His glance darted about the silent playground.

"Nothing like a routine," he murmured, "to settle a lad down."

Two blasts: four boys ran to stand beneath us, spacing themselves about ten feet apart.

"House Captains," explained Uncle Arthur.

Three blasts: the motionless boys churned into a mob and then shuffled themselves out into four lines. He allowed a few seconds to elapse as they dressed ranks and then blew one long blast.

Silence was rigid.

As each boy, House by House, called out *Present, Uncle Arthur!* in response to his surname, Uncle Arthur ticked the mimeographed sheet. When numbers were tallied and initialled, Churchill House and Hanover moved off first to the showers.

"Never initial anything," said Uncle Arthur, "until you've double-checked personally. Best advice I can give you. I learned that in the Service and it's stood me in good stead ever since." Stripped of their grey overalls, the boys looked even more horribly anonymous, buttocks, pubic hair, feet. I glanced down the line of naked bodies trying not to show my embarrassment and distaste. I looked down at Uncle Arthur's mauve socks in the brown openwork sandals. At the further end of the line, a mutter of conversation was rising. Uncle Arthur's whistle burbled, a sound almost meditative.

"Careful you don't lose your pea, Uncle Arthur," said one of the tallest boys.

All the boys laughed.

"It won't be *me*, lad," said Uncle Arthur, nodding slowly, ponderous work with his eyebrows, "it won't be *me* as'll be losing my pea."

I recognized this as ritual joke.

The laughter grew louder, wilder, ragged at the edges.

Order was restored by a single blast.

He advanced to a position facing the middle of the line.

Into the silence, he said,

"Cleanliness, Mr. Cresswell, as the Good Book says, is next to Godliness. So at Eastmill here it's three showers a day *every* day. We get lads in here that come from home conditions you wouldn't credit. Never had contact with soap and water, some of them. Last time some of this lot touched water was when they was christened. *If* they was christened. *Sewed* into their underclothes, some of them are. And dental decay? Horrible! Turns the stomach, Mr. Cresswell. Athlete's foot. Lice. Scabies and scales. Crabs of all variety. Crabs, Mr. Cresswell, of every stripe and hue."

He surveyed the silent line.

"Start with little things, you see, Mr. Cresswell, because little things lead to big things. That's something that in the Service you *quickly* learn. And talking of *little things*," he bellowed suddenly, his face flushing, "what are *you* trying to hide, lad? *Stand up STRAIGHT!*"

Half turning to me, he said from the side of his mouth,

"A rotten apple if ever I saw one. Attempted rape was the charge. Got off with interference."

I nodded and avoided looking at the boy.

In spite of all the showering, there was a close smell of sweat, feet, sourness.

While Uncle Arthur raked the naked rank with his flushed glare, I made a pretence of reading the mimeographed names on the clipboard. I found myself thinking of the strange civil service gentleman, somehow connected with the Home Office, who'd interviewed me a month earlier.

We like our chaps to have rubbed along a bit with other chaps.

Boxing, eh? The Noble Art, hmm?

Excellent. Excellent.

My role, he had informed me, would be both educational and diagnostic.

Uncle Arthur's keys clinked in the awful silence. He selected one, and the captain of Churchill stepped out of line to receive it. The boy unlocked a metal cupboard and took out a square ten-pound tin and an aluminum dessert spoon.

Upon command, the boys began to file past holding out a cupped hand and Uncle Arthur spooned in grey tooth-powder.

"Better than paste," he confided. "What's paste but powder with the water added?"

The boys were crowding round the racks of tagged toothbrushes, bunching round the six long sinks, dribbling water onto the powder, working it up in their palms with the brushes.

"What about the others?" I said. "The other boys?"

"They'll be at their exercises in the yard with Mr. Austyn. In the quadrangle. Stuart House and Windsor tonight. Anyone who goes on report, you see, the whole House suffers. Ginger them *all* up. Doesn't make the offenders popular. Discourages them as likes to think of themselves as hard cases."

A scuffle was starting around the last sink. The sounds of hawking, gobbing, gargling, were becoming melodramatic.

"Right! Let's have you!" bellowed Uncle Arthur. "Lather yourselves all over paying special attention to all crevices—and no skylarking!"

He turned on the showers and the dank room filled with steam. The pale figures slowly became ghostly, indistinct. Conversation was difficult above the roar of the water.

When the showers were turned off, the boys dried themselves, fixed the soggy towels round their waists, and formed a single line facing the far door. Uncle Arthur unlocked the door and the line advanced. The first boy stopped in front of us, stuck his head forward, contorted his features into a mocking grimace. I stared at him in amazement, fearing for him. Uncle Arthur inspected the exposed teeth and then nodded. Face after snarling face, eyes narrowed or staring, flesh-stretched masks, until the last white towel was starting up the stairs.

"Here's a tip for you just in passing," said Uncle Arthur as he double-locked the door and we followed them up, "a wrinkle, as you might say, that they wouldn't have taught you in the university. Tomorrow, in the morning showers, keep your eyes skinned for any lad as has a tattoo. Right? Then you have a read of his file. Right? Any young offender, as they're now called, any young offender that's got a tattoo, you be on the *qui vive* because sure as the sun shines you've got trouble on your hands. Right?"

I nodded.

"Most particularly," said Uncle Arthur, stopping, puffed by the stairs, "if it says 'Mother.'"

There were forty beds in the dormitory, twenty on each side of the room. On each bed was a single grey blanket. Hanging from the end of each iron-frame bed was a grey cloth drawstring bag. The boys, now in pyjamas, stood at attention at the foot of the beds.

Uncle Arthur surveyed them.

Then nodded.

The boys opened the cloth bags, taking out rolled bundles of *Beano* and *Dandy, Hotspur, Champion,* and *The Wizard.*

"Providing there's no undue noise," said Uncle Arthur, "comics till nine."

I followed him down the sounding stairs and along another blank corridor until he stopped and said,

"Here we are, then—our home away from home."

The Common Room contained six shabby Parker-Knoll armchairs, two coffee tables, and a low bookcase stacked and heaped with pamphlets and old newspapers. In one of the armchairs sat a morose middle-aged man whose spectacles were wrapped at the bridge with a Band-Aid. By the side of his chair stood a wooden crate of beer. He was wearing slippers, his feet stretched out towards the electric fire where imitation flames flickered.

"Mr. Grendle," said Uncle Arthur, "our metal-work teacher. Our new English teacher, Mr. Cresswell."

"How do you do?" I said.

Mr. Grendle did not look up and did not reply.

"Well . . ." said Uncle Arthur.

The yellowing muslin curtains stirred in the breeze.

"Coffee," said Uncle Arthur, "tea," pointing to an electric kettle and some unwashed cups and spoons. "Ale you'll have to organize for yourself."

Mr. Grendle tapped out his pipe on the arm of the chair, swept the ash and dottle onto the floor, wiped his palm on his cardigan.

"Perhaps," said Uncle Arthur, "you'd better come along and see your room, get yourself settled in."

"A scriber!" said Mr. Grendle, staring at the imitation flames. "A scriber in the back. Or battered with a ball-peen hammer. That's how *I'll* end."

As we went out into the fading light of the summer evening, Uncle Arthur said, "Get's a bit low, sometimes, does Henry. Since his accident."

"Accident?"

"Yes," said Uncle Arthur. "That's right. Now this is a view I've *always* been partial to."

We stood looking at the screen of trees, at the long gravel drive which turned down through tended lawns and shrubs to the Porter's Lodge, a single-storey brick building beside the gate in the tall mesh fence which was topped by angled barbed-wire.

Far below us, a man was wandering over the lawns spiking up scraps of paper.

"Often comes out for a constitutional around this time," said Uncle Arthur.

"Pardon?"

"The Old Man."

The figure disappeared behind a clump of rhododendrons.

"Well," said Uncle Arthur, consulting his watch, "no rest for the wicked, as they say. Time for me to relieve Mr. Austyn. Now over *here's* where you are, in the West Building."

My room was featureless. A red printed notice on the inside of the door said: Please Keep This Door Locked At All Times. On the iron-frame bed were two grey blankets. I hung up clothes in the small varnished wardrobe, stacked shirts and underwear in the varnished chest of drawers, stowed the suitcase under the bed. I set my small alarm-clock for six-thirty.

The toilet paper was harsh and stamped with the words: Not For Retail Distribution.

Lying in bed under the tight sheets, I found myself thinking of the boys in the dormitory, found myself wondering if the serials *I'd* read as a boy were still running in the comics, the adventures of Rockfist Rogan, the exploits of Wilson the Amazing Athlete. Was it *Hotspur* or *The Wizard?* I could feel the rough paper, smell the smell of the paper and print. I found myself wondering if the Wolf of Kabul with his lethal cricket-bat bound in brass wire was still haunting the Frontier.

And as I drifted into sleep, I remembered the name of the cricketbat. The Wolf of Kabul. He'd called it "Clickee-baa."

Tick-tock of the clock.

Clickee-baa.

* * *

When I entered the Staff Dining Room next morning with my tray, one of the two men at the long table called, "Do come and join us! Austyn. With a 'Y.' Sports and Geography."

He was tall and boyish, dressed in a white shirt and cricket flannels.

"My name's Cresswell," I said, shaking his hand, "and I'm supposed to be teaching English."

"And my surly colleague," he said, "is Mr. Brotherton. Woodwork."

I nodded.

"You're a university man, I understand?" said Mr. Austyn as I unloaded my tray. "Something of a *rara avis* in Approved School circles."

"Oh, I'm just a novice," I said.

"I, myself," he said, "attended Training College. Dewhurst. In Surrey."

Mr. Brotherton belched.

"Well, look," said Mr. Austyn, rising, draining his cup, consulting his watch in a military manner, "time marches on. I'd better be getting my lads organized. I'll look forward to talking to you later."

I watched him as he walked out. He was wearing white plimsolls. He walked on his toes and seemed almost to bounce.

Mr. Brotherton explored his nose with a grimy handkerchief and then started to split a matchstick with his horny thumbnail.

I drank coffee.

He picked his teeth.

"'I *attended* Training College!'" he said suddenly.

"Pardon?"

"I've 'attended' a symphony concert at the Albert Hall but it doesn't mean I played first sodding violin."

"What do you mean by that?"

"You wouldn't likely think it," he said, getting to his feet and tossing a crumpled paper napkin onto the table, "but I was once a sodding cabinet-maker."

In the quadrangle, the boys, lined up House by House, were standing silent but at ease facing the steps of the North Building. It was five minutes to eight. Uncle Arthur and Mr. Austyn were supervising two House Captains who were positioning on the top step a record-player and two unhoused speakers. Uncle Arthur adjusted the height of the microphone stand. Not knowing what exactly to do, I sat on the low wall by the side of the East Building.

The microphone boomed and whined. One of the House Captains touched the needle of the record-player and a rasp sounded through the speakers. Mr. Grendle hurried out of the East Building bearing large plywood shields. He propped them against the low wall beside me and hurried back into the building. The outer shield said: STUART. A man I hadn't seen before strode up and down the lines rearranging a boy or two here and there to establish an absolute descending order of height.

Uncle Arthur looked at his watch.

He blew a single blast.

In a long shuffle of movement, the boys dressed ranks.

Mr. Austyn said something urgently to Uncle Arthur and Uncle Arthur turned to one of the House Captains, jabbing his finger in my direction.

The boy sprinted towards me.

"Is it these you want?" I said, fumbling together the awkward sliding shields.

"Oh, fucking hell!" said the boy, grabbing them from me, nearly dropping them, bumping me in his urgency.

"Sssssst!" said a voice behind me.

Turning, I saw Mr. Grendle on top of the East Building steps urging me in clenched pantomime to stand at attention.

Mr. Brotherton, his face expressionless, stood sentry on the top step of the South Building.

The whistle shrilled again; the boys stiffened; the shields, HANOVER, STUART, WINDSOR, and CHURCHILL, were steadied by the captains. Mr. Austyn lowered his outstretched arm as though applying a slow-match to a touch-hole. At this signal, the crouching boy lowered the needle onto the record. There was a loud preliminary hissing before the music rolled forth. The awful volume and quality of sound brought to mind fairgrounds and gymkhanas. Uncle Arthur held wide the North Building's heavy door. The brass and massed choir worked their way through "Land of Hope and Glory."

Nothing happened.

The crouching boy put on another record.

The National Anthem blared.

At

Long to reign over us

the shadowed doorway darkened and a large man in a brown suit walked out past Uncle Arthur and stood before the microphone. His chest was massive. He seemed almost without a neck. He was wearing mirrored sunglasses. Stuck at the angle of his jaw was what looked like a small piece of toilet-paper. What could be seen of his face was red and purple.

As the Anthem concluded, the boy lifted off the hissing needle.

Our Father Which Art in Heaven

Hallowed Be Thy Name

said the Headmaster.

And stopped.

The silence extended.

And extended.

Mr. Austyn was quivering at attention.

The Headmaster cleared his throat. The head moved, the mirrored lenses scanning the four ranks.

"If I find a boy," he said slowly, his voice heavy with menace, "*not* pulling together, I'm going to be very sorry for that boy. Very sorry indeed. But not half as sorry as that boy is going to be."

There was another long silence.

He brought out a packet of cigarettes and a box of matches and looked down at them and then put them back in his jacket pocket.

He then buttoned the jacket.

Uncle Arthur moved to his side and the microphone picked up the murmured prompting.

Thy Kingdom Come . . .

"What do you say, Arthur?" boomed the microphone.

The head and torso turned ponderously to the left; he seemed to be staring at the shield that said WINDSOR.

For ever he suddenly said *and ever. Amen* and his brown bulk broke from the microphone and strode past the taut white figure of Mr. Austyn into the shadows of the doorway and disappeared.

Roll-call followed.

Followed by morning showers.

My classroom was less than a quarter the size of a normal classroom and the twenty boys were jammed along the benches. There was somewhere, Uncle Arthur believed, a set of readers. I issued each boy with a sheet of paper and a pencil, and, as I had been instructed by Uncle Arthur, wrote on the blackboard:

When I grow up, I want to—

These papers were to be read by Dr. James, described by Uncle Arthur with a wink and a finger pressed to the side of his nose as "the old trick cyclist."

I watched the boys writing, watched the way the pencils were gripped or clasped. I curbed the use of the wall-mounted pencil-sharpener after a couple of boys had managed to reduce new pencils to one-inch stubs. I denied nine requests to go to the lavatory. At the end of the allotted time, I collected and counted the pencils and glanced through what Uncle Arthur had called the "completions."

They were brief, written in large, wayward script, and violent in spelling. Some of the papers were scored almost through. Deciphered, they expressed the wish "to be pleeceman," "to have big mussels," "to go Home," etc.

One paper was blank except for the name sprawled huge.

"Who's Dennis Thompson?"

A boy put up his hand. He looked about eleven or twelve.

"Why didn't you complete the sentence, Dennis?"

"Well, I don't do writing, do I?"

The accent was south London.

"Why's that?" I said.

"Well, I'm excused, aren't I?"

"Excused?"

Uncle Arthur bustled in. I was to meet the Old Man. Immediately. The boys were left with dire threats. I was hurried through the North Building and out of the rear door. The brown-suited figure was standing some two hundred yards distant with his back to us looking at the vast area given over to garden.

"Word to the wise," puffed Uncle Arthur, laying his hand on my arm, "sets great store, the Old Man does, by being called 'Headmaster.'"

As we drew nearer, Uncle Arthur cleared his throat.

The Headmaster's hand was large and moist.

Uncle Arthur was dismissed.

The Headmaster returned to his contemplation of the large floral bank which spelled out:

EASTMILL RECEPTION CENTRE.

I stood beside him looking at the greyish plants of the lettering, the green and red surrounding stuff.

"The letters," he said, after a long silence, "of the display are Santalima Sage. A hardy perennial."

I nodded.

"The red," he said, pointing, "the green, the contrasting foliage, known as the filler, is called Alternamthera."

I nodded again and said,

"It's extremely impressive, Headmaster."

"A tender annual," he said.

"Pardon?"

"Alternamthera."

"Ah!" I said.

"I am proud of our record here at Eastmill, Mr. Cresswell. In eleven years, *three*—"

The mirrored glasses were turned upon me.

"—only *three* absconders."

I nodded slowly.

"Two," he said, "were caught before they'd gone five miles."

He paused.

"The third was apprehended in Pontypool."

There was a long silence.

We studied the floral display.

Eventually, he cleared his throat in a manner which I took to be a sign that the interview was concluded.

"Thank you, Headmaster," I said.

The long day bore on with three more "completions," lunch supervision, midday roll-call and showers. The cricket match between Windsor and Stuart with twenty boys on each side was interminable. The shepherd's pie and jam-roll with custard weighed upon me. Uncle Arthur seemingly tireless, drove the boys on through the afternoon's hot sun. An occupied boy, he held, was a happy boy. As we stood joint umpires at the crease his public exhortations were punctuated by *sotto voce* asides:

"Don't ponce about, lad! Hit it square!"

Stole a Morris Minor.

"Come on, lad! That's not the spirit that won the war!"

Had half a ton of lead off of a church roof

The game lasted for more than three hours.

After evening meal supervision, roll-call, and evening showers, I settled down in the empty Common Room with the files of those names I'd managed to remember. I'd scarcely got myself arranged, coffee, ashtray, cigarettes, when the door opened and I looked up at a man of about forty who was wearing a blue suit with a Fair Isle pattern pullover.

"Good evening," I said. "My name's Cresswell."

"James," he said, nodding his head almost as if ducking, and then plugged in the electric kettle.

"Not *Dr.* James?"

"Well, not really. It's a Ph.D. You're from a university. I did *try* to explain . . ."

He came over and sat facing me. The blue shoulders were dusted with dandruff. He began to fiddle with a tiny bottle of saccharine tablets, trying to shake out just one.

"I'm about to make a start on your files," I said.

"Were you interviewed by the Home Office?"

"For this job? I'm not sure really. Some sort of civil service character."

"They *all* call me 'Doc,'" he said. "Even the boys."

I watched him trying to funnel saccharine tablets back into the bottle.

"Have you spoken to the Headmaster? Since you've been here?"

"Yes," I said. "This morning."

"Did he by any chance say anything to you about me? In any way?"

"No," I said. "He . . ."

"Or imply anything?"

He started nibbling at his thumbnail.

"No. He didn't say *anything*, really. Just warned me about boys absconding. He seemed to want me to look at his flower-bed-thing. Actually," I said, "he seemed rather *odd*."

"Odd!" said Dr. James. *"Odd!* The Headmaster—"

He got up and went to close the door.

"Files," he said, guiding the boiling water into his mug, "files and expert opinion are obviously the centre of any such organization as this. The heart. The very core."

He looked up, spectacles befogged by steam.

I nodded.

The teaspoon was stuck to the newspaper.

"The Headmaster," he said, "the Headmaster ignores my reports. He rejects all my recommendations. He deliberately undermines the efforts of all my work. Deliberately. And he openly influences the staff against me."

"Why?" I said.

Seating himself again, he took off his spectacles and stared at me with naked eyes.

"There have been countless ugly incidents. He's incapably alcoholic, but of course you must have realized that. And for all this, accountable to no one, of course, we have the Home Office to thank."

"But why would he undermine your... ?"

"Because he perceives me as a threat."

The naked eyes stared at me. He rubbed the spotty spectacles on the Fair Isle pullover.

"Threat in what way?"

"The man has no education whatever beyond elementary school. Yes! Oh, yes! But there's more you should know, Mr.... er..."

"Cresswell," I said.

"For your own protection."

He peered again towards the door.

"Before he became Headmaster, he was employed—I have access to the files—the man was employed by the City of Eastmill—"

He bent his head and hooked the springy wire side-pieces of the spectacles around the curves of his ears and looked up again.

"—employed as a *municipal gardener*."

"No!" I said.

He nodded.

"But how on earth..."

"Ask our masters at the Home Office."

"Good God!" I said.

He carried the mug of coffee to the door.

"Mention to no one," he said, "that we have spoken."

I settled down to read.

The files contained condensed case histories, I.Q. scores, vocabulary scores, reports from previous schools, reports from social workers and probation officers, family profiles, anecdotal records, recommendations. The files were depressingly similar.

Thompson, Dennis.

I remembered him, the London boy from the morning who'd claimed to be excused from writing, the waif's face, the dark lively eyes. Fifteen years of age. According to the scores he'd received in the *Wechsler-Bellevue, Stanford and Binet, Terman and Merrill,* etc., his achievements and intelligence were close to non-existent. His crime was arson. Three derelict row-houses in Penge had been gutted before the flames had been brought under control.

He claimed not to know why he had done it.

He said he liked fires.

* * *

I soon lost my nervousness of these boys under my charge. As the days passed, I stopped seeing them as exponents of theft, rape, breaking and entering, arson, vandalism, grievous bodily harm, and extortion, and saw them for what they were-working-class boys who were all, without exception, of low average intelligence or mildly retarded.

We laboured on with phonics, handwriting, spelling, reading.

Of all the boys, I was most drawn to Dennis. He was much like all the rest but unfailingly cheerful and co-operative. Dennis could chant the alphabet from A to Z without faltering, but he had to start at A. His mind was active, but the connections it made were singular.

If I wrote CAT, he would stare at the word with a troubled frown. When I sounded out C-A-T, he would say indignantly: Well, it's *cat,* innit? We had a cat, old tom-cat. Furry knackers, he had, and if you stroked 'em ...

F-I-S-H brought to mind the chip shop up his street and his mum who wouldn't never touch rock salmon because it wasn't nothing but a fancy name for conger-eel.

C-O-W evoked his Auntie Fran-right old scrubber *she* was, having it away for the price of a pint ...

Such remarks would spill over into general debate on the ethics of white women having it off with spades and Pakis, they was heathen, wasn't they? Said their prayers to gods and that, didn't they? *Didn't* they? Well, there you are then. *And* their houses stank of curry and that. You couldn't deny it. Not if you knew what you was talking about.

These lunatic discussions were often resolved by Paul, Dennis's friend, who commanded the respect of all the boys because he was serving a second term and had a tattoo of a dagger on his left wrist and a red and green hummingbird on his right shoulder. He would make pronouncement:

I'm not saying that they are and I'm not saying that they're not but what I *am* saying is ...

Then would follow some statement so bizarre or so richly irrelevant that it imposed stunned silence.

He would then re-comb his hair.

Into the silence, I would say,

"Right. Let's get back to work, then. Who can tell me what a vowel is?"

Dennis's hand.

"It's what me dad 'ad."

"What!"

"It's your insides."

"What is?"

"Cancer of the vowel."

The long summer days settled into endless routine. The violent strangeness of everything soon became familiar chore. Uncle Arthur left me more and more on my own. Showers and the inspection of teeth. Meal supervision. Sports and Activities. Dormitory patrol.

The morning appearances of the Headmaster were predictably unpredictable. The Lord's Prayer was interspersed with outbursts about what would happen if boys did not pull their weight, the excessive use of toilet-paper, an incoherent homily concerning the flotilla of small craft which had effected the strategic withdrawal of the British Army from Dunkirk, and, concerning departures from routine, detailed aphasic instructions.

Every afternoon was given over to Sports and Activities.

Cricket alternated, by Houses, with gardening. Gardening was worse than cricket. The garden extended for roughly two acres. On one day, forty boys attacked the earth with hoes. The next day forty boys smoothed the work of the hoes with rakes. On the day following, the hoes attacked again. Nothing was actually planted.

The evening meals in the Staff Dining Room, served from huge aluminum utensils, were exactly like the school dinner of my childhood: unsavoury stews with glutinous dumplings, salads with wafers of cold roast beef with bits of string in them, jam tarts and Spotted Dick accompanied by an aluminum jug of lukewarm custard topped by a thickening skin.

Uncle Arthur always ate in his apartment with the wife referred to as "Mrs. Arthur" but always appeared in time for coffee to inquire if we'd enjoyed what he always called our "comestibles." Mr. Austyn, referred to by the boys as "Browner Austyn," always said:

May I trouble you for the condiments?

Between the main course and dessert, Mr. Brotherton, often boisterously drunk, beat time with his spoon, singing, much to the distress of Mr. Austyn:

Auntie Mary
Had a canary
Up the leg of her drawers.

Mr. Grendle drizzled on about recidivists and the inevitability of his being dispatched in the metal-work shop. Mr. Hemmings, who drove a sports car, explained the internal-combustion engine. Mr. Austyn praised the give and take of sporting activity, the lessons of co-operation and joint endeavour, The Duke of Edinburgh's Awards, Outward Bound, the beneficial moral results of pushing oneself to the limits of physical endurance.

But conversation always reverted to pay scales, overtime rates, the necessity of making an example of this boy or that, of sorting out, gingering up, knocking the stuffing out of etc. this or that young lout who was trying it on, pushing his luck, just begging for it etc.

The days seemed to be growing longer and hotter; clouds loomed sometimes in the electric evenings promising the relief of rain but no rain fell. The garden had turned to grey dust; cricket-balls rose viciously from patches of bald earth. Someone stole tobacco; there was a fight in the South Building dormitory. Comprehension declined; pencils broke. Showerings and the cleaning of teeth measured out each day.

One afternoon at the end of my fifth week, I was in charge of thirteen boys, seven having been commandeered by Mr. Grendle to do something or other to his forge. At the shrill of my whistle, the boys halted outside Mr. Ausryn's shed while I drew and signed for the necessary cricket gear.

I unlocked the gate in the wire-mesh fence, locked it behind us. The cricket bag was unpacked; two boys were detailed to hammer in the stumps. The rest stood in a listless group grumbling about bleeding sunstroke and bleeding running about all bleeding afternoon for bleeding nothing.

There were only three bails; I had signed for four, had watched them go into the bag.

"Bail?" repeated a boy in vacant tone.

"What's he mean, 'bail?'" said another voice.

"It's money what you have to pay to get out the nick."

"You stupid berk!" said another voice.

The laughter grew louder, jeering.

I shrilled on the whistle, confronted them.

"I will give you," I said, "precisely five seconds to produce the missing bail."

"What's he going on about?"

"If the bail," I said, "is *not* produced . . ."

A flat voice said,

"Oh fuck the fucking bail."

Lunging, I grabbed a handful of the nearest denim, swung the boy off his feet. He fell on one knee. I jolted him backwards and forwards ranting at him, at them.

"Sir!"

Dennis's voice penetrated.

"'Ere! Sir!"

The boy fell slack; he was making noises.

My hand was like a claw.

I wandered away from them, crossing the limed line of the boundary, and sat waiting for my heart to stop the thick hammering. The close-mown grass was parched and yellow. Beyond the mesh fence yards in from of me were thick woods a quarter of a mile deep before the beginning of the houses of the East Point subdivision. In the afternoon heat the trees were still. I watched the unmistakable dance of Speckled Wood butterflies over the brambles, dead leaves, and leaf-mould at the wood's dappled edge. As a child, I'd chased them with my green muslin net. I stared beyond them into the darkening, layered shade.

Time had passed without my noticing. The missing bail had appeared; the game had got under way without the usual squabbling; was now winding down to a merely formal show of activity.

Dennis wandered over and in a pretence of fielding, crouched down a few yards away from me.

"It's all right, Dennis," I said.

He nodded. He sat down.

"It's all right," I said again.

Soon all the boys were sprawled in the grass.

"Wish we could play in there," said Dennis, staring into the woods.

I lay back and closed my eye listening to their voices.

You could make a house in a tree like on the telly. That family. They had this house . . .

You haven't got no hammer and you haven't got no nails. And you haven't got no bits of old wood neither.

What about Tarzan, then? He didn't have no hammer neither.

Red suns behind my closed eyelids glowed and faded.

'Ere! Know what I'd be doing right now if I was Tarzan? Do you? I'd be having a bunk-up, having a crafty one with Jane.

Get lost! With a face like yours, wanker, you'd be lucky to cop a feel off his bleeding monkey.

I sat up and forced the key around the double ring until it was free. I tossed it to Dennis.

"Be back here," I said, "in one hour. Understand?"

As I lay back in the grass, I heard their yells and laughter, the sounds of their passage through the undergrowth, sounds which grew fainter. Later, a thrush started singing.

At three o'clock, I walked back towards the four main buildings.

* * *

Well, even that, I suppose, could do as an ending.

Of sorts.

Lacking in drama, some might say.

Pastel colours. Too traditional.

I know all about that.

. . . marred in its conclusion by an inability to transcend the stylistic manner of his earlier work . . .

If I were interested in finishing this story, in cobbling it up into something a bit more robust, it's here that I ought to shape the thing towards what would be, in effect, a *second* climax and denouement. It's at this point that I should make slightly more explicit the ideas which have been implicit in the detail and narrative matter, treating them not baldly *as ideas*, of course, but embodying them, in the approved manner, in incident. (As a story-writer, I'm concerned, needless to say, with feelings, with moving you emotionally, not sermonizing.) And what is it exactly, then, that I would wish to emerge a touch more explicitly were I interested in rounding the story off for your entertainment? Certainly nothing intellectually stunning. Platitudes, some might say. That the guard is as much a prisoner as those he guards; that the desire to conform, to fulfill a role, distorts and corrupts; perhaps, to extend this last, that the seeds of Dachau and Belsen are dormant within us all.

And how, in the approved manner, might I have effected these ends? Dramatically, perhaps. A confrontation with the deranged Headmaster, the mirrored sunglasses worn even in his dim room, the venetian blinds permanently shuttered.

David and Goliath.

Or, more obliquely, affectingly, by an encounter at a later date with the recaptured Dennis.

Simple enough to do.

But I can't be bothered.

It was while I was writing this story that something happened which disturbed me, which made the task of writing not only tedious but offensive.

What happened was this.

It was Open Evening at the public school my son and daughter attend. My wife and I dutifully turned out, watched the entertainment provided, the thumping gymnastics, the incomprehensible play written and performed by the kids in Grade Seven, renditions by the choir, two trios, a quartet, and the ukulele ensemble. We then inspected our children's grubby exercise books which we see every day anyway, admired the Easter decorations, cardboard rabbit-shapes with glued-on absorbent-cotton tails etc. Smiled and chatted to their teachers. A necessary evening of unrelieved dreariness.

And driving back home along the dark country roads replying to my children's back-seat interrogation—Which did you like best? The gymnastics? The choir? What about the play? Wasn't the play funny?—and assuring my wife that I wasn't driving too fast, that the road wasn't icy, I passed the township dump. The dump was on fire. I looked down on the scene for only a few seconds. Twisting above the red heart of the fire, yellow tongues of flame. In the light thrown by the flames, grey smoke piling up to merge with the darkness of the night. Two figures. And high in the night sky, a few singing sparks. Then the sight was gone.

At that moment, my heart filled with a kind of—it's a strange word to use, perhaps, almost embarrassing, but I *will* say it—filled with a kind of *joy*.

What disturbed me, upset me, was that the feeling was so violent, so total. No. No, that's not what upset me. In the aftermath of that feeling, what upset me was its *strangeness*, the realization that I'd felt nothing like it for so many years.

Since then, and during the time I've been trying to finish up this story, I've been thinking about Dennis, for there *was* a Dennis, though I have no idea now what his name was. Let's call him Dennis and be done with it. Those events, in so far as they're at all autobiographical, happened more than twenty years ago in a country which is foreign to me now. So. Dennis. I've been thinking about him. And me.

And the vision of fire at night.

Fire at night seen through winter trees.

Drifting into sleep or lying half-awake, I picture fire. And I'm filled with an envious longing. Though I ought to qualify "envious." As I qualify most things. This isn't making much sense, is it? But listen. This is difficult for me, too. I want to make clear, you see, that I'm in no way romanticizing Dennis. I think that's important.

I know his life quite intimately. Much to my parents' distress, I admired his local counterparts and played with them for much of my childhood. I can imagine the pacifier smeared with Tate and Lyle's Golden Syrup when he was a baby, the late and irregular hours as an infant. On the casually wiped oilcloth of the kitchen table, the buns with sticky white icing and the cluster of pop bottles. I can imagine him and his brother and sister like a litter of hot-bellied puppies squabbling, gorging, sleeping where they dropped oblivious to the constant blare of the TV and radio. I can see his sister, off to school in a party frock, his snot-blocked brother with the permanent stye. And as Dennis grew a little older, ragtag games that surged in the surrounding streets till long past dusk.

I know his mother, warm and generous but too busy and always too tired. Too soft with him, too, after his father died. Not a stupid woman but slow and easy-going. I can see her dressing herself up on Friday nights in a parody of her youth, a few too many at the local, and after the death of her husband, consoling herself with a succession of uncles who'd give Dennis a couple of bob to go to the pictures to get him out of the way.

And then the drift into playing where one should not play, railway-yards perhaps, bouncing on the lumber in timberyards, the pleasures of being chased. And as the world of school closed against him—hand-me-downs, incomprehension, hot tears in the school lavatories—the more aggressive acts. Street lights shot out, bricks through windows, feuds in the parks, and running stone-fights with rival gangs across the bomb-sites where willow herb still grew. Webley air-pistols, sheath knives, an accident involving stitches. Shoplifting in Woolworth's. Padlocks splintered from a shed. And edging towards the adult world, packets of *Weights* and *Woodbines* bought in fives, beer supplied by laughing older brothers, and, queasily, the girl up his street they all had, the girl from the special school.

And, years past the year I knew him, I can see him in the pub he's made his local, dressed to kill, his worldly wealth his wardrobe, dangerous with that bristling code of honour which demands satisfaction outside of those whose eyes dare more than glance . . .

No. I'm not romanticizing Dennis.

I wonder what became of him. Did he become a labourer perhaps? Carrying a hod "on the buildings," as he'd say? Or is he one of an anonymous tide flowing in through factory gates? Difficult to imagine the Dennis I knew settling down to that kind of grind. More probably he's on unemployment or doing time for some bungled piece of breaking and entering.

Dennis.

I *did* see Dennis again after I'd left the Approved School that afternoon. I saw him after he'd been recaptured. I know I'm not organizing this very well. It's difficult for me to say what I want to say.

It happened like this. I'd got another job in Eastmill almost immediately in a Secondary Modern School. Dr. James—let's call him that anyway—got the information from my parents, whose address was on the application I'd filed at the Reception Centre. He phoned me at the school and told me that Dennis had been caught in London, had been held down naked over a table by Uncle Arthur and Mr. Austyn and savagely birched by our friend in the sunglasses, was in the Eastmill Sick Bay, was feverish, and kept on asking for me. Dr. James, with considerable bravery given his personality and circumstances, smuggled me in one evening to see the boy. He was obviously in pain, his face gaunt, the eyes big and shadowed, but he smiled to see me and undid his pyjama jacket carefully, slowly, lifting it aside to show me his chest. His brother, the one in the army who'd been home on leave, had paid for it. It was just possible to distinguish the outlines of a sailing ship through the crust of red and blue and green, the whole mess raised, heaving, cracking in furry scabs.

I can't remember what we said. I do remember the way he undid the jacket as though uncovering an icon and the tremendous heat his infected chest gave off.

This incident, now I come to think about it, would have made a suitable ending to the story. Touching. The suggestion of a kind of victory, however limited, over the force of evil. David and Goliath. Readers like that sort of thing. But it would have been a sentimental lie.

Dennis was no hero. He was a bloody nuisance then and he's doubtless a bloody nuisance now. And the staff of that school weren't evil, though at one time, my mind clouded by the prating of A.S. Neil and such, I doubtless thought so. They were merely stupid. Their answer to the problem of Dennis was crude, but it was at least an answer. I just don't *know* any more. Time and experience seem to have stripped me of answers.

My life has been what most people would call "successful." I have a respected career. My opinions on this and that are occasionally sought. Sometimes I have been asked to address conventions. I love *my* wife. I love my children. I live a pleasant life in a pleasant house.

What, then, is the problem?

Fire at night seen through the forms of winter trees.

That is the problem.

You see, what I'm trying to get at, Dennis, is this. They told you all your life, the Wechsler-Bellevue merchants, the teachers, the guardians of culture, and, yes, me, I suppose, that you were wrong, stupid, headed for a bad end. But you had something, *knew* something they didn't. Something *I* didn't. Do you see now why it's so important for me to stress that I'm not romanticizing your life, Dennis, or the lives of the ignorant yobs and louts who were your friends? You can't even begin to grasp how appalling it is for me to attempt to say this. Say what? That my life, respectable, sober, industrious, and civilized, above all civilized, has at its core a desolating emptiness. That, quite simply, you in your stupid, feckless way have enjoyed life more than I have.

I've never escaped, you see, Dennis. I've never lived off hostile country.

Did you burn down houses in Penge? I don't know, can't remember if I invented that. But if you *did,* the blood gorging you with excitement, the smoke, the roar as the whole thing got a grip—I can hardly bring myself to say this, *must* say this—if you did, *Christ!* it must have been wonderful.

You don't understand, do you, what it means for me to make these confessions? To *have* to make these confessions, to face the death I feel inside myself?

Let me try to put this in a different way. Let me try to find words that perhaps you'll understand. Words! Understand! Good Christ, will it never end, this blathering!

Dennis. Dennis. Listen!

Dennis, I envy you your—

Christ, man! Out with it!

Dennis. Listen to me.

Concentrate.

Dennis, I wish *I* had a tattoo.

GENTLE AS FLOWERS MAKE THE STONES

FISTS, teeth clenched, Jim Haine stood naked and shivering staring at the lighted rectangle. He must have slept through the first knocks, the calling. Even the buzzing of the doorbell had made them nervous; he'd had to wad it up with paper days before. The pounding and shouting continued. The male was beginning to dart through the trails between the *Aponogeton crispus* and the blades of the *Echinodorus martii*.

Above the pounding, words: "pass-key," "furniture," "bailiffs."

Lackey!

Lickspittle!

The female was losing colour rapidly. She'd shaken off the feeding fry and was diving and pancaking through the weed-trails.

Hour after hour he had watched the two fish cleaning one of the blades of a Sword plant, watched their ritual procession, watched the female dotting the pearly eggs in rows up the length of the leaf, the milt-shedding male following; slow, solemn, seeming to move without motion, like carved galleons or bright painted rocking-horses.

The first eggs had turned grey, broken down to flocculent slime; the second hatch, despite copper sulphate and the addition of peat extracts, had simply died.

"I know you're in there, Mr. Haine!"

A renewed burst of doorknob rattling.

He had watched the parents fanning the eggs; watched them stand guard. Nightly, during the hatch, he had watched the parents transport the jelly blobs to new hiding places, watched them spitting the blobs onto the underside of leaves to hang glued and wriggling. He had watched the fry become free-swimming, discover the flat sides of their parents, wriggle and feed there from the mucous secretions.

"Tomorrow... hands of our lawyers!"

The shouting and vibration stopped too late.

The frenzied Discus had turned on the fry, snapping, engulfing, beaking through their brood.

A sheet of paper slid beneath the door.

He didn't stay to watch the carnage; the flash of the turning fish, the litter floating across the surface of the tank, the tiny commas drifting towards the suction of the filter's mouth.

He went back into his bedroom and worked himself into the sleeping bag. Four more weeks and they would have lost their tadpole look, growing towards their maturity, becoming disc-shaped.

He studied the All-Island Realties notice. Nasty print. Two months rent: $72.50 per month; $145.00. And two more months before he could apply for the last third of his Arts Bursary. He reached for the largest butt and, staring into the flame of the match, considered his position. A change of abode was indicated. And preferably by evening.

Taking his night-pencil, his Granby Zoo pencil with animal-head pictures, he wrote on the back of the notice *God Rend You, All Island Realties*. And then doodled. And then found himself writing out again from memory what he had completed the day before.

Into your hands, my father and my mother, I commend
My darling and delight, my little girl,
Lest she be frightened by the sudden dark
Or the terrible teeth of the dog who guards your world.

"Your world" was exactly right. No use in fucking about with "Hades" or "Tartarus."

Parvula ne nigras horrescat Erotion umbras
Oraque Tartarei prodigiosa canis.

"Sudden dark" wasn't bad, either.

There was a sense of rightness, too, in dividing the sentences of the original into stanzas.

The night had produced no advances on stanza two.

She would have been but six cold winters old if she had lived
Even those few days more;

That could stand. But

Inter tam veteres ludat lasciva patronos.... "Patronos," that was the bugger. "Protectors" was impossible; "guardians" too custodial. Something grave was needed, grave yet tender.

"veteres patronos"

His pencil worked loops and curlicues on the paper.

The muffled phone in the kitchen rang twice, stopped, rang again. Pulling on his jeans, he went to answer it.

"Jim? It's Jackie, man."

Jackie's voice dropped to a whisper.

"The Desert Express Is In."

"Good shit?" said Jim.

"Up a tree—you know? A real mindfuck, man."

"Far out," said Jim.

"Hey, and that Gold, man. What a taste! Two tokes and you're wasted!"

"Tonight, man," said Jim.

He hung up the phone and sighed.

"veteres patronos"

veteres patronos

His possessions, by design, fitted into two large cardboard cartons. Kettle and mug. Sleeping bag and inflatable mattress. Clothes. One picture. Writing materials. An alarm dock. The few books he had not sold.

He stirred the coffee and Coffeemate together and wandered into the front room. On the table there lay the medium felt pen, the fine, and the fountain pen. Beside them, the three pads of paper, white, yellow, and pale blue, the porcelain ashtray, the square of blotting paper, the Edwardian silver matchbox.

He sat at the table drinking the coffee. He tried to visualize the three stanzas of the completed poem on the page. He'd have to supply a title; and at the end, in brackets, "The poet commends the soul of a pet slave girl to his parents who are already in the lower world. Adapted from Martial. *Epigrams. Book V. 34.*" Less distracting than under the title.

"veteres patronos"

He stared at the aquarium; had only a half of the fry survived a little half of all his pretty ones—growing to the size of a dime, a quarter, a silver dollar, he could have sold them through Réal to Ideal Import Aquariums for twelve to fifteen dollars each.

With the medium felt pen on white paper he wrote:

Sixty *Symphysodon discus* at a conservative $12.00 = $720.00
Minus $25.00 for the tank
$10.00 for the pump and filter
$30.00 for the breeding fish
$15.00 for weed, tubifex worm, whiteworm, brine shrimp, and *daphnia*.

An inevitable profit of $640.00.

Work was impossible.

He needed money; he needed a place to live.

He began packing his belongings into the two cartons. The $3,500 of his Canada Council grant eroded by child-support payments, eroded by the cling of old habits. He would have to abandon the aquarium and hope that Réal could get it out.

The last of the air from the mattress.

Pevensey!

Pevensey might be good for a $30.00 review. Maybe even $60.00 for a round-up. If he could be trapped. He rolled the mattress and sleeping bag brooding about the toadish Pevensey. Who had promised to review *The Distance Travelled* and lied.

Lack of space, old boy. Hands were tied.

In his Toad-of-Toad's-Hall tweeds and deerstalker.

In his moustache.

Who weekly reviewed *English Formal Gardens of the Eighteenth Century* or *The Rose Grower's Vade Mecum*, toadish Memoirs of endless toadish Generals.

Opening the freezer compartment of the fridge, he took out the perspex map-case which contained his completed poems and work sheets and wiped off the condensation; he kept them there in case of fire.

The kipper and the cardboard cup of Bar-B-Q Sauce he would leave to All-Island Realties as quit claim and compensation.

"Montreal *Herald*," said the girl. "Entertainments."

"Charles Pevensey, please."

"I'm sorry. He's not in this morning."

"Oh. That's strange. I'd understood he's been trying to contact me. Something about the length of my review."

"Oh," said the girl. "I see. Well, he might be in later. If you could call back at about eleven?"

Could one, he wondered, "beard" a toad?

Hefting his Air Canada bag, he stood looking around the bare white room. He'd shift the cartons after nightfall. The picture. The sleeping bag would protect it.

A potato-shape in black crayon. A single red eye near the top. Seven orange sprouts. He'd typed underneath:

"Daddy" by Anna Haine (age 2½)

The newsprint was yellowing, the expensive non-glare glass dusty; the top edge of the frame was furred. He wiped it clean with his forefinger.

Orange arms and legs of course, silly Jim.

He tried to recall the name of the girl who'd got it framed for him. A painter sort of girl. Black hair, he remembered.

Frances?

Sonia?

But it was gone.

* * *

The Montreal *Herald* building reared concrete and glass. As he walked along towards the main entrance, past the emporia of used office-furniture, the pawn shops, the slum side streets, he wondered, as he often wondered, why he always had a compulsion to lie about his occupation to the people who gave him lifts; why he claimed to be a professor at McGill, a male nurse, a pest-control officer, a journalist.

The escalator conveyed him to the potted palms of Third Floor Reception, the elevator to the Fourth. Below him on the first and second floors, the giant drums and rollers of the *Herald* presses. He smiled at the memory of a wrench-brandishing Charlie Chaplin swimming through the cogs. He turned down the corridor to Entertainments and pushing through the swing doors, walked up the aisle between the desks to Pevensey's corner. The desk was piled with review copies, a hundred more stacked in the window embrasure behind.

He stood irresolute for a few moments and then went into the pen and sat in Pevensey's chair. The clattering typewriters paid no attention. Opposite, on the other side of the room, he noticed another set of swing doors. Glass portholes. He glanced at the top copy-sheet in the folder; a review of *Heraldry and You.* He took three cigarettes from the open package on the desk.

A tall blonde girl was walking up the aisle, looked about twenty, shoulder bag, shades. Legs too thin. She went into the next pen and dropped her bag on the desk. A plaque on the desk said Youth Beat. Her typewriter cover was dotted with stick-on flowers and butterflies. He felt her staring at him.

"Excuse me, sir."

"Umm?"

"Are you looking for someone?"

"What an attractive pendant!" he said, staring at her breasts.

"Oh, thank you."

He turned back to the file of copy.

"Excuse me..."

He did his blank look.

"If you're waiting for Mr. Pevensey, I'm afraid..."

"Mr. Pevensey!" called Jim.

A tactical blunder.

Pevensey, what looked like a teapot in his hand, glanced, pushed back through the swing doors, disappeared. Jim hurried after him.

"Mr. Pevensey!" he shouted to the echo of the footsteps on the concrete stairs. He ran down and found himself in an empty corridor facing two doors.

"PEV-EN-SEY."

One door led to the cafeteria, the other to the library. The cafeteria was nearly empty; the library girl claimed not to know who Pevensey was. He walked back up the corridor, past the foot of the stairs, found a washroom. Locking himself into a cubicle, he took the Magic Marker from his Air Canada bag and wrote on the wall:

"Charles Pevensey has a PERSONAL subscription to *Reader's Digest*."

He lowered his trousers and sat.

He needed money.

He needed breakfast.

He needed a place to live.

A downtown breakfast would be more expensive than the Budapest where he usually ate; he liked the Budapest because George, the owner, had gold teeth and always said, "For you, gentlemans?" Today, he decided, would have to be a toast day.

Toast reminded him that it was Monday. He added a note to his list:

Cantor's Bakery 11:30 PM (if poss.).

The woman there sold him Friday's Kaiser rolls for two cents each. He also needed more tins of Brunswick sardines. Holding steady at twenty-nine cents a tin.

Moving upset him. And he was fond of the Victoria Manor Apartments. He would miss the conversations with Mrs. McGregor who gave him milk and who, on the day he'd moved in six months or so ago, had slipped a note under his door which read:

> They are all FLQ in this building. Signed:
> the Lady Next Door. (Scottish)

And Bernie who ran the FCI Detective Agency on the first floor. He'd miss the stairways which were always jammed with struggling furniture; the conversations with the basement owner of the Harold Quinn School of Music; the showcase outside the Starkman Orthopedic Shoe Company which was full of plaster casts of deformed feet.

The rest of the list read:

Call Réal.

Call McCready.

Night of the Jewish Ladies.

Staying with Myrna would be impossible; she'd want to screw all the time which was wasteful and irritating when he was nearing a possible form. Alan was still shacked up with the Bell Telephone girl.

Carol?

He remembered the last time he'd been forced to use her place. No. Not even for a few days could he live in the maelstrom of *her* emotional life. He remembered how, at her last gasp, she'd sobbed a stanza of Sylvia Plath. Nor, come to think of it, could he stomach her brown rice with bits in, wheat germ salad, and other organic filth. And he definitely wasn't inclined to endure lectures on the power of Sisterhood and the glories of multiple clitoral orgasm.

Remembering a glimpse of her naked in the bathroom, one foot on the rim of the tub, thigh, hip, the creases of her waist suffused in morning sunlight. Pure Bonnard stuff. Painter's work. He wondered if she still brushed her teeth with twigs, still washed her hair with honey.

He strained and grunted.

veteres patronos

He was being too literal. Again. He needed to get further from the text. To preserve. Intact. The main line of. Intent. But let. The.

The outer door banged shut; the bolt of the next cubicle slotted home. Checkered trousers rumpled over a pair of brown shoes.

Inter tam veteres ludat lasciva patronos
Et nomen blaeso garriat ore meum.

"Care!" said Jim.

The brown shoes cleared his throat.

Yes.
Expand it.

She would have been but six cold winters old if she had lived
Even those few days more; so let her walk
And run a child still in your elder care

"You beautiful, inevitable bastard!" said Jim.
"Are you okay?" said the brown shoes.
"What?"

* * *

Breakfasted on toast and coffee (twenty-five cents) now 12:35 and his guts hollow. Used the counter phone. Professor McCready was teaching; would he care to leave a message? The white globes above the length of the counter reminded him of a night scene. A cafe. A woman singing. Degas? Renoir?

Just beyond, in that place between night and twilight, not to be pried at, not to be forced, the words were moving in his head.

He walked up towards Dorchester and the Queen Elizabeth Hotel weighing his chances in the lottery of grant renewal. His other two references were certain to be good. He'd sent McCready a Xerox of the central poems of *Marriage Suite* now nine days ago along with the Letter of Reference form. Sixteen days to the deadline.

He strolled into the foyer of the Queen Elizabeth and wandered around looking for the notice board. Conventions, Annual Meetings, Associations of. Sometimes, wearing shirt and tie, under buffet conditions, it was possible to lunch or dine with Travel Agents, Furniture Retailers, Pharmaceutical Sales.

In the hardcover Classic Book Store on St. Catherine Street, he checked the number of copies of *The Distance Travelled*, arranged them more advantageously. He was classified under "Canadiana" and surrounded by Esquimaux and whales.

He strolled back on the other side of the street to the paperback store and browsed through the literary magazines, off-set and mimeo, looking for work by his contemporaries. *Edifice, Now, Ssip*, another new thing from Vancouver called *Up Yours.*

He walked up to the Sheraton and consulted the notice board; looked in at Mansfield Book Mart; checked the Sonesta Hotel.

The same girl answered the phone again. Professor McCready had just left for the day; would he care to leave a message?

Ten cents.

He copied down McCready's home number from the directory.

Academe—Intercede for us

Standing closed in the phone booth, he stared out at the flow of cars along Sherbrooke.

Jury of Experts—Compassionately Adjudicate us

Significance of Past Contribution—*Justify us*

Selling the drugs for Jackie would probably bring him $40.00 or $50.00 but he resented the waste of time, the endless phone calls.

The Desert Express Is in.

Poor glazed bastard.

He wondered what peyote looked like; what one *did* with it? Smoked it? Made an infusion? Ate it? He went back towards Classics to find out. For all he cared, they could stuff it up their collective fundament. As he walked along, he constructed arguments:

Look, man. You've dropped acid. You've done chemicals. Okay. But this is pure, it's like ORGANIC.

Or, for the carriage trade,

It's like acid, but SMOOTH. It's the difference between a bottle of Brights and a bottle of wine.

In Classics he gleaned the necessary sales information. You ate it.

Devotees of the cactus cult are said to be "following the Peyote Road"—he copied the expression into his notebook. The practice had spread from Mexico to the Kiowa, Comanche, and Apache Indians. Ingestion put one in touch with *mana*—the LIFE FORCE. Introspection resulted. Visions of God, Jesus, and those on the Other Side were vouchsafed.

The prospect of being forced to stay with Jackie was depressing. In the gloom of obligatory candles he would have to listen to the latest fragment of Jackie's novel—the action of which all took place in Jackie's head during a seven hour freak-out on top of Mount Royal and involved him in varieties of Cosmic Union with stars, planets, and a bi-sexual Cree Guide called Big Bear.

And he, in turn, would have to pay tribute by giving Jackie a copy of his latest verse. He'd already chopped *Howl* into tiny sections. He considered Gerard Manley Hopkins.

O the mind
MIND
has mountains
   cliffs
   of
   fall
   SHEER
nomanfathomed.

It's like a lyric, man. They write themselves.

He resolved to call Carol.

For an hour or more, he stood watching the work on a construction site on Dorchester. He watched the tamping of the dynamite in the rock, watched the crane swing the coir nets and matting into place, waited for the dull *crump* and the heave of the matting and then the buckets grubbing out the boulders and the scree. He could feel the words edging closer. He watched until he no longer saw the yellow helmets, the clanking bulldozers, the trucks churning up the muddy slope, until his eyes grew unfocused.

The end of the afternoon was growing cold. The words hurried him across the approach of the Place du Canada where the wind was clacking the wire halyards against the aluminum flagpoles.

He found an empty table at the back of the Steerarama and sat warming his hands on the coffee cup. Shapes of figures passing beyond the net-curtained windows. Light on the chrome of the cash register. A sheen of light across the polished lino below the cash register, a green square, a red square, part of a green square before the carpet edge.

Et nomen blaeso garriat ore meum.

The horns were long, buffed and lacquered, the colours running from grey through beige to jet at the points. From the astrakhan middle where the horns were joined hung a card which read:

Our "Famous" Steerburger (6 oz. of Prime Beef)

As he tilted his head, the light ran the horns' curved length.

blaeso garriat demanded "lisping," "stammering."

The gloss had given him: "And lisp my name with stammering tongue."

Which made the child sound like a cross between a halfwit and Shirley Temple.

"lisping"

"prattle"

"babble"

He stared at the cinnamon Danish in the glass case on the counter. But the Night of the Jewish Ladies had promised refreshments.

Although a bending of the text, a real distortion of meaning even, and swaying on a tightrope over sentimentality, "baby talk" might.

Might.

If it was somehow balanced off.

He smoothed the paper place mat with the edge of his hand and sat staring at the drawing of the smiling waitress.

Bienvenue

He gave her spectacles, a moustache, gaps in her teeth. Suddenly he started to write.

She would have been but six cold winters old if she had
lived
Even those few days more; so let her walk
And run a child still in your elder care
And safely play, and tease you with my name in baby talk.

Nodding at what he'd written, he stretched and leaned back. Everything depended now on the resolution of the final stanza. Blondin poised over Niagara had little on this. Lips working, he read the lines through again and again.

Precarious.

The *ands* repetition wasn't bad, wasn't *too* obtrusive in its suggestion of the child. But it was the tension in "tease"; it was only "tease" and its implications that were keeping him aloft.

He found that he was gazing at the cinnamon Danish; he wanted the cinnamon Danish very much. He could feel the pressure of the final stanza, the bulge and push of it in his head. The hunger had turned to hollow pain. Half an hour to his meeting Mrs. Wise on the mezzanine in her russet linen pant suit and carrying a copy of the Montreal *Herald*. A group of young wives, she'd said, meeting in each other' houses, quite informally, to discuss, to listen to speakers, to be stimulated, to broaden horizons.

Now you mustn't be modest, Mr. Haine. Quite a few of the girls saw your photograph and the piece about you in the Gazette.

He hoped they'd pay him the $25.00 after the reading and not at some polite interval; he hoped it was sandwiches and not cakes. Sandwiches with meat in.

Or egg.

Or cheese.

He felt an urge to delete the inverted commas on the *Our "Famous" Steerburger* sign with his Magic Marker.

He hoped that payment would be made in cash.

The last time had been cakes.

Seventeen members of the Canadian Authors' Association had gathered in a salon of the Laurentian Hotel. The president had asked everyone to stand one after another to announce their names. Most were hyphenated ladies.

Against their rising conversation, he had read from *The Distance Travelled*. During the last two poems a waiter had wheeled in a trolley of iced cakes and an urn of coffee.

The president, a large lady, had called the meeting to order.

When he'd finished reading, sudden silence ensued.

Answering the president's call for questions, a lady with aggressive orange hair had said:

"Am I right in assuming you've had your work published?"

"Ah, yes."

"And you didn't pay for it?"

"Pay for it?"

"To have it published."

"Oh. No."

"Well, my question is—who do you know?"

"Know?"

"In Toronto."

* * *

Alone in the cream and gold sitting room, he examined the mantelpiece with its tiny fluted columns, shelves, alcoves, its three inset oval mirrors. He examined the silver-framed bride and groom. He examined the Royal Daulton lady in her windblown crinolines, the knickknacks, the small copper frying-pan-looking thing that said *A Gift from Jerusalem*, the Royal reclining Doulton lady. Glancing round at the open door, he turned back and peered into the centre mirror to see if hairs were sticking out of his nose.

He sank for a few minutes into the gold plush settee.

The doorbell kept ringing; the litany continued.

Bernice! It's beautiful!

We only finished moving in three weeks ago.

The pair of brass lamps which flanked the settee were in the form of huge pineapples. He touched the prickly brass leaves. The lampshades were covered in plastic. On the long table at the far end of the room, a white tablecloth covered food; he stared at the stacked plates and cups and saucers, at the tablecloth's mysterious humps and hollows. He took a cigarette from the silver box. Which of the little things on the occasional tables, he wondered, were ashtrays? Each time the front door opened, the chandelier above him tinkled.

Oh, Bernice! And quarry-tile in the kitchen, too!

Would you like the tour?

And as the tramplings went upstairs, faintly:

master-bedroom . . .

cedar-lined . . .

A plump woman wandered in. He nodded and smiled at her. She hesitated in the doorway staring at him. The green Chinese lady gazed from her gilt frame. The plump woman went around the other end of the settee and stood fingering the drapes. He tried to remember the painter's name; Tetchi, Tretchisomething—a name that sounded vaguely like a disease.

"Are you the poet?" said the plump woman.

"Yes, that's right."

He smiled.

"We had a nudist last week," she said.

* * *

Panty-hose. Stocking-top. The whites of their thighs.

Seated in the centre of the room on the footstool provided, he read to the assembled ladies. He read from his first Ryerson chapbook.

He read his Dylan orotundities:

In a once more summer time than this.

His Auden atrocities:

Love, now, like light.

He read for forty minutes, giving them Nature, Time, and Love.

The pièce de résistance proved to be lox.

With rye bread. And cream cheese. Salami. Half-sours. Parma ham. Lima bean salad with mint. Devilled eggs and sculptured radishes. The cheese-board afforded Limburger, Gouda, Cheddar, Danish Blue, Feta, and Gruyere.

Are poets different than other people?

Salami.

... or do you wait for inspiration?

Potato salad.

"No, of course not. It's my pleasure. For...?"

"Bernice."

Jenny. Helen. Shirley. Joan. Ruby.

WITH BEST WISHES.

Nine Distance Travelled *at $6.00 (Author's Discount $2.00 = $18.00 Profit).*

"Well, I don't want to sound pompous, but I suppose you'd call it vision."

Radish.

"Pardon?"

"... was wondering if Bernice had arranged a lift down-town for you? Because I'm leaving soon if you'd like a ride?"

* * *

"Over there," she said, as they crunched across the gravel. "What my dear husband calls 'the Kraut bucket.'"

He wondered how old she was. Thirty-five. Expensively styled black hair. A year or two more maybe. Her strained skirt rode higher as they slammed the doors. He glanced at the nylon gleam of her thighs. She seemed unconcerned.

"Cigarette?" she said.

He leaned towards the flame. Her perfume was heavy in the car.

She blew out smoke in a long sigh.

"I liked your poems," she said.

"Thank you."

"I'm not just saying that. I thought they were really good."

"I really appreciate that."

"You're very polite—a very polite person, aren't you?"

She turned the key and roared the motor.

"What makes you say that?" he said.

She shrugged.

"Nothing."

As they turned out of the drive, she said, "How do you stand it?"

"Stand what?"

"Oh, for Christ's sake!" she said.

He stared at her profile.

"Why do you go then?" he said.

"Stand *what!*" she said.

"What the hell did you expect me to say?"

She shrugged and then crushed the cigarette into the ashtray.

"Are you married?"

"No," he said. "Why?"

She turned onto the access road to the Trans-Canada.

"Kids," she said. "My dear husband's dinners. Even Bernice Wise is a vacation."

She snapped on the radio.

They settled into the drive back from Pointe Claire. She drove with angry concentration. The nylon sheen of her thighs green in the glow from the radio dial. The winding and unwinding notes of a harpsichord, the intricate figurings, absolved him from conversation. Mesmeric the rise and fall of headlights, the steady bore of the engine, the weaving patterns of the lanes of traffic; mesmeric the play of light and shadow, the approach and fall of overpasses, the rush of concrete void. The heater was making him drowsy. The words were drifting.
Her gloved hand moved on the gear-shift.

Trying to break free, the swell of words lifting and stirring like pan ice.

Mollia non rigidus caespes tegat ossa, nec illi,
Terra, gravis fueris: non fuit illa tibi.

The final movement of the poem, dear ladies, changing direction, *terra*, changing direction, terrain the vocative.

All, all, dear ladies, a question of balance.

"rigidus caespes"

"Sod" was ludicrous; he toyed with "rock," "turf," and "stones." He was being trapped into the literal again; the morning at the Montreal *Herald* was repeating itself.

"Charles Pevensey has a PERSONAL subscription to *Reader's Digest.*"

Pleasing.

There was something about the toad-like Pevensey that had been working on his mind all day. An echo of the name's sound. *Epitaph on Salomon Pavy.* Because it was an echo too, he knew, of Ben Jonson. *Epitaph on Elizabeth L. H.*

Pevensey. Pevensey.

Penshurst.

COUPLETS.

It needed couplets. *That* was the connection. The bastard needed couplets. He sat up and patted his pockets, finding a pencil stub in his shirt. His pad was in the Air Canada bag on the back seat. Removing the cigarettes from his package, wrapping them in the silver paper.

"Yes, please," she said.

"What? Oh, sorry."

"Will you light me one?"

As she took it from him, she said, "I'm sorry I was bitchy before."

"That's okay."

"Just one of those days," she said.

He spread the inner part of the packet on his knee and started to write, then scribbled over the words.

The car stopping and starting now. Neon signs. Salada Tea. Traffic lights. Uniroyal Tire.

They turned south onto Decarie heading downtown. Past the first of the restaurants.

"Mr. Haine?"

She glanced in the rear mirror and then smiled at him.

"If you want to write it down," she said.

"What?"

"It's 743-6981."

Gentle as flowers . . . he wrote.

"And if a man answers?"

She laughed.

Gentle as flowers make the stones

She pulled into the right-hand lane and took the exit to Queen Mary Road.

"You know something?" she said.

He grunted enquiry, crossing through a word he'd written.

"You've got a cruel mouth. I bet a lot of women have told you that."

"Me, cruel? I'm nice," he said.

"James Haine," she said. "Does anyone call you 'James?'"

"No. Nor Jimmy."

Dare he use "comfort?"

"Actually," she said, "my name isn't Rena. Well, it *is*, but my friends call me Midge."

"Midge?"

"Short for Midgicovsky—from school."

"That's a nice name," he said. "I like that."

"And you *have* got a cruel mouth."

"Oh, Grandmama!"

"What's that meant to mean?"

A girl's name—two syllables.

"You're making me sound like the Big Bad Wolf."

"*What?*"

"You know. All the better to bite you with sort of stuff."

She laughed.

"Well, you *have*," she said. "And anyway, you don't hear me screaming for help."

That comfort . . .

"Anyway, I like it," she said. "You're different."

He glanced at the Due de Lorraine bakery as they turned onto Cote des Neiges. He used to buy warm croissants there in his richer days. Surprise her with coffee, cognac, croissants. After writing all night, walking up in the early morning with the dog before she was awake.

Two syllables.

She braked and changed lanes.

Gentle as flowers make the stones
That comfort Liza's tender bones.

Turning off Cote des Neiges, she took the road leading up to the Mountain.

"It's so beautiful up here at night," she said. "You don't mind, do you? I always come this way on the way home."

On the left the cemetery spreading up the slope for acres behind the black railings; mausoleums, statues, crosses, the dull glimmer of the endless rows of polished marble headstones.

Past Beaver Lake. On to the summit.

She parked the car at the Mount Royal Lookout, silence settling as they gazed over the lights of the city. A ghostly wedge from the revolving sweep of the searchlight on top of Place Ville Marie shone against the cloudbank to their left, shone, disappeared, shone.

"I never get tired of this view," she said.

He nodded.

She sighed.

"Jim?"

As he turned, she stretched across, her arms reaching out for him. She kissed his chin, the corner of his mouth, found his lips. Twisting towards her in the awkwardness of the seat, the gear-shift, he put his arms round her, one hand on a breast.

"Hold me," she whispered.

His back was hurting.

Her mouth was hot and open. Squirming, she reached up and unhooked her brassiere. After a few moments, she pushed her face into his neck.

"That's the sad thing about getting old," she said, her breath hot and moist on his flesh, "having your breasts fall."

"Not old," he mumbled.

She kissed him open-mouthed, then biting gently at his lower lip. She was breathing heavily.

"Get in the back," she whispered.

As they kissed again, her legs were stirring restlessly. His hand moved over nylon. She lifted herself, pulling up her skirt.

She stretched out one leg and drew the other up, gasped as his fingers found her.

"We can't," she whispered. "We mustn't."

Her breathing was throaty.

"I'm off the pill and I haven't got anything with me."

His fingers were moving.

"You don't mind?"

She moved her bottom further off the edge of the seat; she was gripping his other arm and making noises.

The side of his face was sweaty against the shiny plastic upholstery.

She was arching, arching herself towards him.

Suddenly her body went rigid and she clamped his hand still. They lay quiet, the race of her breathing slowing. Her eyes were closed; her face slack. He watched the sweep of the searchlight against the cloudbank.

Lie lightly, Earth . . .

No.

After a minute or so she moved her legs, easing herself up.

"Mmmm," she sighed.

She pushed him towards the other side. Her hands undoing his belt buckle, she whispered, "Go on, lie back." She was pushing up his shirt. She lay with her cheek against his stomach and then he felt the heat of her mouth on him. Her hand moving too.

Her hair was stiff, lacquered.

He grunted and she moved her head; sperm pumped onto his stomach.

They lay in silence.

He could feel the sperm getting cold, running down his side, cold on his hip.

"There's some Kleenex in my purse," she said.

She wiped his thigh and stomach, and pulling down his shirt, snuggled up against him, kissing his mouth, his chin, his neck. He stroked her shoulders, back, running his hand down to her buttocks and up again. She pulled herself higher until her cheek was against his.

"Was it good for you, too?" she whispered.

"Mmm."

He felt a mounting excitement.

All, all, dear ladies, a question of balance.

And he'd found it.

His balancing pole, as it were, commas.

COMMAS

No risk of falling now; no staggering run up the incline of a sagging rope.

Earth COMMA *lie lightly on her* COMMA *who* COMMA *Living* COMMA *scarcely burdened you.*

Tears were welling in his half-shut eyes, the lights of the city lancing gold and silver along his wet lashes, the poem perfect.

Gentle as flowers make the stones
That comfort Liza's tender bones.
Earth, lie lightly on her, who,
Living, scarcely burdened you.

Feeling his hot tears on her cheek, she lifted her head to look at him.

"You're crying," she whispered. "Don't cry."

She brushed the backs of her fingers against his cheek.

"Jim?"

He stirred, shifting himself of some of her weight.

"Jim?"

She nestled against him.

"You know something?" she said. "You're very sweet."

DANDELIONS

GEORGE KENWAY straightened his shoulders and sat upright to ease the pang of heartburn. He breathed deeply until the pain began to fade, its sharpness settling into a dull ache in his teeth on the left side. He took the bottle of aspirins from the centre drawer of the desk and shook a couple out onto his palm. When the pains had first started he had thought he was suffering heart attacks.

It was probably lack of exercise. That, and sitting hunched over the desk. When the spring came again he would really try to get himself into shape. He pulled his stomach in and looked down, but the grey cardigan Mary had knitted him still bulged. Tennis might do the trick. He stared down at the mother-of-pearl buttons. Or walking. Walking was quite pleasant. He pushed his spectacles higher on the bridge of his nose.

On both sides of the central aisle, the shelves stretched down the length of the narrow shop. There were no customers. In the silence, he could hear the sounds of the old beams and floor boards. On the desk lay *Imprint* and *Book News*; he had not yet read them. The paperback order forms, too, were waiting to be completed. The pencil in his hand doodled over the yellow pad drawing tiny, interlocking circles in endless repetitions.

The bell above the door jangled. A woman with a child came in. He looked at her over his glasses and inclined his head in welcome. He never approached customers now. He did not want to say *Can I help you?* and hear the ritual *I'm just looking, thank you.*

"A book for a boy, madam? This boy? Over in the far corner."

Over in the far corner with all the trains and planes, the fire engines and the spaceships, the brown bunnies and the cuddly bears; with all the fat, pink pigs in trousers, the winsome pups and patient horses. He glanced at his pocket watch. The glass was scratched and yellowed. It had belonged to his father. Mary had made a shammy-leather pocket for it in the waistband of his trousers.

Business was slow, even for a Monday. Twenty-odd paperbacks, a book about the care of budgies, two copies of *Middlemarch* because they were doing it on TV and an enquiry:

I can order it for you.

And the traditional lie:

I especially wanted it for today.

He wrapped the book in brown paper, sticking down the flaps with tape. So much more sensible than string. *Farm Friends.* And change from the tin cash box in his drawer. He walked towards the door with the woman but stopped to straighten the Penguins and Pelicans. He would have to reorder, too, on the new gardening books. A very popular line.

He moved back past Gardening and Cookery, Religion (Common Prayers in white leatherette and Presentation Bibles), Modern Literature (low again on the Cronins and Shutes), Hobbies, Travel, and Adventure, towards his desk.

He had put his sandwiches in the desk drawer. He wondered what they were today. Cheese and tomato, perhaps? He hoped they weren't fish-paste or luncheon-meat. Those always left him so thirsty. She'd promised shepherd's pie tonight. He'd always liked that. It was an attractive name, too. Shepherd's pie. As he put his hand down to open the drawer, he noticed the sticking plaster across the back of his thumb. He thought, as he always did, what an unpleasant colour it was; that unnatural flesh colour, almost salmon, that children produced in their paintings. A nasty scrape on one of the wing nuts of Roy's bicycle. And the wheel still wasn't straight. That would be another job for tonight. He'd probably have to take off the brake blocks. And the front hedge couldn't go much longer. It was silly, though, how upset she got about things like that. He would have to buy a bottle of machine oil for the clippers on the way home.

The sandwiches were wrapped in grease-proof paper and secured with an elastic band. He looked at his watch again and decided to wait until one o'clock. Another ten minutes. Perhaps he could lose weight if, every day, he left one sandwich. But then, he knew that he would eat it with his afternoon cup of tea.

Sometimes, in the long afternoons, after the day had been divided by the sandwiches, he saw the shelves as he had always imagined them, the rows of calf-bound volumes, gilt titles, gilt decoration on the spines, the light hinting on the mahogany richness of the old leather. Standing along the bottom shelves, the massive folios—Heraldry, County Visitations, Voyages, Theological Disputations, and Chronicles. The air would be heavy with the must of old paper. Lying open on his desk, or perhaps propped against his works of reference, would be a sixteenth-century German blackletter with quaint woodcuts of vigorous tortures and martyrdoms, and in the glass-fronted cases behind him a few incunabula and the Aldines and Elzevirs and the volumes with the fore-edge paintings. In the heavy portfolio beside the desk there would be the Speed and Bartholomew maps, single leaves from Caxton, a few autographs, and pages of medieval manuscript brilliant with gold, blue, and scarlet illumination. And to his few customers—for most of his trade would be through his scholarly catalogues—he would say:

"Well, the title's foxed and there's some worming in the last signature, but it's a rare volume. Not recorded in Wing, I believe."

Or he'd say:

"It's a pleasing book. A very representative binding."

He still bought catalogues of the sales and read the report from Sotheby's every week in the *Literary Supplement*. It was Friday's chief pleasure.

He unwrapped the sandwiches, leaving them out of sight in the open drawer in case a customer came in. They were egg and lettuce. The coffee in his thermos flask was the kind without caffeine. She was always worrying about his health. On winter mornings, when he stooped to kiss her goodbye, she always tucked his muffler more firmly inside the old mac.

The afternoon sun was quite strong for September and the narrow room was becoming uncomfortably warm. He got up from his desk and walked down to the window where he lowered the Venetian blind. He checked to see that the sign on the door said Open and then went back to his desk.

He took out his fountain pen, a gift from Mary eleven years ago, and unscrewed the cap. He took the bottle of Permanent Black from its place in the left-hand drawer and filled the pen, wiping it clean on a piece of rag he kept with the ink bottle. He placed the pen beside his memo pad on the blotter and then started to work his way through *Book News* but it was difficult to concentrate; his eyes jumped lines of print and he had to keep on going back to grasp what he was reading. He did not like to admit it, but he often felt quite sleepy after lunch. It would have been most refreshing to stretch out, just for a few minutes.

With the blind down, the room was rather dim, except for a single patch of sunlight where a slat in the blind was buckled. He took off his glasses and rubbed his eyes. The bridge of his nose, too, was sore from the pressure.

He raised his head and stared down the warm gloom towards the window. His eyes were caught and dazzled in the burst of light. As he stared, the light seemed to grow brighter like a climbing candle flame, and larger, until he saw nothing else. Then, slowly, in the white centre of the light, a picture grew.

He saw a small boy standing in a familiar room looking towards the window. The boy was himself. He was standing alone in the big stone-flagged kitchen. He could feel the coolness of the stone through his stocking-feet. Behind him, on the mantelpiece, the black clock was ticking.

On the red-tiled windowsill stood a jam jar full of dandelions. The window burned. Between the lace curtains, sunlight, sunshine glittering off the silver tap, gleaming in the white sink, glowing on the crowded yellow heads.

He had picked them in the orchard.

The details of the picture faded, faded until he saw only the burning flowers in the jam jar, and then, blinking, he found that he was staring at the sunpatch, the Venetian blind with its buckled slat, the shelves of books, and his desk in front of him with his glasses lying on the green blotter. For a few moments, he stared at the glasses as though he did not know what they were for. Then he reached out and picked them up, settling them cautiously on his nose. He sat motionless in his chair and the afternoon ebbed quietly away.

The bell above the door jangled. A young man, an untidy young man in jeans and a sweater, a student, walked up the shop towards him and stood in front of the desk.

"*Economic Theory* by Woodall? I don't believe I have ... no, I'm sure ... I beg your pardon? Order it for you? Oh, yes. *Order* it. Certainly, sir. Certainly."

When the young man had gone, he took out his watch and, looking at it, shook his head. He felt rather fuzzy; a cold coming on perhaps, or possibly the aspirins. He put the thermos flask into his briefcase and snapped shut the clasp. His raincoat was in the cupboard behind the desk and he took it out and shrugged his shoulders into it. He pulled the belt tighter and stood looking round the shop.

He was surprised to see his fountain pen still lying on the blotter. He put it in the right-hand drawer in its proper place in the *Castañeda* cigar box.

He put the lock down on the door and turned the Open sign around. He pulled the door shut after him and shook the handle to make sure, as he always did. And as he always did, he looked up at the sign above the door: Geo. Kenway: Bookseller.

Because he was earlier than usual, there was not such a long queue at the bus stop and when the bus came he managed the luxury of a seat to himself. The familiar landmarks passed in their usual order and he got automatically to his feet just before his stop.

The fresh air seemed to clear his head as he walked down Cherril Avenue and turned into The Grove. Down at the far end, by the bowling green, a group of boys were straddling their bikes and talking. He recognized Roy, and Peter from next door.

He had forgotten to empty the tin cash box.

The painters were at work at number fifty-three. He hoped the green they were using was an undercoat. Mr. Glover waved to him.

"How are you keeping, Mr. Glover ?"

"Sprightly for an old one. Keeping busy, you know. And yourself?"

"Oh, very well, thank you," he called.

"Yes, it's been a beautiful afternoon."

He turned in at number forty-seven. The front door was ajar. As he hung up his raincoat and pushed his briefcase under the hall table, he called, "Hello? Mary?"

She came out from the kitchen and as he bent to kiss her she said, "Is anything wrong, George?"

"Wrong?"

"You're so early."

"Oh, no. I had a bit of a headache and things were quiet. I just thought I'd come home."

"Would you like a cup of tea?"

"Yes," he said. "Yes, that'd be nice."

"It was so lovely this afternoon," she said, "just like summer, so I made a salad for you. With salmon. And Roy's off somewhere playing speedbike."

"Speedway," he said.

He had forgotten the oil for the clippers.

"Whatever he calls it," she said.

"I think I'll do the hedge before supper," he said, as he followed her into the kitchen.

It was still warm, although, as the sun set, a breeze was springing up. He moved gradually into the rhythm of the work. It became enjoyable and he frequently stepped back to see if the line was straight. The higher sprigs would have to be tackled from the other side. But he had managed a smooth curve towards the crown of the hedge. Very smooth, in fact. He stepped back to look again and then moved in to trim a straggling spray.

His hands were hot and sweaty and a heavy pulse beat in his neck. Leaning on the front gate, he rested for a few minutes before starting on the other side.

The light was thickening and the houses opposite were becoming shapes against the flushed sky. Shepherd's delight. Shepherd's pie. Another fine day tomorrow. He could hear the distant whirr and clack of a lawnmower, and across the road the Romilly girl was practising scales on the piano, the notes falling softly into the evening.

There was a light, sharp scent in the air, a faintly acid smell. The smell of sap and bruised privet leaves. It seemed to move a memory in him . . . a recollection . . . but he could not remember what it was.

THE YEARS IN EXILE

Although it is comfortable, I do not like this chair. I do not like its aluminum and plastic. The aluminum corrodes, leaving a roughness on the arms and legs like white rust or fungus. I liked the chairs stacked in the summer house when I was ten, deckchairs made of striped canvas and wood. But I am an old man; I am allowed to be crotchety.

By the side of my chair in the border are some blue and white petunias. They remind me, though the shade is different, of my youngest grandson's blue and white running shoes, Adidas I believe he calls them. They are one of this year's fads. He wears them to classes at the so-called college he attends. But I must not get excited.

It is one of her days. The voice of the vacuum cleaner is heard in the land. But I should not complain. I have my room, my personal things, the few books I still care to have about me. Before moving here, life was becoming difficult; the long hill up to the shopping centre for supplies I neither wished to cook nor eat, sheets, the silence broken only by the hum and shudder of the fridge.

Strange that this daughter of my first marriage, a child of whom I saw so little, should be the one who urged this home upon me. Or not so strange perhaps. I am old enough to know that we do not know what needs compel us.

The cartons were mentioned again this morning, those in my room and those in the basement. She calls them "clutter," and perhaps she is right. The papers are promised to Queen's University but I cannot bring myself to sort through years of manuscript and letters from dead friends. Much of the order of things I couldn't remember and it is a task which smacks too much of some finality.

I am supposed to be resting today, for this evening a man is coming to interview me for some literary journal or review. Or was it a thesis? I forget. They come quite often, young men with tape recorders and notebooks. They talk of my novels and stories, ascribe influences I have never read, read criticism to me. I nod and comment if I understand them. I am not an intellectual; I am not even particularly intelligent. I am content to sit in my aluminum chair and stare at the weeping-willow tree in the next-door garden.

I have lived in Canada for sixty-one years covered now with honours yet in my reveries the last half century fades, the books, the marriages, the children, and the friends. I find myself dwelling more and more on my childhood years in England, the years when I was nine and ten. My mind is full of pictures.

My sleeplessness, the insistence of the pictures, are familiar signs. Were I younger, I would be making notes and outlines, drinking midnight coffee. But I will not write again. I am too old and tire too easily; I no longer have the strength to face the struggle with language, the loneliness, the certainty of failure.

I remember my own grandfather. I wonder if I seem to Mary and her children as remote as he appeared to me, talking to himself, conducting barely audible arguments in two voices, dozing, his crossed leg constantly jiggling, the dottle from his dead pipe falling down his cardigan front.

I remember the bone-handled clasp-knife, its blade a thin hook from years of sharpening. I can see his old hands slicing the rope of black twist into tiny discs, rubbing them, funnelling the prepared tobacco from the newspaper on his lap into his wooden box which stood on the mantelpiece. The mantelpiece had a velvet fringe along its edge with little velvet bobbles hanging down at intervals. I can see his old hands replacing the gauze mantle in the gas lamp, the white-yellow incandescence of the light.

Many might dismiss such meaningless particulars of memory.

I know that I am lost in silence hours on end, dwelling on another time now more real to me than this chair, more real than the sunshine filtering through the fawn and green of the willow tree.

Summerfield, Hengistbury Head, Christchurch, with their rivers, the Avon and the Stour, and always central in my dream and reverie, the spoiled mansion, Fortnell House. Were I younger, I would attempt to frame its insistence.

Fortnell House.

A short story could not encompass it; it has the weight and feel about it of a novella. But the time for such considerations is past.

I have not read much in late years; I lack the patience. But of the younger writers I have read Cary. Thinking of my rivers, my Headland and estuary, the bulk of my great grey Priory above the salt marsh, I looked again not a week since at a remembered passage in his novel *To Be a Pilgrim*. Old Wilcher speaking. It has stayed in my mind:

> The English summer weighs upon me with its richness. I know why Robert ran away from so much history to the new lands where the weather is as stupid as the trees, chance dropped, are meaningless. Where earth is only new dirt, and corn, food for animals two and four-footed.

I must go, too, for life's sake. This place is so doused in memory that only to breathe makes me dream like an opium eater. Like one who has taken a narcotic, I have lived among fantastic loves and purposes. The shape of a field, the turn of a lane, have had the power to move me as if they were my children, and I had made them. I have wished immortal life for them, though they were even more transient appearances than human beings.

I, too, have thought myself a pilgrim.

In the summer, dilapidated farmhouses in the Eastern Townships; in the winter, Montreal's cold-water flats. My mother's letters to me when I was young, how they amused yet rankled: "living like a gypsy," "a man of your age," "not a stick of furniture to your name." My early books returned. All so many years ago.

A blue night-light burns on my bedside table. Mary put it there in case I have need of the pills and bottles which crowd the table-top, Milk of Magnesia, sedatives, digitalis, the inhaler, the glycerine capsules.

Yes, I have thought myself a pilgrim, the books my milestones. But these recent weeks, the images that haunt my nights and days...

I have seen the holy places though I never knew it. I have travelled on, not knowing all my life that the mecca of my pilgrimage had been reached so young, and that all after was the homeward journey.

Fortnell House.

The curve of the weed-grown drive, the rank laurels, the plaster-fallen crumbling portico. Lower windows blind and boarded.

I read once in a travel book of an African tribe, the Dogan, famed for their masks and ancestor figures. They live, if I remember aright, south of Timbuctu under the curve of the Niger. Their masks and carvings are a part of their burial rites;

the carvings offer a fixed abode for spirits liberated by death. The figures are placed in caves and fissures where the termites soon attack the wood and the weather erodes.

I have seen such weathered figures in museums.

I stare at my wrist as it lies along the aluminum arm of the chair, the blue veins. The left side of the wrist might be the river Avon and its estuary, the right side the sea. And then my fist, the bulge of the Headland.

* * *

Away from the Southbourne beach, away from the sand, the bathers, and the beach games onto the five miles of crunching pebbles towards Hengistbury Head. Scavenging, I followed the line of seawrack, the tangles and heaps of seaware, kelp, and bladderwrack. In my knapsack I carried sandwiches, pillboxes for rare shells, and a hammer.

Sometimes among the tarred rope and driftwood branches, the broken crates, the cracked crab shells, and hollowed bodies of birds, were great baulks of timber covered with goose barnacles stinking in the sun. Scattered above and below the seaweed were the shells, limpet, mussel, periwinkle, whelk and cockle, painted top and piddock. Razor shells. The white shields of cuttlefish, whelks' egg cases like coarse sponge, mermaids' purses.

At low tide, the expanse of firm wet sand would shine in the sun, the silver smoothness broken only by the casts of lugworms.

The halfway point of my journey was marked by The Rocks. I always thought of them as a fossilized monster, the bulk of its body on the beach, its lower vertebrae and tail disappearing into the sea. The rocks in the sea were in a straight line, water between them, smaller and smaller, and almost invariably on the last black rock stood a cormorant.

I always liked the cormorant's solitary state. As I climbed up the rocks, it would usually void in a flash of white and fly off low over the water. My favourite birds were ravens; they nested on the Headland strutting on the turf near the dangerous cliff edge. Cormorant in Latin means "sea raven." I liked the sound of that; it might have been a name for Vikings.

I climbed among the rocks looking in the rock pools where small green crabs scuttled and squishy sea anemones closed their flowered mouths at a touch. I usually rested in the shadow of the rocks and used my hammer on the larger pebbles, often those with a yellowish area of discolouration; they broke more easily. I sometimes found inside the fossils of sea-urchins. I dug, too, at the cliff face dreaming of finding the imprint of some great fish.

Two or three miles past The Rocks I scrambled up where the cliff dipped to perhaps twenty feet before beginning its great rise to the Headland. At this point the Double Dykes met the cliff edge. The Dykes ran across the wrist of land to the estuary on the other side. They were Iron Age earthworks designed to cut the Headland off from attack by land, built presumably by the people whose barrows still rose above the turf and heather high up on the hill. They were perhaps twelve or fifteen feet high from their ditch, still a struggle up slippery turf to gain the other side.

They must have been much higher 2,000 years ago but were eroded now by time and rabbits; they formed a huge warren and the fresh sandy diggings were visible everywhere. The land beyond the Dykes was low on the estuary side and rose to 180 feet at the point of the Headland. On the estuary side there were woods and pools and marsh and then, as the land rose, short turf, bracken, and heather.

At the far end of the Dykes, the estuary end, stood the keeper's cottage. Mr. Taylor was of uncertain temper and had a collie with one eye, and ferrets, and an adder just over three feet long pickled in alcohol. On his good days he showed me the adder or gave me owl pellets; once he let me help with the ferrets.

Before going along the curve of the estuary into the woods, it was part of my ritual to climb the height of the land and sit beside the larger of the two burial mounds to eat my sandwiches. The Headland behind the Dykes had been a camp for many peoples. Before the legions arrived, some British king or chieftain had even established a mint here. Later, the Vikings, penetrating up the Avon and Stour, had used the Headland as a base camp. Although I knew that the larger barrow was of the Iron Age, or even earlier, I preferred to connect it with Hengist and Horsa, legendary leaders of the first Anglo-Saxon settlers in Britain. According to Bede, Hengist and his son Aesc landed and eventually reigned in far-away Kent. But for me, Hengistbury Head was Hengist's fort and I imagined inside the larger mound the war-leader's huge skeleton lying with his accoutrements. An axe and shield, a sword, spears, and his horned helmet. I knew that he was huge because I had read in the encyclopedia that Hengist was probably a personal name meaning "stallion." I gave alliterative names to his weapons.

"Bone-Biter" was one, I seem to remember.

I always poured a trickle of lemonade, wishing I had wine.

This was my Valley of the Kings.

Sitting by the burial mound I looked out over the estuary. It curved in at both sides where it met the sea, a narrow run of water between two spits of beach, the salmon run, and then white breakers beyond. On the far side of the estuary mouth was the village of Mudeford, eight or nine houses, one painted black. It was called, simply, The Black House, and in the eighteenth century had been a meeting place for smugglers. It had once been an inn, I believe, but now served teas to summer visitors.

I used to imagine moonless nights, a lugger standing off, the rowing boats grating up the shingle. The brandy, wine, and lace were taken by the winding paths across the saltings to Christchurch where it was rumoured they were hidden in a false tomb in the Priory graveyard.

Across the estuary sailed and tacked the white yachts like toys but at Mudeford the fishermen netted the salmon run or put out to sea with lobster pots. Although the run was less than fifty yards across there was no way of getting over and Mudeford could only be approached from the Christchurch side. I used to walk to Christchurch sometimes and then set out for Mudeford at low tide across the saltings, jumping from tussock to tussock, always getting plastered with mud. The knowledge of the paths was lost or they had eroded with the shifting tides. Sometimes I imagined myself a smuggler, sometimes a revenuer, but after I got the cutlass with its brass guard and Tower of London stamp near the hilt from Fortnell House I was always an excise man.

Behind Mr. Taylor's thatched cottage, on a triangular patch of land between the back of the house and a shed, grew teazles. After the death of the purple flowers the brown, spiky teazles stood tall and dry in the autumn. Every autumn I cut teazles for my mother. They stood in the Chinese dragon vase in the hall.

I often wondered if they were chance-sown behind the house so thickly, or if for centuries the cottage people had grown them specially to card and comb the wool from sheep they grazed on the Headland.

I can still remember the maps I used to draw marking the cottage and the teazle patch, the burial mounds and Dykes, the wood, the estuary and salmon run, The Black House, dotted lines marking the smugglers' routes across the saltings, to Christchurch Priory and the river Avon in its tidal reaches to Wick Ferry, the nesting sites of the ravens.

I can see those childish maps now as clearly as I see the petunias by my chair or the willow in the next-door garden. I can remember the names I gave to various areas: "The Heron-Sedge," "Badger's Sett," "Lily-Pad Pond," "Honeysuckle Valley."

Dear God. I can smell the honeysuckle!

* * *

A pair of Monarchs chasing each other about the leaves of the apple tree; the lawn is strewn with fresh windfalls. The sun is higher now. The Monarchs will not find milkweed in this garden. Will you, my beauties? No weeds here for you. Robert doesn't like weeds. Roots them out. Weed-killer and trowel.

Were it my garden, I would sow it thick with milkweed so that you would always grace me with your presence.

The windfalls surprise me; Robert will doubtless gather them this evening. He has an oblong wooden basket of woven strips, cotton gloves, a pair of secateurs. He does not know that such a basket is called a "trug."

I hug the word to myself.

Earlier, Mary brought me lemonade. My bladder will not hold liquid as it once did. I have to suffer the indignity of struggling from this reclining chair like a wounded thing to go indoors to the lavatory. She's still vacuuming, now upstairs. It is cool and dim in the bathroom. I urinate without control and when I have finished and zipped up my trousers, I can feel a dribble of urine wetting my underpants.

I wonder if my room smells, if I smell? I often remarked it in old people when I was younger. I can remember still the smell of my grandmother. Thank God I will never know. I can, at least, still bathe without assistance though she insists I do not lock the door. Some I remember smelled medicinal, some of mothballs, some just a mustiness. I have not shaved today. I must remember to shave before evening for the young man is coming to ask me questions.

The cushion for the small of my back.

The Monarchs have disappeared in search of ground less disciplined.

I have always disliked Wordsworth. Once, I must admit, I thought I disliked him for his bathos, his lugubrious tone.

But now I know that it is because he could not do justice to the truth; no philosophical cast of mind can do justice to particularity.

I am uncomfortable with abstraction, his *or* mine.

I stood one morning in the fierce heat by the Lily-Pad Pond. Two frogs were croaking and then stopped. A dragonfly hovered and darted, blue sheen of its wings. Then I, too, heard it. The continuous slither of a snake moving through dead grass and sedge at the pond's edge. I knew, being by water, that it would be a grass snake. I stood rooted, staring at the yellow flags where the faint sound seemed to be coming from.

I had caught grass snakes and adders by the dozen, yet for unknown reasons felt upon me again that awful sense of intrusion, that feeling of holy terror. I stood waiting to see the snake curve into the water and swim sinuous through the lily pads, its head reared. But nothing happened. The snake did not move again. I stepped away backwards from the margin of the pond, placing my feet silently until I was at a distance to turn and walk downhill towards the wider sky and the open light of the estuary.

Again.

In the valley of the honeysuckle it was full noon; the bordering wood was dim. As I stepped into the wood's overgrown darkness over a fallen tree and brushing aside some saplings, the air suddenly moved and above my head was a great shape. I never knew what it was. I was afraid to turn. I felt my hair ruffle in its wind.

A holiday in Dorset in my tenth year in the Purbeck Hills outside the haven of Poole. The cottage was called "Four Winds," I remember, and in the garden stood a sundial. I remember the collection of Marble Whites and variants I was netting. I went out every day with net and cyanide jar, happy to wander for hours along the cliff path and across fields.

The fields were separated by dry-stone walls and where stones had fallen I pulled them up from the gripping turf in search of slow worms. I carried the slow worms inside my shirt and kept them in a large box in the cottage garden.

One day I prised up a large stone by its corner. The earth beneath was black. A few white threads of roots. Three bright red ants. And there lay the largest slow worm I had ever seen. It was over twelve inches long, strangely dark on its back, almost black, and fat. It was as fat as two of my fingers together. It started to move. Its belly was fawn. I was filled with terror. It started to burrow into the grass roots surrounding the oblong of black earth, the length of its body slowly disappearing.

The sky was blue, the wind blowing over the grass from the sea. I knew I had seen the slow worm king. Filled with an enormous guilt, I ran from the place, my heart pounding, the killing-jar thumping against my back in the knapsack. I ran for three fields before the terror quieted and I remember then sitting on a pile of rocks emptying out the limp, closed Marble Whites from the cyanide jar; I remember the greenish veins of the underside of their wings as they lay scattered on the grasses.

* * *

Mary has brought me a tuna sandwich and a peeled apple cut into slices and has moved my chair back into the sun. She is still wearing a headscarf ready to attack another part of the house. As I eat the sandwich, I crave for all the things I am forbidden—cucumber, strong cheese, radishes, tomatoes in vinegar. Pork. Especially pork. I cannot abide this blandness. Like an old circus lion with worn down teeth.

Mounting the centre box, cuffing at the trainer.

Words on paper. Words on paper.

With my chair in this position I can see her through the kitchen window. The hair pulled back, framed in the scarf, the shape of her face seems to change; she has, surprisingly, my looks about her.

I always wanted to own a piece of land so that the children could grow up in the country or visit me in a place they could make their own. True, we lived in a variety of rural slums during the summers, but the children were always too young to begin to learn and appropriate things and place. It was only in the city I could hawk my largely unwanted talents. Hand to mouth for so many years as the books and dry times bore on, the struggle to make ends meet thwarted me. And by the time I could have afforded land, the time and the children were gone.

I have spent so many hours dreaming of that place. A stream running over rocks sweeping into deep, silent trout pools. Honeysuckle in the evenings. Near the house, clumps of brambles which in the late summer would be heavy with blackberries. A barn filled with hay for the children to run and jump in, sunlight filtering in through broken boards, swimming down in shafts of dust-motes.

I can hear their voices calling.

Would they, too, have made maps with magic names?

Once I felt bitter.

A memory of Mrs. Rosen fills my mind. She is sitting on a park bench holding a grey poodle on her lap and gazing across the baseball field.

I worked for Mr. Rosen for over five years. I taught English in the mornings in his private school trying to drill the rudiments into dense and wealthy heads and toiled over my typewriter in the afternoons and on into the early evening.

He is now long dead.

Rosen College Preparatory High School occupied five rooms on the floor above the Chateau Bar-B-Q Restaurant and Take-Out Service. There were three classrooms, the Library, the supplies locker, and the Office. The staff was all part-time and so in my five years I came to know only the morning shift—Geography, Mathematics, and Science. At recess, the four of us would huddle in the supplies locker and make coffee.

Mr. Kapoor was a reserved and melancholy hypochondriac from New Delhi who habitually wore black suits and shoes, a white shirt, and striped college tie. His only concession to summer was that he wore the gleaming shoes without socks. I remember his telling me one day that peahens became fertilized by raising their tail feathers during a rain storm; he held earnestly to this, telling me that it was indeed so because his grandmother had told him, she having seen it with her own eyes in Delhi. He taught Science in all grades.

Mr. Gingley was a retired accountant who taught Mathematics and wore a curiously pink hearing aid which was shaped like a fat human ear.

Mr. Helwig Syllm, the Geography teacher, was an ex-masseur.

Mrs. Rosen, who drew salaries as secretary, teacher, and School Nurse, would sometimes grip one by the arm in the hall and hiss: "Don't foment. My husband can fire anyone. *Anyone*."

Exercising my dog one morning some three years or more after Mr. Rosen's death and some five years after I'd left the school, I saw his widow in the park. Bundled in an astrakhan coat against the weak spring sunshine, she was holding a grey poodle on her lap and gazing across the baseball field. Queenie, who was in heat, pulled towards her but I did not recognize her until I had passed and she did not notice me. I kept Queenie busy on the far side of the park and, throwing sticks for that ungainly dog, I suddenly felt loss, an absurd diminishment.

I wonder if this coming March I will be sitting across the desk from Mr. Vogel? When I first went to see him he was just a sprig but is now a portly middle-aged man. Even then, he made me feel a little like a truant youth before the principal. He shakes his head over the mysteries, his spectacles glint as he reproves me for lack of receipts. His fingers chatter over his adding machine.

His manner is dry; his inventions are fantastical.

"And now," he always says, "we come to Entertainment."

Flashing a glance of severe probity.

"A very *grey* area."

I do not want to be seen laughing aloud in the garden. I stifle the laughter and cough into my handkerchief.

Will Mr. Vogel and I invent my taxes this coming March?

Only the cartons of papers for Queen's await my attention; my other papers are in order. My will is drawn up, insurance policies in force, assigns of copyright assigned. I should not pretend any longer. I remember the papers in that outer room of Fortnell House, a scullery perhaps. I do not want my papers abandoned in that way, stored in the damp to rot. But if I do not put them in order perhaps they will be consigned to some air-conditioned but equal oblivion. Tomorrow, after the young man, I must start to sort them, the manuscripts, the journals, the letters from dead friends.

The doors had been nailed up.

That outer room in the rear of Fortnell House whose iron window bars we forced with a branch must have been a scullery or pantry. It was stone-flagged and whitewashed, green mould growing down the walls and on some of the damp papers. After the awful noise of screws being wrenched and wood splintering, we stood in the cold room listening.

Stacked in boxes were bundles of letters, newspapers, parchment deeds with red seals, account books, admiralty charts, and municipal records. The papers littered the floor, too, in sodden mounds where other boys had emptied boxes searching for more exciting things.

I stuffed my shirt.

I took bundles of parchment deeds, indentures, wills and leases, documents written in faded Latin.

THIS INDENTURE *made the second day of May in the seventeenth year of our Sovereign Lord George the Third by the Grace of God of Great Britain France and Ireland King Defender of the Faith and so forth and in: the Year of Our Lord . . .*

I remember, too, the half-leather ledger of the clerk of the Christchurch magistrate's court. The dates ran from 1863-65. The handwriting was a faded sepia copperplate, the name of the defendant in one column, the offence in a second, the fine in a third.

For bastardy, the commonest charge, the fine was five shillings.

The cover was, yes, mottled pink and white. The end papers were marbled. The leather spine was mildewed. The front lower corner was bruised, the cardboard raised and puffy with damp.

I can feel it in my hands.

* * *

The salmon fishers who netted the run between Mudeford and Hengistbury Head—the hours I have sat watching the two rowing boats laying the cork-bobbing net across the incoming tide. Mostly they came up empty, the net piling slack and easy. Perhaps twice a day the net would strain, a flash of roiling silver, and then the great fish hauled in over the side to be clubbed in the boat bottom.

The name for a bludgeon used to kill fish is a "priest." How I hug these words to myself, savouring them. "Priest" was not a local usage; I have seen it in print. It is not recorded in the *Shorter Oxford.*

One of Mr. Taylor's ferrets was brown, the other albino. I swung a stake with him one day on the Double Dykes despatching rabbits as they bolted into the nets pegged over their holes. The albino ferret eventually reappeared masked in blood. The ferrets frightened me; Mr. Taylor handled them with gauntlets. Some of the dead rabbits were wet underneath with trickles of thick, bright yellow urine which stood on the fur.

Over the two stone bridges and beyond Christchurch, along the New Forest road towards the Cat and Fiddle Inn, we cycled sometimes on our new Raleigh All-Steel bicycles to Summerfield. The Summerfield Estate stretched for miles over heath, farmland, and woods. We visited the roadside rookery where in late spring we gathered the shiny twelve-bore cartridge cases that the gamekeeper had scattered blasting into the nests from underneath. Beyond lay the heath where adders basked and kestrels circled the sky. We visited the hornets' nests in the trees in the dead wood and the pools where the palmated newts bred and we walked down the stream-bed to attach leeches to our legs. And always, past the cottages and the wheat fields and pasture, we headed down for the woods and coverts.

The gamekeeper was our invisible enemy; he was rumoured to have shot a boy in the behind. The raucous calls of pheasant held us in strained silence; rootling blackbirds froze us.

We trespassed into the heart of the wood where in a clearing we would stare at the gamekeeper's gibbet—a dead, grey tree hung with the corpses of rats, crows, owls, stoats and weasels, hawks and shapeless things. Some of the bodies would be fresh, others rotted to a slime. There in the still heat of the afternoon we stared. Over the bodies in a gauze of sound crawled the iridescent flies.

Children are, I think, drawn towards death and dying. I remember the ambivalence of a young girl of eight or nine to a litter of puppies at suck, the blind mouths and puddling forepaw at the swollen dugs—she, too, it seemed to me, sensed a relationship between herself and the bitch. I remember it—vividly. The daughter of a friend. I seem to remember attempting a story once on that but as with so many of my stories, I could find no adequate structure.

* * *

The cutlass was about three feet long and slightly curved. The guard was brass and the Tower of London armoury mark was stamped on the blade near the hilt. The hilt was bound in blackened silver wire. I got the cutlass from one of the older boys—I forget his name—in exchange for six Christmas annuals and a William and Mary shilling. It was from him, too, that I learned the secret of Fortnell House.

I went there first on my own. The house was an eighteenth century mansion on the outskirts of Christchurch. It was invisible from the road; large padlocked gates marked the entrance to the drive. On the gate-pillars weathered heraldic beasts stood holding shields. The details of the quartering within the shields were little more than lumps and hollows. I think the beasts were griffins but time and the weather had so eroded the soft grey stone that the outlines of the carving were indistinct.

I climbed the iron spears of the railings and forced my way through the rank laurels onto the drive. The wood and the drive were overgrown and dark; the gravel had reverted to grass and weeds. The bottom windows of the house were blind and boarded; the front door was padlocked. Pink willowherb and weeds sprouted from the guttering. Some of the second storey windows were broken.

Around the back of the house were extensive grounds and a spinney, the lawns and terraces overgrown, the garden statuary tumbled. The windows were boarded and the doors nailed shut. I tried the doors with my shoulder. Inside, according to report, upstairs, room after room was filled with swords and spears and armour, guns, statues, strange machines, old tools, pictures, books—a treasury. The silence and the rank growth frightened me.

To one side of the house at the back, next to the coach house, stood three wooden sheds, their doors smashed open to the weather. Two were empty except for a rusted lawn-mower and an anchor but in the third I found a broken mahogany cabinet full of shallow drawers. It had contained a collection of mineral specimens, many of which were scattered about the floor. I filled my pockets with strange and glittering stones. In a corner of the shed were stacks of plates and dishes; many had been smashed. I found intact two large willow-pattern plates, meat chargers. The blue was soft and deep. I told my parents I had traded something for them.

Fortnell House had been built in the 1720s. The last Fortnell, Sir Charles, had left the house and his collections to the town of Christchurch as a museum. The town had accepted the gift but was disinclined or unable to raise the money to refurbish the building and install a curator.

Sir Charles had served for many years in India, the Middle East, and Africa. He was one of that vanished breed like Burton, Speke, and Layard—romantic amateurs who were gentlemen, scholars, linguists, and adventurers. Fortnell House became the repository of collections of minerals, fossils, books, weapons, tribal regalia, paintings and carvings. On his retirement, Sir Charles had devoted his energies to Christchurch and the county, collecting local records, books, memorabilia, and the evidences of the prehistoric past.

It has become the fashion to decry such men as wealthy plunderers but we shall not see their like again. My youngest grandson, he of Adidas College, has called me fascist and them racist. I forbear to point out that his precious victims of oppression and colonialism despoiled their ancestral tombs for gold and used the monuments of their past for target practice. My heart does not bleed for the Egyptians; I do not weep for the Greeks.

It is, I suppose, natural to clash with those younger, natural this conservatism as one grows older; one has learned how easily things break.

What will the young man say to me this evening? And what can I say to him? It is difficult to talk to these young college men whose minds no longer move in pictures. Had he been here this morning I could, like some Zen sage, have pointed to the Monarchs about the apple leaves and preserved my silence.

Particular life. Particular life.

All else is tricks of the trade or inexpressible.

I have often wondered, I wonder still, what became of those willow-pattern plates I stole from Fortnell House. I brought them to Canada with me when I was a young man and they survived endless moves and hung on an endless variety of kitchen walls. They disappeared when June and I were divorced. She was quite capable of breaking them to spite me. Or, more likely, selling them. She had little aesthetic sense. She would have called them dust-gatherers or eyesores—some such thin-lipped epithet. So do they now hang on some Westmount wall or decorate an expensive restaurant?

I liked to be able to glance at them while I was eating; I used to like running my fingertips over that glaze. It comforted me. That deep lead glaze, the softness of the blue—one did not need to check pottery marks to know such richness was eighteenth century work.

I remember reading that Wedgwood used to tour the benches inspecting work. When he found an imperfect piece he smashed it with a hammer and wrote on the bench with chalk: *This will not do for Josiah Wedgwood.* I have always liked that story. We would have understood each other, Josiah and I.

As the years passed, I thought more often, and with greater bitterness, of those two large plates than I did of June. She is now the dimmest of memories. Strange that I cannot recall her features or her body; strange that she was Mary's mother. Alison, too, has receded now so far that I must concentrate to see her features, strain to hear her voice. She sends me Christmas cards from Florida.

Far clearer and more immediate is Patricia Hopkins. I see the scene like an enlarged detail from a great canvas. We are hidden in the laurel bushes in her garden; it is gloomy there though light hints on the glossy leaves. In the far distance the sunshine sparkles on the greenhouse. In the immediate background is a weed-grown tennis court along whose nearest edge the wire netting sags in a great belly. Patricia's knickers are round her knees. I am staring at the smooth cleft mound of her vagina. I am nine and she is eight.

Better remembered than the bodies of two wives.

I have always detested photographs. There was an article in Robert's *Time* magazine about that fellow Land and his Polaroid cameras. He called photography "the most basic form of creativity." So obscenely wrong.

But I must not get excited.

My third visit to Fortnell House was my last.

We got in through the bars of the scullery window and both lingered, turning over the sodden papers and documents that littered the floor, unwilling to go further into the dark house. Eventually we crept along a short passage into the kitchen.

One wall was taken up by a vast black range, another by two long sinks. In the middle of the room was a long wooden table. On the wall above the door that led out of the kitchen was a glass case of dials. Inside the dials were numbers and beneath the case hung two rows of jangly bells on coiled strips of metal—a device, we decided, for summoning servants to the different rooms.

A passage led from the kitchen through two doors to the hall. The hall was dark and echoey. On the walls hung the dim shapes of mounted heads and antlers. All the doors off the hall were closed. The staircase was uncarpeted. We started up it towards the first landing.

A few thin rays of light came through chinks in the boards that covered the landing window. A line of light ran up the handrail of the banister. We spoke in whispers and walked on the outside edges of the stairs.

A board creaked; a shoe cap knocked hollow on a riser.

It was just as my hand was turning on the huge carved acorn of the newel post on the landing that a door opened below and a man came out. He was a black shape with the light of the room behind him, shelf after shelf of books. He called us down and demanded our names and addresses. He was cataloguing the library. He was sick of boys breaking in and was giving our names to the police. He fumbled the front door open and ordered us out.

Secure in our aliases, we walked away down the drive.

Now, in my dreams, I have returned.

Nightly I brave the weathered griffins, the rank laurels; nightly I climb those uncarpeted stairs; nightly my hand grasps the great carved acorn of the newel post. But my dream does not continue.

Perhaps one night I will not awaken in the blue dark to turn and stare at the blue night-light on the bedside table. Perhaps one night soon—I have that feeling—I will round the dark oak acorn and reach the rooms above.

The sun has long since passed over the house and I am sitting in the shade. Soon Robert will return from his office and change into his gardening clothes; he will gather the windfalls in his oblong wooden basket. Soon the garage will sound as my grandson, returning from his college, roars his motorbike into the narrow space; soon the kitchen will be full of noise. Then Mary will call me for dinner. I should go and shave. But I will sit a little longer in the sunshine. Here between the moored houseboats where I can watch the turn of the quicksilver dace. Here by the piles of the bridge where in the refracted sunlight swim the golden-barred and red-finned perch.

THE NIPPLES OF VENUS

ROME stank of exhaust fumes and below our hotel room on the Via Sistina motor bikes and scooters snarled and ripped past late into the night rattling the window and the plywood wardrobe. The bathroom, a boxed-in corner, was the size of two upright coffins. It was impossible to sit on the toilet without jamming your knees against the wash-basin. In the chest of drawers, Helen discovered crackers, crumbs, and Pan Am cheese.

I'd reserved the room by phone from Florence, choosing the hotel from a guidebook from a list headed: Moderate. We would only have to put up with it for Saturday and Sunday and would then fly home on Monday. After nearly three weeks spent mainly in Florence and Venice, I had no real interest in looking at things Roman. I felt . . . not tired, exactly. Couldn't take in any more. I'd had enough. "Surfeited" was the word, perhaps. I was sick of cameras and photographs and tourists and tourism and disliking myself for being part of the problem. I felt burdened by history, ashamed of my ignorance, numbed by the succession of *ponte, porta, piazza,* and *palazzo.* I was beginning to feel like . . . who was it? Twain, I think,

Mark Twain, who when asked what he'd thought of Rome said to his wife:

Was that the place we saw the yellow dog?

Helen was bulged and bloated and the elastic of her underpants and panty-hose had left red weals and ribbing on the flesh of her stomach. She'd been constipated for nearly two weeks. I'd told her to stop eating pasta, to relax, to stop worrying about whether the children would leave the iron switched on, about aviation disasters, devaluation of the lira, cancer of the colon, but at night I heard her sighing, grinding her teeth, restless under the sheets, gnawing on the bones of her worries.

That waiter in—where was it? Milan? No. Definitely not in Milan. Bologna?—a waiter who'd worked for some years in Soho in the family restaurant—he'd told us that the tortellini, the tiny stuffed shells of pasta in our soup, were commonly called "the nipples of Venus."

Fettuccine, tuffolini, capelletti, manicotti, gnocchi …

Mia moglie è malata.

Dov'è una formacia?

Aspirina?

Bicarbonato di soda?

… polenta, rigatoni, tortellini …

Praaaaaaaaap …

Scooters on the Via Sistina.

Praaaaaaaaap …

Helen passing gas.

* * *

The Spanish Steps were just at the top of the street anyway and at the very least, Helen said, we had to see the Trevi Fountain and St. Peter's and the Pantheon.

They all looked much as they looked in photographs. Not as attractive, really. The Spanish Steps were littered with American college students. The sweep of St. Peter's Square was ruined even at that early hour by parked coaches from Luton, Belgrade, Brussels, and Brighton. Knowing that St. Peter's itself would be hung with acres of martyrdom and suchlike, I refused to set foot in it. The Trevi Fountain was rimmed with people taking its photograph and was magnificent but disappointing.

Places of historical interest often make me feel as if I'm eight again and the sermon will never end. I enjoyed the *doors* of the Pantheon—I always seem drawn to bronze—but the hushed interior struck me as lugubrious. Helen, on the other hand, is an inveterate reader of every notice, explication, plaque, and advisement.

Straightening up and taking off her reading glasses, she says,

"This is the tomb of Raphael."

"How about a coffee?"

"Born 1483."

"Espresso. You like that. In the square."

"Died in 1520."

"Nice coffee."

And then it was back to the Spanish Steps because she wanted to go jostling up and down the Via Condotti looking in the windows—Ferragamo, Gabrielli, Bulgari, Valentino, Gucci. And then in search of even more pairs of shoes, purses, scarves, gloves, and sweaters, it was down to the stores and boutiques on the Via del Tritone.

For lunch I ate *funghi arrosto alla Romana.* Helen ordered *risotto alla parmigiana* and had to go back to the hotel. She said she'd just lie there for a bit and if the pains went away she'd have a little nap. She asked me if I thought it was cancer, so I said that people with cancer *lost* weight and that it was *risotto, manifestly* risotto, *risotto first and last.*

"There's no need to shout at me."

"I am *not* shouting. I am speaking emphatically."

"You don't mind?" she said. "Really?"

"I'll go for a stroll around," I said.
"You won't feel I'm deserting you?"
"Just rest..."

* * *

I strolled up the Via Sistina and stood looking down the sweep of the Spanish Steps. Then sauntered on. Some seventy-five yards to the right of the Steps, seventy-five yards or so past the Trinita dei Monti along the stretch of gravel road which leads into the grounds of the Villa Borghese, tucked away behind a thick hedge and shaded by trees, was an outdoor cafe hidden in a narrow garden. The garden was just a strip between the road and the edge of the steep hill which fell away down towards the Via Condotti or whatever was beneath. The Piazza di Spagna, perhaps. Houses must have been built almost flush with the face of the hill because through the screening pampas grass I could glimpse below the leaning rusty fence at the garden's edge the warm ripple of terra cotta roof tiles.

The garden was paved with stone flagstones. Shrubs and flowers grew in low-walled beds and urns. In the centre of the garden was a small rectangular pond with reeds growing in it, the flash of fish red and gold. The tall hedge which hid the garden from the road was dark, evergreen, yew trees.

It was quiet there, the traffic noises muted to a murmur. Round white metal tables shaded by gay umbrellas, white folding chairs. Two old waiters were bringing food and drinks from the hut at the garden's entrance. There were only three couples and a family at the tables. The yew hedge was straggly and needed cutting back. The shrubs and flowers in the stone-walled beds were gone a little to seed, unweeded.

I sat at the only table without an umbrella, a table set into a corner formed by the hedge and a low stone wall. The wall screened the inner garden a little from the openness of the entrance and from the shingled hut-like place the food came from. All along the top of the wall stood pots of geraniums and jutting out from the wall near my corner table was the basin of a fountain. The basin was in the form of a scallop shell. The stone shell looked much older than the wall. It looked as if it had come down in the world, ending up here in this garden cafe after gracing for two hundred years or more some ducal garden or palazzo courtyard. The stone was softer than the stone of the wall, grainy, the sharpness of its cuts and flutes blurred and weathered.

I sat enjoying the warmth of the sun. The Becks beer bottle and my glass were beaded with condensation. Sparrows were hopping between tables pecking crumbs. Water was trickling down the wall and falling into the stone scallop shell from a narrow copper pipe which led away down behind the wall and towards the hut at the garden's entrance. Where the pipe crossed the central path feet had squashed it almost flat. The small sound of the water was starting to take over my mind. The glint and sparkle of the sunlight on the water, the tinkling sound of it, the changes in the sound of it as it rose and deepened around the domed bronze grate before draining—it all held me in deepening relaxation.

Somewhere just below me were famous guidebook attractions—the Barcaccia Fountain, the Antico Caffe Greco, the rooms where John Keats died now preserved as a museum and containing memorabilia of Byron and Shelley—but all I wanted of Rome was to sit on in the sunshine drinking cold beer and listening to the loveliness of water running, the trill and spirtle, the rill and trickle of it.

Watching the sparrow, the small cockings of its head, watching the little boy in the white shirt and red bow-tie balancing face-down over his father's thigh, I was aware suddenly at the corner of my eye of flickering movement. I turned my head and there, reared up on its front legs on the rim of the stone scallop shell, was a lizard. It stood motionless. I turned more towards it. Its back was a matte black but its throat and neck and sides were touched with a green so brilliant it looked almost metallic, as if it had been dusted with metallic powder.

Set on the stone surround of the scallop shell were two pots of geraniums and from the shadow of these now appeared another lizard, smaller than the first, not as dark in colouring, dun rather than black and with not a trace of the shimmering peacock green—compared with the male a scrawny creature drab and dowdy.

This lizard waddled down into the curve of the stone basin where she stopped and raised her head as if watching or listening. Or was she perhaps scenting what was on the air? I'd read somewhere that snakes "smelled" with their tongues. Were lizards, I wondered, like snakes in that? Would they go into water? Was she going to drink?

I was startled by loud rustlings in the hedge near my chair. A bird? A bird rootling about in dead leaves. But it wasn't that kind of noise quite. Not as loud. And, I realized, it was more continuous than the noise a bird would have made—rustling, twig-snipping, pushing, scuffling. The noise was travelling along *inside* the hedge. Slowly, cautiously, not wanting to frighten away the lizards on the stone scallop shell, I bent and parted branches, peering.

And then the noise stopped.

As I sat up, I saw that the stone bowl was empty, the brown lizard disappeared behind the geranium pots again. The green lizard was still motionless where he'd been before. Every few seconds his neck pulsed. Suddenly I saw on the wall level with my knee a lizard climbing. Every two or three inches it stopped, clinging, seeming to listen. It too was green but it had no tail. Where its tail should have been was a glossy rounded stump.

Lacking the tail's long grace, the lizard looked unbalanced, clumsy. About half the tail was gone. It was broken off just below that place where the body tapered. The stump was a scaleless wound, shiny, slightly bulbous, in colour a very dark red mixed with black. The end of the stump bulged out like a blob of smoke-swirled sealing-wax.

Just as its head was sticking up over the edge of the stone shell, the other lizard ran at it. The mutilated lizard turned and flashed halfway down the wall but then stopped, head-down, clinging. The pursuing lizard stopped too and cocked its head at an angle as if hearing something commanding to its right.

Seconds later, the stubby lizard skittered down the rest of the wall, but then stopped again on the flagstones. The pursuing lizard pursued but himself stopped poised above the wall's last course of stones. It was like watching the flurry of a silent movie with the action frozen every few seconds. And then the damaged lizard was negotiating in dreamy slow motion dead twigs and blown leaves on his way back into the hedge. He clambered over them as if they were thick boughs, back legs cocked up at funny angles like a cartoon animal, crawling, ludicrous. His pursuer faced in the opposite direction intently, fiercely.

Peculiar little creatures.

I signalled to the waiter for another beer.

I sat on in the sunshine, drifting, smelling the smell on my fingers of crushed geranium leaves, listening to the sounds the water made.

And then the noises in the hedge started again.

And again the lizard with the stump was climbing the wall.

And again the lizard on the top was rushing at it, driving it down.

By the time I was finishing my third beer, the attacks and retreats were almost continuous. The stubby lizard always climbed the wall at exactly the same place. The defending lizard always returned to the exact spot on the stone surround of the scallop shell where the attacking lizard would appear. The stop-frame chases flowed and halted down the wall, across the flagstones, halted, round an urn, into the hedge.

But with each sortie the damaged lizard was being driven further and further away. Finally, the pursuing lizard hauled his length into the hedge and I listened to their blundering progress over the litter of twigs and rusty needles in the hedge-bottom, the rustlings and cracklings, the scrabblings travelling further and further away from my chair until there was silence.

The sun had moved around the crown of the tree and was now full on me. I could feel the sweat starting on my chest, in the hollow of my throat, the damp prickle of sweat in my groin. I glanced at my watch to see how long she'd been sleeping. I thought of strolling back to the hotel and having a shower, but the thought of showering in the boxed-in bathroom inside the glass device with its folding glass doors like a compressed telephone booth—the thought of touching with every movement cold, soap-slimy glass . . .

I lifted the empty Becks bottle and nodded at the waiter as he passed.

A dragon-fly hovered over the pond, its wings at certain angles a blue iridescence.

I wondered about my chances of finding a Roman restaurant or trattoria serving *Abbracchio alla Romana*, a dish I'd read about with interest. And while I was thinking about restaurants and roast lamb flavoured with rosemary and anchovies and about poor Helen's risotto and about how long I'd been sitting in the garden and Helen worrying there in that plywood room heavy with exhaust fumes . . .

you might have been killed . . . you know I only nap for an hour . . . I got so scared . . .

. . . while I was thinking about this and these and listening to the water's trickle and looking at the white, heavy plumes of the pampas grass, there on top of the wall, my eye caught by the movement, was the lizard with the stump.

I studied the face of the wall, scanned the bottom of the hedge, looked as far around the base of the urn as I could see without moving, but there was no sign of the other lizard, no sound of pursuit.

He stood motionless on top of the wall just above the scallop shell where the scrawny brown female still basked. The stump looked as if blood and flesh had oozed from the wound and then hardened into this glossy, bulging scab.

The coast's clear, Charlie!

Come on!

Come on!

He was clinging head-down to the wall inches above the stone shell.

The female had raised her head.

Now he seemed to be studying a pale wedge of crumbling mortar.

Come on!

And then he waddled down onto the stone surround and seized the female lizard firmly about the middle in his jaws. They lay at right angles to each other as if catatonic. The female's front right leg dangled in the air.

Come on, you gimpy retard! Let go! You're biting the wrong one. It's the GREEN ones we bite. The brown ones are the ones we . . .

The waiter's voice startled me.

I smiled, shook my head, picked up the four cash-register slips, leaned over to one side to get at my wallet in my back pocket. When he'd gone and I turned back to the stone scallop shell, the female had already vanished and the end of the stump, somewhere between the colour of a ripening blackberry and a blood blister, was just disappearing into the shadows behind one of the pots of geraniums.

I got up slowly and quietly. I was careful not to scrape my chair on the flagstones. I set it down silently. I looked down to make sure my shoe wasn't going to knock against one of the table's tubular legs. One by one, I placed the coins on the saucer.

* * *

No, I told Helen on Sunday morning, not the Forum, not the Colosseum, not the Capitoline, the Palatine, or the Quirinal. I wanted to be lazy. I wanted to be taken somewhere. But not to monuments. Trees and fields. But not *walking*. I didn't want to *do* anything. I wanted to see farmhouses and outbuildings. What I wanted—yes, that was it exactly—a coach tour! I wanted to gaze out of the window at red and orange roof tiles, at ochre walls, poppies growing wild on the roadsides, vines.

At 10 AM we were waiting in a small office in a side street for the arrival of the coach. The brochure in the hotel lobby had described the outing as Extended Alban Hills Tours-Castelli Romani. Our coach was apparently now touring some of the larger hotels picking up other passengers. The whole operation seemed a bit makeshift and fly-by-night. The two young men running it seemed to do nothing but shout denials on the phone and hustle out into the street screaming at drivers as coach after coach checked in at the office before setting out to tour whatever they were advertised as touring. Commands and queries were hysterical. Tickets were counted and recounted. And then recounted. Coaches were finally dispatched with operatic gesture as if they were full of troops going up to some heroic Front.

As each coach pulled up, we looked inquiry at one or other of the young men. "This is not yours," said their hands. "Patience." "Do not fear. When your conveyance arrives, we will inform you," said their gestures.

We were both startled by the entry of a large, stout man with a shaved head who barged into the tiny office saying something that sounded challenging or jeering. His voice was harsh. He limped, throwing out one leg stiffly. Helen sat up in the plastic chair and drew her legs in. Something about his appearance suggested that he'd survived a bad car-crash. He leaned on an aluminum stick which ended in a large rubber bulb. He was wearing rimless blue-tinted glasses. His lip was permanently drawn up a little at one side. There was a lot of visible metal in his teeth. He stumped about in the confined space shouting and growling.

The young man with the mauve leather shoes shouted "no" a lot and "never" and slapped the counter with a plastic ruler. The other young man picked up a glossy brochure and, gazing fixedly at the ceiling, twisted it as if wringing a neck. The shaven-headed man pushed a pile of pamphlets off the counter with the rubber tip of his aluminum stick.

A coach pulled up and a young woman in a yellow dress got down from it and clattered on heels into the office. They all shouted at her. She spat—*teh*—and made a coarse gesture.

The young man with the mauve leather shoes went outside to shout up at the coach driver. Through the window, we watched him counting, pulling each finger down in turn.

... five, six, *seven*.

Further heart-rending pantomime followed.

Still in full flow, he burst back into the office brandishing the tickets in an accusatory way. Peering and pouting into the mirror of a compact, the girl in the yellow dress continued applying lipstick. They all shouted questions at her, possibly rhetorical. The horrible shaven-headed man shook the handle of his aluminum cane in her face.

She spat again—*teh*.

The bus driver sounded his horn.

The other young man spoke beseechingly to the potted azalea.

"Is that," said Helen, "the Castelli Romani coach? Or isn't it the Castelli Romani coach?"

There was silence as everyone stared at her.

"It *is*, dear madam, it *is*," said the horribly bald man.

"Good," said Helen.

And I followed her out.

We nodded to the other seven passengers as we climbed aboard and seated ourselves behind them near the front of the coach. They sounded American. There were two middle-aged couples, a middle-aged man on his own, rather melancholy-looking, and a middle-aged man with an old woman.

"Here he comes goosewalking," said Helen.

"Stepping," I said.

The shaven-headed man, leg lifting up and then swinging to the side, was stumping across the road leaning on the aluminum cane. His jacket was a flapping black-and-white plaid.

"Oh, *no!*" I said. "You don't think *he's* . . ."

"I told you," said Helen. "I told you this was going to be awful."

The shaven-headed man climbed up into the bus, hooked his aluminum cane over the handrail above the steps, and unclipped the microphone. Holding it in front of his mouth, he surveyed us.

"Today," he said with strange, metallic sibilance, "today you are my children."

Helen nudged.

"Today I am taking you into the Alban Hills. I will show you many wonders. I will show you extinct volcanoes. I will show you the lake of the famous Caligula. I will show you the headquarters of the German Army in World War II. Together we will visit Castel Gandolfo, Albano, Genzano, Frascati, and Rocca di Papa. We will leave ancient Rome by going past the Colosseum and out onto the Via Appia Antica completed by Appius Claudius in 312 before Christ."

He nodded slowly.

"Oh yes, my children."

Still nodding.

"Before Christ."

He looked from face to face.

"You will know this famous road as the Appian Way and you will have seen it in the movie *Spartacus* with the star Kirk Douglas."

"Oh, God!" said Helen.

"Well, my children," he said, tapping the bus driver on the shoulder, "are you ready? But you are curious about me. Who *is* this man, you are saying."

He inclined his shaved head in a bow.

"*Who* am I?"

He chuckled into the microphone.

"They call me Kojak."

Cypresses standing guard along the Appian Way over sepulchres and sarcophagi, umbrella pines shading fragments of statuary. Tombs B.C. Tombs A.D. Statuary contemporaneous with Julius Caesar, of whom we would have read in the play of that name by William Shakespeare. It was impossible to ignore or block out his voice, and after a few minutes we'd come to dread the clicking on of the microphone and the harsh, metallic commentary.

You will pay attention to your left and you will see . . .

A sarcophagus.

You will pay attention opposite and you will see . . .

"Opposite what?"

"He means straight ahead."

"Oh."

. . . to your right and in one minute you will see a famous school for women drivers . . .

Into view hove a scrap-metal dealer's yard mountainous with wrecked cars.

You will pay attention . . .

But despite the irritation of the rasping voice, I found the expedition soothing and the motion of the coach restful. The landscape as it passed was pleasing. Fields. Hedges. Garden plots. The warmth of terracotta tiles. Hills. White clouds in a sky of blue.

The Pope's summer residence at Castel Gandolfo was a glimpse through open ornate gates up a drive to a house, then the high encircling stone wall around the park.

Beech trees.

In the narrow, steep streets of the small town, the coach's length negotiated the sharp turns, eased around corners, trundled past the elaborate facade of the church and through the piazza with its fountain by Bernini.

The famous Peach Festival took place in June.

At Lake Albano we were to stop for half an hour.

No less, my children, and no more.

The coach pulled into the restaurant parking lot and backed into line with more than a dozen others. The restaurant, a cafeteria sort of place, was built on the very edge of the lake. It was jammed with tourists. Washrooms were at the bottom of a central staircase and children ran up and down the stairs, shouting. There was a faint smell of disinfectant. Lost children cried.

In the plastic display cases were sandwiches with dubious fillings, tired-looking panini, and slices of soggy pizza that were being reheated in microwave ovens until greasy.

The man from our coach who was travelling with the old woman sat staring out of the plate-glass window which overlooked the lake. The old woman was spooning in with trembling speed what looked like a huge English trifle, mounds of whipped cream, maraschino cherries, custard, cake.

Helen and I bought an ice cream we didn't really want. We stood on the wooden dock beside the restaurant and looked at the lake which was unnaturally blue. There was a strong breeze. White sails were swooping over the water. I felt cold and wished we could get back in the coach.

"So this was a volcano," said Helen.

"I guess so."

"The top blew off and then it filled up with water."

"I suppose that's it."

The man from our coach who was on his own, the melancholy-looking man, wandered onto the other side of the dock. He stood holding an ice-cream cone and looking across the lake. He looked a bit like Stan Laurel. We nodded to him. He nodded to us and made a sort of gesture at the lake with his ice cream as if to convey approval.

We smiled and nodded.

The engine of the coach was throbbing as we sat waiting for the man and the old woman to shuffle across the parking lot. The stiff breeze suddenly blew the man's hair down, revealing him as bald. From one side of his head hung a long hank which had been trained up and over his bald pate. He looked naked and bizarre as he stood there, the length of hair hanging from the side of his head and fluttering below his shoulder. It looked as if he'd been scalped. The attached hair looked like a dead thing, like a pelt.

Seemingly unembarrassed, he lifted the hair back, settling it as if it were a beret, patting it into place. The old woman stood perhaps two feet from the side of the coach smiling at it with a little smile.

And so, my children, we head now for Genzano and for Frascati, the Queen of the Castelli . . .

We did not stop in Genzano which also had Baroque fountains possibly by Bernini in the piazzas and a palazzo of some sort. Down below the town was the Lake of Nemi from which two of Caligula's warships had been recovered only to be burned by the retreating Adolf Hider.

The famous Feast of Flowers took place in May.

"Why do I know the name Frascati?" said Helen.

"Because of the wine?"

"Have I had it?"

I shrugged.

"I had some *years* ago," I said. "Must be thirty years ago now—at a wedding. We drank it with strawberries."

"Whose wedding?"

"And I don't think I've had it since. Um? Oh . . . a friend from college. I haven't heard from him—Tony Cranbrook . . . oh, it's been *years*."

"There," said Helen, "what kind of tree is that?"

I shook my head.

Frascati.

The wine was dry and golden.

Gold in candlelight.

The marriage of Tony Cranbrook had been celebrated in the village church, frayed purple hassocks, that special Anglican smell of damp and dust and stone, marble memorials let into the wall:

... departed this life June 11th 1795 in the sure and certain hope of the resurrection and of the life everlasting ...

Afterwards, the younger people had strolled back through deep lanes to the family house for the reception. I'd walked with a girl called Susan who turned out to be the sister of one of the bridesmaids. She'd picked a buttercup and lodged it behind her ear. She'd said:

Do you know what this means in Tahiti?

Late in the evening they'd been wandering about the house calling to us to come and eat strawberries, calling out that I had to make another speech.

Jack?

We know you're there!

Susan?

Jack and Su-san!

The larger drawing-room was warm and quick with candlelight. In the centre of the dark polished refectory table stood a gleaming silver épergne piled with tiny wild strawberries. By the side of it stood octagonal silver sugar casters. The candelabra on the table glossed the wood's dark grain. Reflected in the épergne's curves and facets, points of flame quivered.

You will pay attention to your right ...

Traffic was thickening.

Fisher!

The bus was slowing.

Susan Fisher!

. . . above the piazza. The Villa is still owned by the Aldobrandini family. You will notice the central avenue of box trees. The park is noted for its grottos and Baroque fountains.

"Doubtless by Bernini," I said.

"Is that a *palm* tree?" said Helen.

The Villa is open to tourists only in the morning and upon application to the officials of the Frascati Tourist Office. If you will consult your watches, you will see that it is now afternoon so we will proceed immediately to the largest of the Frascati wine cellars.

The aluminum cane with its rubber bulb thumping down, the leg swinging up and to the side, Kojak led the straggling procession towards a large grey stone building at the bottom end of the sloping piazza. A steep flight of steps led down to a terrace and the main entrance. Kojak, teeth bared with the exertion, started to stump and crab his way down.

"Oh, look at the poor old thing, Jack," said Helen. "He'll never manage her on his own down here."

I went back across the road to where they were still waiting to cross and put my arm under the old woman's. She seemed almost weightless.

"I appreciate this," he said, nodding vigorously on the other side of her. "Nelson Morrison. We're from Trenton, New Jersey."

"Not at all," I said. "Not at all. It's a pleasure."

The old woman did not look at either of us.

"That's the way," I said. "That's it."

"She's not a big talker. She doesn't speak very often, do you, Mother?"

Step by step we edged her down.

"But she enjoys it, don't you, Mother? You can tell she enjoys it. She likes to go out. We went on a boat, didn't we, Mother?"

"Nearly there," I said.

"Do you remember the boat in Venice, Mother? Do you? I think it's a naughty day today, isn't it? You're only hearing what you want to hear."

"One more," I said.

"But she did enjoy it. Every year you'll find us somewhere, won't he, Mother?"

Inside, the others were sitting at a refectory table in a vaulted cellar. It was lit by bare bulbs. It was cool, almost cold, after coming in out of the sunshine. In places, the brickwork glistened with moisture. Kojak, a cigarette held up between thumb and forefinger, was holding forth.

The cellars apparently extended under the building for more than a mile of natural caves and caverns. In the tunnels and corridors were more than a million bottles of wine. Today, however, there was nothing to see as the wine-making did not take place until September. But famous and authentic food was available at the cafe and counter just a bit further down the tunnel and bottles of the finest Frascati were advantageously for sale. If we desired to buy wine, it would be his pleasure to negotiate for us.

He paused.

He surveyed us through the blue-tinted spectacles.

Slowly, he shook his head.

The five bottles of wine on the table were provided free of charge for us to drink on its own or as an accompaniment to food we might purchase. While he was talking, a girl with a sacking apron round her waist and with broken-backed men's shoes on her feet scuffed in with a tray of tumblers. Kojak started pouring the wine. It looked as if it had been drawn from a barrel minutes before. It was greenish and cloudy. It was thin and vile and tasted like tin. I decided to drink it quickly.

I didn't actually see it happen because I was leaning over saying something to Helen. I heard the melancholy man, the man who was travelling alone, say, "No thank you. I don't drink."

Glass chinking against glass.

"No thank you."

A chair scraping.

And there was Kojak mopping at his trouser leg with a handkerchief and grinding out what sounded like imprecations which were getting louder and louder. The melancholy man had somehow moved his glass away while Kojak was pouring or had tried to cover it or pushed away the neck of the bottle. Raised fist quivering, Kojak was addressing the vaulted roof.

Grabbing a bottle-neck in his meaty hand, he upended the bottle over the little man's glass, wine glugging and splashing onto the table.

"Doesn't drink!" snarled Kojak.

He slammed the bottle down on the table.

"Doesn't drink!"

He flicked drops of wine onto the table off the back of his splashed hand.

"Mama mia! Doesn't drink!"

Grinding and growling he stumped off towards the cafe.

He left behind him a silence.

Into the silence, one of the women said,

"Perhaps it's a custom you're supposed to drink it? If you don't it's insulting?"

"Now wait a minute," said her husband.

"Like covering your head?" she added.

"Maybe I'm out of line," said the other man, "but in my book that was inappropriate behaviour."

"I never did much like the taste of alcohol," said the melancholy man.

His accent was British and glumly northern.

"They seem to sup it with everything here," he said, shaking his head in gloomy disapproval.

"Where are you folks from?" said the man in the turquoise shirt.

"Canada," said Helen.

"You hear that, June? Ottawa? Did we visit Ottawa, June?"

"Maybe," said June, "being that he's European and ..."

"It's nothing to do with being European," said Helen. "It's to do with being rude and a bully. And he's not getting a tip from *us*."

"Yeah," said June's husband, "and what's with all these jokes about women drivers? I'll tell you something, okay? *My wife drives better than I drive.* Okay?"

He looked around the table.

"Okay?"

"I've seen them," said the melancholy man, "in those little places where they eat their breakfasts standing up, I've seen them in there first thing in the morning—imagine—taking raw spirits."

The old woman sat hunched within a tweed coat, little eyes watching. She made me think of a fledgling that had fallen from the nest. Her tumbler was empty. She was looking at me. Then she seemed to be looking at the nearest bottle. I raised my eyebrows. Her eyes seemed to grow wider. I poured her more and her hand crept out to secure the glass.

"Jack!" whispered Helen.

"What the hell difference does it make?"

I poured more of the stuff for myself.

June and Chuck were from North Dakota. Norm and Joanne were from California. Chuck was in construction. Norm was on a disability pension and sold patio furniture. Joanne was a nurse. George Robinson was from Bradford and did something to do with textile machinery. Nelson and his mother travelled every summer and last summer had visited Yugoslavia but had suffered from the food.

I explained to June that it was quite possible that I sounded very like the guy on a PBS series because the series had been made by the BBC and I had been born in the UK but was now Canadian. She told me my accent was cute. I told her I thought her accent cute too. We toasted each other's accents. Helen began giving me looks.

June had bought a purse in Rome. Joanne had bought a purse in Florence. Florence was noted for purses. June and Chuck were going to Florence after Rome. Helen had bought a purse in Florence—the best area of Florence for purses being on the far side of the Ponte Vecchio. In Venice there were far fewer stores selling purses. Shoes, on the other hand, shoe stores were everywhere. Norm said he'd observed more shoe stores in Italy than in any other country in the world.

Nelson disliked olive oil.

George could not abide eggplants. Doris, George's wife who had died of cancer the year before, had never fancied tomatoes.

Nelson was flushed and becoming loquacious.

Chuck said he'd had better pizza in Grand Forks, North Dakota, where at least they put cheese on it and it wasn't runny.

George said the look of eggplants made him think of native women.

Joanne said a little pasta went a long way.

Milan?

After Venice, Norm and Joanne were booked into Milan. What was Milan like? Had anyone been there?

"Don't speak to me about Milan!" said Helen.

"Not a favourite subject with us," I said.

"We got mugged there," said Helen, "and they stole a gold bracelet I'd had since I was twenty-one."

"'They,'" I said, "being three girls."

"We were walking along on the sidewalk just outside that monstrous railway station . . ."

"Three *girls*, for Christ's sake!"

"They came running up to us," said Helen.

"Two of them not more than thirteen years old," I said, "and the other about eighteen or nineteen."

"One of them had a newspaper sort of folded to show columns of figures and another had a bundle of tickets of some sort and they were waving these in our faces ..."

"And talking at us very loudly and quickly ..."

"... and, well, *brandishing* these ..."

"... and sort of grabbing at you, pulling your sleeve ..."

"*Touching* you," said Helen.

"*Right!*" said Norm. "Okay."

"*Exactly,*" said Joanne. "That's *exactly* ..."

"And then," I said, "I felt the tallest girl's hand going inside my jacket—you know—to your inside pocket ..."

"We were so *distracted,* you see," said Helen, "what with all the talking and them pointing at the paper and waving things under your nose and being *touched* ..."

"So anyway," I said, "when I felt *that* I realized what was happening and I hit this girl's arm away and ..."

"Oh, it was *awful!*" said Helen. "Because *I* thought they were just beggars, you see, or kids trying to sell lottery tickets or something, and I was really horrible to Jack for hitting this girl ... I mean, he hit her *really hard* and I thought they were just begging so I couldn't believe he'd ..."

"But the best part," I said, "was that I probably wasn't the main target in the first place because we walked on into the station and we were buying tickets—we were in the line—and Helen ..."

"I'd suddenly felt the weight," said Helen. "The difference, I mean, and I looked down at my wrist and the bracelet was gone. I hadn't felt a thing when they'd grabbed it. Not with all that other touching. They must have pulled and broken the safety chain and ..."

"Of course," I said, "I ran back to the entrance but ..."

I spread my hands.

"Long gone."

"With us," said Joanne, "it was postcards and guidebooks they were waving about."

"Where?"

"Here. In Rome."

"Girls? The same?"

"Gypsies," said Norm.

"Did they get anything?" said Helen.

"A Leica," said Joanne.

"Misdirection of attention," said Norm.

"Were they girl-gypsies?" I said.

"Misdirecting," said Norm. "It's the basic principle of illusionism."

"I was robbed right at the airport," said Nelson.

"It must be a national *industry,*" said George.

"They had a baby in a shawl and I was just standing there with Mother and they pushed this baby against my chest and well, naturally, you . . ."

"I don't *believe* this!" said Norm. "This I do not *believe!*"

"And while I was holding it, the other two women were shouting at me in Italian and they had a magazine they were showing me . . ."

"What did they steal?"

"Airplane ticket. Passport. Traveller's cheques. But I had some American bills in the top pocket of my blazer so they didn't get that."

"Did you feel it?" said Joanne.

He shook his head.

"No. They just took the baby and walked away and I only realized when I was going to change a traveller's cheque at the cambio office because we were going to get on the bus, weren't we, Mother?"

"A baby!" said June.

"But a few minutes later," said Nelson, "one of the women came up to me on her own with the ticket and my passport."

"Why would she give them back?" said Helen. "Don't they sell them to spies or something?"

"I paid her for them," said Nelson.

"Paid her?" said June.

"Paid her!" said Norm.

"PAID!" said Chuck.

"Ten dollars," said Nelson.

"They must have seen you coming!" said George.

"They must have seen *all* of you coming," said Chuck.

Nelson poured himself another murky tumbler of Frascati. "It wasn't much," he said. "Ten dollars. She got what she wanted. I got what I wanted."

He shrugged. Raising the glass, he said,

"A short life but a merry one!"

We stared at him.

"I got what I wanted, didn't I, Mother? And then we went on the green and red bus, didn't we? Do you remember? On the green and red bus?"

The old woman started making loud squeak noises in her throat.

It was the first sound we'd heard her make.

She sounded like a guinea pig.

"It's time for tinkles!" sang Nelson. "It's tinkle time."

And raising her up and half carrying her to the door of the women's malodorous toilet, he turned with her, almost as if waltzing, and backed his way in.

* * *

... not entirely without incident.

Don't mention Milan to us!

... except for Helen's getting mugged

It all made quite a good story, a story with which we regaled our friends and neighbours. We became quite practised in the telling of it. We told it at parties and over dinners, feeding each other lines.

But the story we told was a story different in one particular from what really happened—though Helen doesn't know that.

The scene often comes to mind. I see it when the pages blur. I see it in my desk-top in the wood's repetitive grain. I see it when I gaze unseeing out of the window of the restaurant after lunch, the sun hot on my shoulder and sleeve. I see it when I'm lying in bed in the morning in those drowsy minutes after being awakened by the clink and chink of Helen's bottles as she applies moisturizing cream, foundation, blush, and shadow.

Chuck from Grand Forks, North Dakota, had been right. They *had* seen all of us coming. Easy pickings. Meek and nearing middle age, ready to be fleeced, lambs to the slaughter.

She'd been the first female I'd hit since childhood. I hadn't intended to hit her hard. I'd moved instinctively. Her eyes had widened with the pain of it.

I'd noticed her even before she'd run towards us. Good legs, high breasts pushing at the tight grey cotton dress, long light-brown hair. She was wearing bright yellow plastic sandals. She had no makeup on and looked a bit grubby, looked the young gamine she probably was.

I'd been carrying a suitcase and felt sweaty even though it was early in the morning. Her hand as it touched the side of my chest, my breast, was cool against my heat.

When I struck her arm, there was no panic in her eyes, just a widening. There was a hauteur in her expression. Our eyes held each other's for what seemed long seconds.

When Helen discovered her bracelet gone, I hurried out of the vast ticket hall but under the colonnade and out of sight I slowed to a walk. There is no rational, sensible explanation for what followed.

I stood in the archway of the entrance. The two small girls had gone. She stood facing me across the width of the curving road. It was as if she'd been waiting for me.

We stood staring at each other.

Behind her was a sidewalk cafe. The white metal chairs and tables were screened by square white tubs containing small, bushy bay trees. The bays were dark and glossy. Dozens of sparrows hopped about on the edges of the tubs. Pigeons were pecking along the sidewalk near her feet. Among them was a reddish-brown pigeon and two white ones. In the strong morning light I could see the lines of her body under the grey cotton dress. She was gently rubbing at her arm.

Sitting there in Reardon's restaurant, drowsy in the sunshine after eating the Businessman's Luncheon Special ($4.95), the cream of celery soup, the minced-beef pie with ginger-coloured gravy, the french fries, the sliced string beans, waiting for the waitress to bring coffee, sitting there with the winter sun warm through the window on my shoulder and sleeve, I walk out of the shadow of the arch and stand waiting on the edge of the sidewalk. She nods to me. It is a nod which is casually intimate, a nod of acknowledgement and greeting. I wait for a gap in the sweeping traffic.

She watches me approaching.

CEAZER SALAD

THE REVIEW of *Chamber Music* had appeared in the Saturday edition of the *Calgary Clarion*, which arrived in Ottawa at Magazines International on Wednesday. The tone of the review was hostile and oddly aggrieved. The reviewer—"a Calgary writer"—suggested that Albertans, commonsensical and down-to-earth as they were, would only be repelled by the book's so-called sophistication, a sophistication which might be lauded by Brahmins in the East but which was elitist and effete. "Tony" had been one of the reviewer's words. He went on to attack Forde's contempt for his readers, as evidenced in his pretentious use of the word "ziggurat," and the book's alleged humour which he, Calgarian, found brittle if not epicene.

Forde rattled the pages of the *Clarion*.

"'Picasso COMMA the famous Spanish painter COMMA.' Well, I suppose you can't go far wrong assuming ignorance in Albertans."

He smacked the sheets with the back of his hand.

"Christ! Here's an amazing one. 'Napoleon COMMA the Emperor of the French COMMA.'"

The sections, Sports, Classified, Wheels, Entertainment, fluttered down the wall to the floor.

"'Brahmins,'" said Forde. "'*Brahmins!*'"

Sheila, who was taking a day off, pulled the lapels of her bathrobe closed and, dipping the brush into the varnish, concentrated on the spread fingers of her left hand. Whenever she took what she called mental health days she sat around in her old terrycloth robe and painted her fingernails and toenails and turned the radio on. She did not listen to the radio. She knew what anguish its bland bonhomie caused him and he was convinced that she turned it on not only to assert her presence but to persecute him.

"One wonders," he said, "why they didn't feel compelled to go on and on and ON. 'Emperor of the French COMMA who lived in olden times COMMA and died in exile on St. Helena COMMA a small island in the South Atlantic Ocean.'"

Sheila tapped the lid of the marmalade jar with a knuckle.

"Please," she said.

"'Unlikely,'" said Forde, "'to be of interest to Western readers.'"

"Do you think this'll still be good, Rob?"

"Hah!" he said. "What," he demanded, "*would* be of interest to Western readers? Eh?"

"It's turned very dark," said Sheila, "almost black."

"Think of the headline that *would* engage the inhabitants of Buttfuck, Alberta . . ."

"*Can* it go bad? Do you think? With all the sugar?"

"ANOTHER COW," said Forde, "FOUND DEAD."

"Mmmm . . ." said Sheila.

"What a sad sad dump. I *hate* Alberta. The whole bloody landscape littered with fun-loving Mennonites and oil pumps on the nod. Bulging, my Lovely, bulging with huge Ukrainians internationally wanted for Nazi war crimes. People dressed up in silly cowboy hats. And boots everywhere that look like skin disease."

"*What?*"

"*Boots.* Lizard-skin boots. Or ostrich or snake or some fucking thing. Nasty *pimply* boots. Remember Ed Lacey? He was teaching in Edmonton and in a letter—now *here's* a turn of phrase—he called Alberta 'that bleak latrine.'"

The acid peardrop smell of the nail polish suddenly brought to him the balsa-wood aeroplane kits of his childhood. Spitfires, RAF roundels. Messerschmitts, swastikas. The clear glue smelled of peardrops and had always been called "aeroplane dope."

Dope! thought Forde.

He watched Sheila fanning her nails with an envelope.

"Did you know—this is absolutely true—there's a town in Alberta called Dog Pound?"

"*Home,* he sang, *home on the range . . .*

"And home to the Aryan Nation and the Northern Guard and home, my winsome marrow, my Dunmow Flitch . . ."

"Who he?" said Sheila.

"What? Where was I? Home to Jim Keegstra and the whatnames, you know, the Heritage Front, and to sturdy Survivalists standing on guard against the encroachment of turban and curry. Yes, my old fruit, when you think about it, it's not very surprising they've got a Eugenics Board. And a Sexual Sterilization Act. And as to the daily round," he said with a wide gesture of his arms, "the amenities, life's little pleasures and refinements—well, there's hardly anything, just to take one example, hardly anything you'd recognize as a restaurant. There were, as I recall, muffins."

He paused.

"Crullers."

Paused again.

"The occasional perogi. But precious little of the old *haute cuisine.* The supermarkets there sell packets of stuff called Tuna-Extender. And when they're not eating Tuna-Extender they eat steaks. They all have barbeques, propane barbeques with dials and switches like airplane cockpits. And they take their gobbets of Alberta Grade A marbled beef and incinerate them on their propane barbeques which is the cause of the yellow dome that sits pudding-shaped over Calgary and which is visible from as far away as Drumheller."

Forde raised a finger.

"Steaks rare would not be requested *saignant* or *bleu*—or even 'rare.' They would be ordered in the Steakaramas, if at all, by those witty rascals in the cowboy hats with, 'Honey, just saw off its horns and wipe its ass.' And to accompany these burnt offerings—do you know what they eat? They eat iceberg lettuce slathered with a concoction called Creamy Cucumber Ranch.

"You think I'm inventing this?

"*Nobody*, my peardrop-smelling inamorata, nobody could invent this.

"And they drink wine that comes in one-and-a-half litre bottles. It is called *Mediterranean Warmth*. That's the carriage trade. The unwashed drink poisonous rye called *Golden Wedding*."

Forde uttered a kind of groan.

"In Alberta," he said, "there is nothing old. The buildings are brutal. The streets merely numbered. Bottle-openers are screwed to the headboards of hotel beds."

He stirred the pages of the *Clarion* with his toe cap.

"There's a drear museum in Calgary that about sums it all up," he said. "Looks like a mothballed factory. Full—are you listening, my fruit of the loom?—full not of the glory that was Greece and the grandeur that was Rome. No, sir! No, siree! Not in Alberta. But furnished with fascinating old scythes and billhooks, patent medicine bottles, Louis Riel's suspenders, pioneer buckets . . ."

Forde paused.

"Christ!" he whispered, as if broken. "Christ! The balls-withering boredom of it all."

* * *

Forde ran his forefinger over the polyurethane on his desktop, hating it. He wished that he could afford an eighteenth-century desk or table. He thought it probable that if he had a beautiful desk it would induce a greater elegance in his writing. He did not necessarily want a piece from the workshop of Robert Adam or Chippendale or Gillow or Hepplewhite. He would have settled for a country piece in applewood or beech, a piece alive with the patina of years.

Pogo clicked along the hall and padded in and subsided across Forde's feet with a sigh, and, following the sigh, arising from the seeping beast, the silent stench of Chunky *God!* Alpo.

And a Turcoman rug would warm the room, a Beshir or a Royal Bokhara. Or a small Persian tribal—his mind drifted on—Baluch or Heriz. He remembered being in London after the overthrow of the Shah when every carpet dealer in town seemed to have shoeboxes of Luristan bronzes for sale, horse bits, adzes, votive axe-heads, finials, harness bells. There had been rumours of sacked museums.

Museums; he thought of the one in Calgary he'd described to Sheila. He'd stayed at a hotel close to that museum. The Palliser. He'd been doing something at the university, what he couldn't now remember, but *did* remember standing on the front steps of the Palliser, the evening sun low, almost blinding, and a barefoot woman came running out of the sun, crossing the road to the sidewalk a yard in front of him. Her blouse had been completely open and her grimy breasts flopped. She ran past and disappeared into a nearby alley. He had stood there waiting, waiting for a pursuer, waiting for a sequel, a motive, a meaning.

And in Edmonton he'd once booked into a hotel near the municipal airport. It was late at night, he remembered. Some disruption of travel plans, Vancouver, fog. The plane had been diverted. The desk clerk gave him a key. As he opened the door a man who was sitting in an armchair watching television turned an astonished head. He was naked except for a dove-grey Stetson and mauve ankle socks.

But it was the foyer of the hotel that had stayed in his mind. There had been a small rectangular pool in the foyer all set about with tubs of ficus trees. A spattering of vomit rode the surface of the pool. In the elevator an empty beer bottle was rolling about on the floor.

A sordid place. He had lain awake half the night, a revolving searchlight washing the ceiling.

Forde wrote on his pad of yellow paper.

"In the elevator an empty beer bottle rolled about on the floor."

Obviously it would be empty. He crossed the word out. The words "about on the floor" were stupidly redundant.

Then he wrote:

"In the elevator a beer bottle rolled."

Ending with "rolled" was pleasing, a strong ending you could *hear*.

"Beer."

"Beer?"

He sat staring at the paper, mouthing the words; considered striking out "beer."

When he had been thinking about the pool in the foyer and the ficus trees in tubs, the words "all set about with ficus trees" had been in his mind, yes, "all set about with." He could see the book's shiny red cloth cover with the gold elephant's head stamped on it, trunk curled up, the adored *Just So Stories*, and he could hear his mother's voice reading, reading about the elephant's child, a child of insatiable curiosity, the two of them waiting for the chanted refrain:

The great, grey, greasy Limpopo River all set about with fever trees.

On his last visit back to England he'd found his mother more stooped, slower. Her flat, though, was just the same. She had insisted on making him a cup of tea, no, no, he didn't know where things were, and from the sitting room he heard her in the tiny kitchen talking to herself, nothing he could understand, a whispery drizzle of words. On the wall, the souvenir plate from Bavaria. On the occasional table, audio cassettes of James Herriot's *All Creatures Great and Small.* A ghastly Alpine scene on the wall above the mahogany bureau, a more than decent piece from the old house. He noticed she had knitted, in turquoise wool, a cover that fitted over the Kleenex box.

She brought the tea to him on a doily-covered tray on which stood a floral cup and saucer, a small cut-glass milk jug, a matching floral bowl of sugar cubes with silver tongs beside.

As the afternoon wore on she suggested they watch on television a programme for children, one of her favourites, none of the violence and goings-on and the things they showed these days. The programme was called *Blue Peter*. The presenter was a particularly nice young man. The co-presenter was a young woman who showed a group of little girls how to make a doll out of the cardboard core of a toilet-paper roll.

Following this they watched a programme involving school teams answering general knowledge questions.

Following this they watched a programme about the rescue of animals in distress and their subsequent treatment and recovery in what looked like a greenhouse.

He had suggested to her that to save them both trouble he would stroll down to the High Street and bring back some fish and chips for dinner. He suggested this not only to forestall efforts on her part to cook, but also to escape from the flat for half an hour. It was not only the children's television that weighed on him. It was her unceasing rehearsal of events in the lives of people he'd never heard of, members of her church, the man who ran the charity shop, the sister of her friend in Eastbourne, who had a little white dog called Penny that rode in a pram, the woman who came to the flat to do her hair, the husband of the woman who came to the flat to do her hair, who, until the accident to his arm in Sainsbury's had had a garden, well, you could scarcely *imagine* the red runner beans . . .

These unending stories oppressed him with a kind of mental pain, the same kind of pain—he cast about—the closest he could come to comparing the pain with any other kind of pain was possibly the pain felt if he were subjected to Lieder or folkfuckery by Benjamin Britten sung by (Oh, poignant Christ!) Peter fucking Pears.

When he came back with the hot package, he heard her in the kitchen, cupboards closing, drawers opening, that same whisper of words. She came out into the sitting room and opened the bureau.

She was looking, she said, for the cutlery canteen. It was a dark leather box. What cutlery, he had wanted to know. There was cutlery in the kitchen drawer. The fish knives and forks, she had said. He said they should use the ordinary forks.

She ignored him and went back into the kitchen. Cupboards again. After a minute or two, an exclamation.

The silver knives and forks were tarnished black and gold. Her eyesight too poor to notice. He rubbed the knife surreptitiously to see if the black came off. He employed the fork gingerly.

"No fish forks, indeed!" she said. "Whatever is the world coming to!"

* * *

Photocopy
Buy stamps
LCBO—Sancerre
Bank

The man in front of him in the line looked to be about sixty years old but was wearing gaudy, unlaced shoes, which swirled in black, white, orange, and blue. Ruby reflectors twinkled on the heels. Forde no longer knew what to call such shoes. They seemed to be moulded, one-piece things made of rubber and canvas, or, for all he knew, of extruded protein, two words he'd once read in a magazine. At school in England, a simpler version of such things had been called tennis shoes or running shoes or sneakers. They had been worn only for sports. Mothers condemned them for daily wear as harmful to the growing foot. The times, thought Forde, condemned one to be cautious in the use of the word "mother."

At *his* school they'd always been called plimsolls. Though, come to think of it, he didn't know why. The Plimsoll Line man? He recalled the almost military inspection of the plimsolls before each gym class, the canvas blancoed to chalky perfection. Gould had been his name. Sergeant Gould. Now, in England, they called such things "trainers."

Forde disliked the technicolour vulgarity of the man's shoes intensely and especially so on a man well past middle age. They were a part of what he thought of as an increasing infantilism, shoes with Velcro tabs instead of laces as though laces had become too complicated to tie, T-shirts with writing and pictures on them. Nursery clothes. Obesity. Saggy sweatpants with elasticized waistbands. No ties, T-shirts, tattooed tits. He deplored this flight from formality. On irritable days, half the people he saw on the streets suggested to him the populations of clinics, mental hospitals, and sheltered workshops.

Forde knew that something had broken. He felt that the world he'd inherited was disappearing. This shift in the world, this slide, had been slow, unremarkable, almost invisible at first, and he, like the frog in cold water brought to the boil, motionless, unaware. He lived now, he often felt, in wreckage, treading water, straining for the feeble cries of other survivors.

Forde was aware of his crankiness. He put it on a bit to amuse himself and to irritate and amuse Sheila but, even if exaggerated, caricatured, at base it represented the way he really felt.

The woman at the teller facing him was conducting an endless transaction; he could tell by the bend of her leg, by the relaxation of her body against the counter, that she was settling in for aeons more of it; probably, thought Forde, cashing in 1945 Victory Bonds.

His attention drifted away. The sentence was wrong; *definitely* wrong. "Beer" had to come out. It weakened the sentence, fudging, blunting. It defeated delivery of the right sound.

"In the elevator a bottle rolled."

His eye lighted on a large poster high on the wall behind the tellers. The poster was red and white and looked professionally printed rather than stencilled or hand-lettered. This suggested that the posters were probably on display in other branches all over Ottawa and possibly in branches of the Bank of Nova Scotia all across Canada.

TRANSFER YOUR MORTGAGE

THE 5% ADVANTAGE

And diagonally across the top left-hand corner:

NO FEE'S

When his turn at last arrived, he said, pointing at the poster, "Why the apostrophe?"

"Apostrophe?" she echoed.

"Where it says 'No Fee's.'"

"I'm sorry?"

Pointing, he said, "Look! Top left."

One of the supervisors seated some way behind her at a desk got up and came to the counter.

"What seems to be the problem?"

"Oh, there's no problem," he said. "I'm just pointing out that the apostrophe in 'No Fee's' is incorrect."

She looked up at the poster.

"Incorrect how do you mean?"

"An apostrophe," he said, "indicates either possession or omission. But 'Fee's,' you see, *doesn't*. Doesn't fit either of those uses."

She considered this.

"Perhaps," she said, "this is a financial meaning."

Forde pursed his lips, shaking his head slightly.

A hectic flush started up her neck.

"The only thing to do," she said, "you'll have to see a Personal Banking Officer."

She opened the wicket and clacked across the marble to a doorless cubicle, in which sat a Personal Banking Officer.

"This gentleman," said the supervisor, "has a complaint."

"More of an observation, really."

The Personal Banking Officer was short and had a ginger crew cut. A little, bulbous nose. He looked just like Josef Lada's line drawings of the Good Soldier Švejk.

The three of them stood in front of his cubicle.

"You see? The top left corner. Says 'No Fee's.'"

The Officer nodded slowly and, after a long pause, said, "So what's your problem?"

Forde launched into it again.

"... and therefore it's simply incorrect."

The Officer frowned.

"That poster," said Forde, "must have been seen by *dozens* of people before it was actually printed."

He shook his head to convey sorrowful amazement at this state of affairs.

The Officer seemed to inflate himself and said, "I have no idea what you're telling me here. Why don't you cut to the chase, fella?"

"I am attempting," said Forde slowly, and with insulting pantomimed patience—deep breaths, slow hand movements—"to explain to you why your poster is illiterate."

Again the Officer frowned.

"... a very bad impression," Forde concluded.

And because he resented being addressed as "fella" by a little ginger prick, added, "You're one of the country's major banks. People—not I, of course—but some might think that if you can't punctuate you might not be able to add and subtract either."

"Listen, fella," said the Officer, turning back into his cubicle, "I go with what I'm given."

Forde rejoined the line. The Victory Bonds woman was still slumped against the counter. At the next wicket another woman was exchanging rolled coins for notes and paying some complex bills. An old man had forgotten his PIN number and lost his bank card and kept opening and closing his wallet in a distraught manner. The man with a business deposit had a cell phone that chirruped *The Bonnie Banks of Loch Lomond*.

Forde did not feel like working—Sheila in her bathrobe, the radio, Pogo seeping, the dailyness of his ugly desk, the draining effort that had gone into *Chamber Music*. He decided on a stroll. He stopped at the corner of Waverly Street to read the densely printed poster in the window of the Nutri-Chem Pharmacy. The store had recently changed hands. Previously it had been an ordinary pharmacy stocking aspirin and Contac-C and toothpaste but now it had been made over into a Centre for Holistic Medicine. They sold elixirs, tinctures, infusions, extracts, and laxatives all derived from leaves and twigs and bulbs and bark.

The poster's headline asked:

WHERE HAS ALL THE GOOD BACTERIA GONE?

Forde considered all the little bottles and boxes and the bundles of twigs and a saucer of cocoa seeds and some leaves gone brown and a big pod. He wondered who would be rash enough to swallow something called Slippery Elm on the advice of people unable to distinguish singular from plural. He thought of going in and trying to make this point to the girl behind the counter, but the ochre hair and the cluster of stainless-steel surgical clamps climbing the cartilage of her right ear dissuaded him.

He paged through some magazines in Magazines International.

He browsed in the bookstore.

He strolled on up Elgin towards Sparks Street. Outside the restaurants the chalkboards advertising daily specials offered the customary mangling of the words Omelette, Spaghetti, and Caesar. The chalkboards were also spattered with quotation marks, dishes being described as "famous," "delicious," "hot," and "juicy," daily examples of the conviction of the semi-literate that inverted commas act as intensifiers.

At the entrance to the Sparks Street Mall reared some fifteen feet high a sheet-metal grizzly bear, its mouth agape, just about to crunch the fish, presumably a salmon, held in its left paw. This travesty of sculpture always caused Forde both anger and cringing embarrassment.

Behind the sheet-metal grizzly bear hung an elaborately framed sign which read:

SPARKS STREET MALL
Great Shops—Services—Parking
ON CANADA'S MOST UNIQUE STREET

Forde thought, with great weariness of spirit, of trying to explain to urban planners, to representatives of community associations, to aldermen, to city councillors, to streetscape specialists, urban renewal specialists, Heritage specialists, specialists in acceptable and non-conforming signage, that the word "Unique" cannot be used with comparatives, that the word means that there is only one of something, that there cannot be more or less of singleness, that "Unique" comes via French from the Latin "unicus," single, akin to "unus" meaning "one."

Overcome by the need for a beer, Forde seated himself in the small outdoor café situated between the sheet-metal grizzly on one side and another monstrosity on the other, a naked and seemingly anorexic family group capering in welded copper and entitled *Joy*.

The waitress offered him the Sandwich of the Day. Forde shrugged and then nodded. The sandwiches, he noted, were kept in a cooler. He read its packaging. It was a Chicken Tikha sandwich and contained, among many other things, gum arabic, sundry citrates, and Stabilizers E 412, E 415, and E 410. It was soggy and tasted faintly of chutney.

To one side of the sheet-metal bear stood W.E. Noffke's main Post Office, its entrances flanked by elegant pairs of heraldic lions supporting shields. The crisp and vigorous carving always pleased Forde. One of the lions had been defaced some years before by a man with a hammer protesting something . . . Forde forgot what. The Royal Family, perhaps. English Canada's domination of Quebec? Canada's colonial status?

As he passed by on his way to the Hill, he glanced at the Second Empire façade of the Langevin Building, the decorative string courses dividing the floors, that horizontal emphasis invigorated by the vertical movements of the windows, large and rectangular on the ground floor but, pulling the eye upwards, smaller and arched on the second and third floors, the arches recessed and set off by flanking columns and capitals, charming little confections of polished pink granite.

On the gates across the tunnel leading into the building's black bowels, an enamel sign presumably directed at chauffeurs waiting to pick up politicians or bureaucrats:

PLEASE SHUT OFF MOTOR'S

* * *

Adrift on the Hill. His mind churning. Wandering past the West Block. Stood regarding the black-and-white enamel sign:

RESERVED PARKING
FOR
MINISTER'S VEHICLES

Past the Info-Tent, where someone had dropped on the path *Discover the Hill: Outdoor Self-Guiding Booklet.* Forde stood staring at the seated statue of Lester B. Pearson. He was portrayed as sitting casually in an office chair with his left leg crossed over his right. It was—Forde struggled with what he was thinking about—it was, it had no life, it was not a sculpture but *an illustration.*

He consulted the *Self-Guiding Booklet.*

Originator of the concept of UN Peacekeeping forces, our 14th prime minister did much to foster the image of Canada as a peaceful nation on the world stage. Thank you, Mr. Pearson!

Pearson's left shoe shone yellow.

In the *Booklet* he read:

People rub Lester B. Pearson's left shoe for good luck.

Like rubbing the left breast of the statue of Juliet in that squalid courtyard in Verona or kissing the exposed brown toe of St. Ignatius in the cathedral in Goa. Though rubbing the left wingtip of a statue of Lester B. Pearson seemed to Forde *desperately* Canadian.

He pottered about the Hill from statue to statue. Those made in more recent years, Diefenbaker, Pearson, Mackenzie King, George Brown, Sir Robert Borden, were stiff, awkward, lacked fluidity. The best statues were all by Louis-Philippe Hébert from Montreal and had been unveiled, Forde noted, either actually in the nineteenth century or within a year of it.

According to the *Booklet*, the young lady on the base of the statue of Queen Victoria is "an allegorical figure of Canada"; the young lady on the statue of Alexander Mackenzie "an allegorical figure of Probity"; on the statue of Sir John A. Macdonald the young lady represents "Confederation."

Allegorical figures! thought Forde. Probity! It was obvious, simply, that Louis-Philippe Hébert had a liking for titty wenches and good for Louis-Philippe thought Forde.

But the more modern statues. It was the same thing he'd been thinking about all morning. The motionless frog in the slowly heating water. When had it become impossible to cast statues of public figures? And why exactly? The dates seemed to suggest the Great War. Those four years seemed to mark...

Louis-Philippe's statues had all been cast in the great bronze foundries of Paris. International sculpture radiated from Paris. Hébert himself had trained and worked there. Most sculptors at this period studied under the same masters at the École des Beaux Arts. And later, in the world of contracts and commissions, sculptors worked as artisans for each other and shared their workmen.

All this was much in Forde's mind because his reading lately had been almost exclusively in the art history and biography of this period. This international language, as it were, of sculpture was silenced by World War I. But the tradition was under attack, too, by the dominance of photography, by surrealism, Dada, Deco, movements away from realism, Rodin, Jacob Epstein, Maillol, the beginnings of modernism, Ossip Zadkine, new ways of looking. And at this time, too, sculpture had split into two camps, monumental sculpture and studio or gallery sculpture, and it was studio sculpture that proved more vital.

Forde was contemplating a novel involving dubious authentications, a corrupting art-dealer based on Lord Duveen, and a scholar based on Berenson. All in a brooding villa like Berenson's *I Tatti*, replete with wife and mistress, secretary, and a sexually ambivalent protégé, the whole seraglio indirectly prompted years earlier by his reading Malamud's *Pictures of Fidelman.*

It was the Berenson-figure he was relishing, patriarchal yet petted, cosseted, food fads, enemas, pompous with precepts and prejudice, a *ridiculous* little man but at the same time something of a genius being lured onto the perilous lee shore of Duveen's dark intentions. The Berenson-man had an ebony cane with a silver pommel in the shape of a skull. He was rarely parted from it. Two half-turns of the pommel released a two-foot blade. The cane was called The Blogue. Forde could hardly wait to get his hands on him.

The cane had transported itself from a biography of Sir Arthur Evans, an imperious and theatrical little man, who all his life carried a walking stick called Prodger.

But *The Blogue*?

He turned away from it. It was a perfect detail, a gift. He did not want to pick at it. He luxuriated in this welling up, the swimming in of detail.

The Blogue. Unexplained. Inexplicable.

Perfect.

But these figures, these statues, his mind worrying at the matter, these neoclassical figures of Louis-Philippe Hébert—he glanced up at the dominating figure of Queen Victoria—they were at the end of the tradition, which had flowered in France in the seventeenth century. He thought almost with anguish of the loveliness of the radiant figures in the sculpture courts of the Louvre, bronze, marble, *terre cuite*, nymphs, warriors, satyrs, bacchantes. Louis-Philippe's work was at home inside that tradition. The rest of the statues were not.

Degenerate—no, that wasn't the word he was looking for—*debased*, that was more what he wanted. The more modern statues were debased—as coinage becomes debased by lowering its gold or silver content. As tribal sculpture becomes debased when it is separated from its people and purpose.

* * *

Forde stood behind the cannon's cascabel, running his fingertip over the Broad Arrow cut into the metal. He patted the sun-warmed bronze and walked around the cannon, looking at the touchhole, trunnions, quoins, and tompion, revelling in this antique terminology. This was the kind of thing he had been taught.

This gun, a nine-pound muzzle-loading ship's cannon, had been cast, the *Booklet* said, in Wales in 1807 and had been used in the Crimean War in the siege of Sevastopol. The British Army presented the cannon to their garrison in Canada as a trophy and commemoration of the Crimean battles.

Far below on an outcropping of bare rocks in the middle of the river, a white myriad of gulls ceaselessly screeched and fluttered. Across in Hull, federal office buildings now dominated the view, sterile hives looking as if they had been stuck together by an unlikeable child. Forde could remember the vast hoarding belonging to the E. B. Eddy Company pulp and paper mills, which from Hull, had faced the Parliament Buildings—a hoarding advertising White Swan Toilet Paper.

In 1698 a law was passed imposing harsh penalties on anyone found in possession of naval stores or other goods marked with the Broad Arrow. Government rope was marked by a coloured strand woven in, a strand called the Rogue's Yarn. In the main dockyard roperies, a yellow strand denoted Chatham cordage, a blue strand, Portsmouth, and a red strand, Devonport. This was the kind of thing he had been taught.

The cannon with its Broad Arrow, the statues of Louis-Philippe Hébert, the Gothic Revival buildings behind him, all spoke the same cultural language, all belonged to the same world, a world for which his education had groomed him, a world now as relevant as potsherds and shell-middens.

His hand on the warm bronze, he stood gazing up the river towards the Chaudière Falls. He remembered standing in the gun embrasures on the parapets of Malakhov Hill and looking down into the harbour of Sevastopol, the sea a strange, almost turquoise green with dark-brown patches further offshore. He remembered the Two-Headed Romanov Eagle on the cannon barrels, the tumbledown revetments, the glacis overgrown with scrub and bushes. Behind the cannon, black painted garlands of shot. Sevastopol had withstood siege for eleven months, during which a hundred thousand Russian soldiers and residents died. Malakhov Hill fell to the French in 1855. It seemed to Forde not long ago.

He remembered, too, the battlefield at Balaclava. The valley was planted now with vines, the leaves limp and yellowing along their wires, fall mists wisping. He had walked along the Causeway Heights to Redoubt No. 4, overlooking the North and South Valleys. The guns Lord Cardigan was supposed to capture were some British-made cannons captured by the Russians from the Turkish redoubts further down the Causeway. They were being hurried away by Russian troops in the South Valley. Lord Lucan, misunderstanding Lord Raglan's orders, instructed Lord Cardigan to ride, not against those skirmishers and stragglers, but against the dug-in positions of the Russians at the head of the North Valley.

After receiving the orders, Lord Cardigan rode out some yards ahead of the first line of cavalry and said, at conversational volume, *The Brigade will advance.*

Later, up on the Sapouné Heights where Lord Raglan had dithered, Forde had overlooked both Valleys. The advance down the North Valley looked to be about a mile, maybe more. What an eternity it must have seemed as the Brigade walked their horses, bits jingling, then trotted into the increasing barrage of nine-pound shot savaging the thinning lines, the crackle of musketry, the bruise-yellow banks of gunpowder smoke, acrid and blinding.

As the pace of the charge picked up, an excited officer rode up alongside Lord Cardigan and Cardigan barred the flat of his sword across the man's chest and called,

Steady! Steady! The 17th Lancers.

Behind him, as the men and horses fell, the squadron commanders, preserving the mass and weight of the charge, shouted repeatedly against the roar of the guns,

Close to your centre!

Look to your dressing on the left!

Close in!

Close in!

Up on the Sapouné Heights, high above the battle, General Bosquet watching the slaughter, murmured

C'est magnifique, mais ce n'est pas la guerre.

Riderless horses bolted out of the smoke, the whites of their eyes wide in terror. Troopers forced forward with knees and rowels as horses baulked at bodies on the ground.

Close in!

Close in to the centre!

Lowering his sword in the signal to charge, Lord Cardigan unleashed into the Russian gun emplacements a thunder of red uniforms, the charge subsiding into individual actions as the horsemen worked their mounts around guns, carts, water butts, fascines fallen from the breastworks. The Russian gunners struck at the cavalry with ramrods or tried to hide or run but were quickly sabred.

Some three or four hundred yards distant, the Russian army was drawn up, but the ranks watched in silence and made no move to engage.

The Light Brigade had suffered some two hundred and twenty killed or wounded. Lord Lucan, Lord Cardigan, and Lord Raglan were all variously incompetent, arrogant, petulantly vicious, or doddering, but no one, thought Forde, could deny the magnificent, imperturbable courage.

He glanced down at the *Booklet*.

From 1869-1994, the cannon was fired at noon to allow all postal employees to synchronize their watches, thereby regulating and ensuring the quality of the postal service.

Christ! thought Forde as he gave the bronze a farewell pat.

* * *

For some time Forde had been aware of a voice behind him. The speaker was French Canadian, his English heavily accented. Forde turned from the gun to look at the old man, who was talking to some obvious tourists.

"Me, I've been here coming on fourteen year. The Catman, they call me. Every day I'm here. Never missed a day. That's a long time."

"Kitty, kitty, kitty," called one of the little girls.

Forde moved closer and looked over the ornamental iron railings at the patch of bare earth spread with squares of filthy old carpet, the wooden hutches raised on bricks, the paper Maple Leaf flags and Stars and Stripes stapled to little sticks—tongue depressors, possibly, or popsicle sticks—and tied to branches and bushes. Two ginger cats were sleeping on the roof of one of the wooden boxes. Their faces were so fat their tongues stuck out. Pictures of cats hung from branches and wires strung overhead. The biggest pictures were of the cartoon cat, Garfield, and looked as if they'd been trimmed from the covers of comics.

"I have thirty now. Two weeks ago there were twenty-five. Too many cats, that's not too good. The houses, it's good for twenty-four. They go in there to the straw, two by two. When I have more they can go four or five in each one. You can't kill a cat with the bad weather. They get close together and they sleep good."

Forde looked at the Outdoor *Self-Guiding Booklet* and read:

Parliament Hill has been home to stray cats for decades. However, it is only since the 1970s that volunteers have paid special care and attention to these animals: creating the "cat sanctuary," maintaining its infrastructure and ensuring that the animals (cats, raccoons, groundhogs, squirrels, pigeons, chickadees and sparrows) are fed on a daily basis.

Maintaining its infrastructure! thought Forde.

Bizarre punctuation to boot, courtesy of the National Capital Commission.

The juxtaposition of the formality, pomp and ceremony of the Parliament Buildings and the modest cat sanctuary reflects the important Canadian values of tolerance and compassion.

The old man fell silent as families, groups, or couples walked on but started up again in a sort of soliloquy with each new passer-by.

"Maybe it's time for me to retire. I put an ad in the paper once and nobody showed up. It's volunteer, that's why. When Irene Desormeaux, she died, I've been the Catman since that day. The government they don't give me any money at all. But you know when you like something? Do it well or don't do it at all. The cats they keep me young. Two weeks ago there were twenty-five. I have thirty now. People, they drop their cats. They're not supposed to drop their cats. But they do it. If they get caught, they're gonna pay a fine. But it's hard to catch them. There's a squirrel. If I put a peanut in my ear they jump out of the tree onto my shoulder here and they take it out. I call them all Charlie because they look the same. I know all these cats. Her—that one sleeping underneath the house—that's Lapout. Lapout and Lulu, that's two sisters. Their mother is Brunette. When I see them, I know right away their name. Fluffy now, Fluffy was here a minute ago. Fluffy, now that's a nice cat. Fluffy's got a long robe. His fur, it's long. Big Mama—her sleeping under that bush—she's big. And Cocoa and Brownie. That one just went in the house. That's Princess. I had four grey but I see only two . . . Timin and Tigris. Here I have Bon Bon. I tell you! That Bon Bon! I bet you every day he's in the bushes."

He started working something bulky out of one of the plastic bags hanging from the railings. He set off with a plastic jerrycan to get water.

Forde drifted closer to the railings and stood regarding the scruffy cats, the squalid squares of carpet weighted at the corners with rocks. A plastic windmill on a stick. Among the paper flags, larger cloth flags on sticks were stuck into cans and toilet-paper cores, which had been worked onto branches as holders. Dozen upon dozen small pictures of cats were tacked to trunks and dangled from bushes, pictures cut from magazines or labels from cans or entire empty packages with cat pictures on them, *Whiskers, Finicky Cat, Nutrition First, Iams, Fancy Feast, Friskies, Meow Mix, Pounce Minouche, No Name Beef and Chicken Dinner.*

A raccoon toiled into the tiny clearing. Cats fled. It was hugely pregnant, its distended dugs leaking on the ground, staining the dust. Its fur was dull. It began eating from the nearest aluminum-foil dish. His presence did not deter it. From time to time it looked up at him with bleak eyes.

Forde stood staring.

On the tops of tree stumps, in rusted cans, wilting posies of flowering weeds. Scattered lids of opened cans. A plastic sunflower on a stick. Copulating flies dizzed on the crusting food and on the beaten earth.

THE MUSEUM AT THE END OF THE WORLD

IN the Pontic Alps high above Trebizond, dug into a sheer cliff face, Sumela Monastery. The last three-quarters of a mile was only possible on foot as the track climbed steep and broken, tree roots crawling out over the plates of rock, in places more scramble than walk. Forde and Sheila were moving at a fair pace to get out of the drizzle.

The quaint pamphlet given out with the tickets—a blurry photo on the second page of a filigreed relic of the True Cross—stated that the last Orthodox monks had left in the Exchange of Populations in 1923, taking with them, to Greece, the icon of the Virgin Mary popularly believed to be one of four painted by St. Luke. Now, after years of neglect, and wanton behaviour by tobacco smugglers, only crumbling Byzantine frescoes remained.

Forde cherished such useless information and relished the English in which it was often written. The "wanton" behaviour of tobacco smugglers expanded in his imagination, scenes of peculiarly Turkish debauchery, tight buttocks and turbans, played out under the gaze of frescoed saints stiff in gold and azure copes.

"Come *on*!" urged Sheila. "I'm getting soaked."

When they reached the tiny forecourt, a ledge cut into the face, one last long flight of steep steps climbed into the building itself. Forde stood leaning against a wall winded and puffing.

"What is it?" said Sheila. "What's wrong?"

Forde shook his head.

"Rob?"

"Just . . . a bit winded."

And closed his eyes again.

"Stop being so bloody British."

"Well, it's in my arm . . ."

"Christ!" said Sheila.

They picked their way back down the broken track and across the scree to the area where the vans were parked. One with its sliding door open, inside Father Keogh and the hulking flannel-mouthed man Forde had come to think of as The Minder.

The Minder proffered his little oval tin of mauve cachous.

Father Keogh was wearing a flat plebeian tweed cap and sat staring straight ahead.

"The monastery didn't attract you?" said Sheila.

He considered her.

"And why," he said, "would I be wishing to visit a nest of schismatics?"

"Mmmm," said Sheila.

The minder started his soothing babble of sound, weaving repeated words and phrases, encompassing the rain, the gloomy foliage, the steepness of the path, the grandeur of that morning's breakfast, his mother and something and soda bread. It was a song almost, an Irish crooning which made little sense. The flow of words did not seem to be directed at the priest personally but seemed rather like oil on generally troubled waters, placatory, a hush-now, hush-now.

Forde tuned out his blather and sat watching, through the van's open doorway the quick picking of a sparrow under a picnic table. He was waiting. He was feeling drawn deep inside himself, cautious, tentative in the world. He was waiting to see if the pain would fill his back teeth, crush his chest, bow and bend him.

He thought back to his last stress test at the Ottawa Heart Institute.

Injection of radioactive material.

Tapping Forde's wedding ring, the technician had said, "The wife'll like this."

"Pardon?"

"It'll make your willie glow in the dark."

Eighteen minutes of scanning photographs.

Injection of Persantine to stress the heart. Five unpleasant minutes later the injection of an antidote. Followed by the injection of more radioactive material. Followed by a chopped-egg sandwich. Followed by eighteen more minutes of photographs.

He fingered through the material of his jacket pocket the shape of the pump-spray of sublingual nitroglycerin.

He sat waiting, breathing shallow.

Father Keogh sat primly in remote silence.

Sheila was frowning as she struggled to understand the Minder's brogue. He was extolling the beauties of County Wexford, the soft, silver sheen of the Slaney's sweet waters, rhapsodizing over the red cows of Leinster, hock-deep in wild flowers—the white in the green—and the gorse, ah, God! the gorse, the scent of the gorse on the noon's heavy heat . . .

Father Keogh produced a silver flask.

The Minder stopped in mid-sentence.

Father Keogh unscrewed the flask's cap, which served as a little beaker.

"It's not yet five o'clock, Father."

"He knows perfectly well what time it is," said Father Keogh.

"Five o'clock was the hour appointed. Five o'clock was the agreed-upon hour."

Father Keogh carefully filled the cap.

"He is not," said Father Keogh, "to be judged by snivellers."

"But. Father . . ."

"He will not be badgered."

Forde turned his head completely and openly stared.

* * *

"*What* was she saying? No. Completely gone. Honestly."

"Not everyone can fit in at the same time so half'll go to the palace first and half to the mosque," said Sheila.

"And then switch over sort of thing?"

"Right."

"Well, let's go to the palace. I've gone off mosques. Taking your shoes off and putting them on again and pottering about with them in dirty plastic bags."

"That one's the palace bus," said Sheila.

"And all those athlete's foot carpets," said Forde.

He soon abandoned the local guide with her insistent "If I may invite you this way here shall you see . . ." and wandered off into the desolate ruins of the palace of the Grand Comneni. Here, where he stood in what had been the palace library, Cardinal Bessarian, as a youth, had read his Homer. Here, in this library, Forde imagined the exquisite Byzantine bindings, ivory plaques carved in bas-relief let into the covers and surrounded by beaten gold set with cameos and gems.

From the corner of his eye, he caught the flicker of a lizard. Seaward were the ruins of the harbour built by the indefatigable Hadrian in the first century, Hadrian, accomplished poet, learned in Greek. Wind from the sea stirred the nettles. Viciously thorned sprays of blue-green caper plants grew from fissures in the tumbled masonry.

Here, eight hundred years ago during the reign of Alexius II, Byzantine court ceremony and splendour reached its apex.

Here, in the imperial court, arts and letters flourished. Here had been the last refuge of Hellenistic civilization.

He remembered having seen some of them, the Greek manuscripts that had belonged in later years to Cardinal Bessarian. In Venice, he'd seen them. In the library of St. Mark's.

He stood staring about him.

capperis spinosa

The clink of rock on rock.

Forde turned, expecting to see Sheila.

It was a woman from the ship stepping over what had been the door sill. Seeing him, she tilted her head and for a second or two hesitated, one foot still in the air. Her held stance suggested a hen. His face half-creased into a polite smile.

Tinny tune cackling rent the silence. She rootled in her purse for the cell phone.

The spell violated, Forde picked his way forward to escape the noise of her.

* * *

The ship people were milling about in the forecourt of the Sultan Mehmet Mosque. Forde stood on the sidewalk waiting for Sheila, who had gone off in search of aspirin. Neatly uniformed school children stared up as they flowed around him. He surveyed the furniture shops with their swollen settees, the jewellers with gold and silver bangles displayed on poles, the pastry shops with savoury pies and borek in the windows. The shops and houses were utilitarian, seemed modern, concrete block and brick slapped together with mortar oozing out of every course.

Forde read a passing teenager's T-shirt: KEEP IT REAL.

In trays, pans, shallow bins, the fish stores displayed the catch of the day; that day in Trebizond the choice was bonito. In clothes stores, child-mannequins, suits and bow ties for three-year-old boys, puffy sleeved froufrou dresses for tiny girls.

Shouting their presence louder than other shops, narrow storefronts selling film, cameras, cell phones, disks, CD-players, calculators, digital pedometers, their windows a blare of posters and logos: SONY, TOSHIBA, SAMSUNG, OLYMPUS, CANON PANASONIC, FUJI, KODAK, HITACHI, NIKON.

"Got some!" called Sheila. "Bayer. *And* Immodium."

"Why, have you. . . ?"

"Just prophylactic. Wouldn't want to get the squitters on, you know, the Odessa Steps or something."

* * *

Forde sat on the low stone wall that retained the flower beds in the forecourt of the mosque. On his right rose a high brick wall, scabby, rotted stucco, with a course of stonework along its top. To his left, the elegantly designed octagonal stone ablutions cistern where men washed before going in to pray. In front of each of the eight stone faces sat three stone stools and in each face three modern taps.

He had a sense that the precincts of the mosque had been encroached upon, the road beyond the present arched entrance having eaten up what had once been garden, houses built within what once had been forecourt. He suspected—the run of the hill down towards the placing of the mosque, the high brick wall climbing up—that in some more gracious times the wall had carried an aqueduct which fed the roofed, faceted cistern. He imagined the water constantly rilling down each face, the tinkle and plash of it as it ran and fell into the surrounding trough of inward-sloping flagstones before gurgling off into drains.

As inconspicuously as possible, Forde was watching three men as they performed their ritual ablutions. He could still see Sheila in the line-up. He watched her for a moment or two.

Had a sudden memory of her standing in the kitchen, frowning as she phoned the plumber on the TV remote, the dark swirling grain of the oak floor, her bare feet in a wide bar of sunlight. The sun was mellow on the brickwork, warm on his back.

Also watching the three men was a girl in jeans and a lighter blue sweater. She looked to be eighteen or so. She was calling out to the men, remarks which, judging from her sexual gestures, were lewd provocations. One of the men was laughing. The others ignored her. Her body was pertly nubile but her face was coarse, her jaw heavy and slightly prognathous, features suggesting some form of retardation.

A man with grey hair and grey beard was trudging across the forecourt towards the cistern. He was paunchy and was wearing old black suit trousers and a white, collarless flannel shirt. Sandals. Over the shirt, a black vest. Most of the shirts Forde had seen on locals and in shops had been nylon or polyester. The man lowered himself with a loud sigh onto a stone stool. He sat with his hands on his knees, staring at the facing stone.

The girl held up a handful of empty, hinged mussel shells and then clacked them on the coping of the flower-bed wall in announcement. She then skittered them across the flagstones, a crinkle of sound.

She launched into the mime of a barnyard rite. Thrusting with her loins, making a jeering, farting noise with her lips, she imitated a man thrusting into a woman.

Then, taking a step forward, she became a man.

The man she had become caught the passing girl—the farmer's daughter?—a servant girl?—by the upper arm and pulled her back against him. His hands came round and cupped her breasts. He nuzzled her neck, nibbled her ear, then stroked and kneaded her buttocks. Letting go of her, he unbuttoned the four buttons of his fly and unshipped a large but flaccid cock. It lay across his left palm. With his right hand, he hauled up her skirts and bending her down piled the skirts onto her back. He stuck two investigating fingers between her legs.

The man at the cistern, surmounting the mound of his paunch, grunting with the effort, strained down over it to unstrap his sandals.

Umph, he grunted, *Umph.*

The barnyard man brought his two wet fingers out, letting the skirts fall, and began to ease back his foreskin, anointing the head of his cock with her stickiness. Slowly the penis stirred, stiffened, rose.

The grey-haired man turned on the tap.

He lifted the skirts again, piled them on her back, pinned them there, pushed her lower. Then with his left boot he tapped the inside of her left ankle, then with his right boot the inside of her right ankle, forcing her to shuffle her legs wider apart. She tried to straighten up a little but he pushed her down again, slapping the side of her head.

He pushed himself into her.

Ahhhhhh!

Gripped her by the hips, pulling her onto him.

Straining over his paunch, the cistern man was rubbing water between his toes.

Left foot. *Uuuh. Uuuh. Uuuh. Uuuh.*

The barnyard man was thrusting, grunting *Aah! Aah! Aah!*

Right foot. *Uuuh. Uuuh. Uuuh. Uuuh.*

Aah! Aah! Aah!

The face carved in concentration.

arrrggul—arrrggul—arrrggul gargled the cistern man.

Splat onto the flagstones.

Doing something with his nose. Snuffling up water from his cupped palm. Nostrils pinched closed. Then *nnnnnnnm* onto the flags.

Coughed.

Retched.

Arr! Arr! Arr! growled the barnyard man.

The cistern man's forefinger wiggling in his ear.

Faster now, faster, frenetic the thrusting.

Ah-ah-ah-ah-oh!

Sudden stillness.

Then a strained cry, almost falsetto, from the barnyard man.

A groan.

Then. Gouts of it. Four separate spasms gripped him rigid.

A soft sigh ended the performance. She seemed to lose interest entirely. She turned her back on them and, plucking a purple dahlia, wandered off across the forecourt, kicking at mussel shells, and out through the arched entrance and disappeared into the street.

* * *

It was Sheila's turn to sit by the window. Across the aisle from Forde sat the man with the Woolly Bear-caterpillar-eyebrows, things rank and gross in nature, thought Forde, and positive tufts sprouting from his ears. He always wore a squashy sun bonnet tied under his chin with a string. It looked like something a toddler might wear. He must have been in his late seventies. He was deaf and carried his antique hearing-aid apparatus hanging around his neck in a custom-made leather case whose size reminded Forde of World War II naval binoculars. A side flap unbuttoned, giving access to knobs. Wires connected it to his ears.

The aluminum gangway steps leading up from the quay to the entry port on the third deck were solid with unmoving passengers and more pooling at the foot of the steps as buses arrived. It was Woolly Bear blocking the inward flow.

He stared at the Indonesian purser like an astonished baby.

"He needs your identity-card thing, Edwin," said his wife.

"My dear fellow!" remonstrated Edwin. "What an extraordinary thing to say!"

"Edwin," said his wife, "are you sure you're switched on?"

"Of *course* I didn't swipe it. I was *given* it."

"What he *means*, Edwin," said his wife. "Oh . . . *God!*" she said, twitching the card from his fingers and handing it to the purser to run through the machine.

As the flow started again, Forde heard Edwin explaining, "One gives them one's passport and they give you this card. One buys things with it. Drinks and so forth. Toiletries."

It was a pleasure to ease off the heavy walking shoes. He washed, enjoyed the starched pleasure of a clean shirt, put on his suit and a pair of black Florsheim dress shoes and, taking his journal, headed for the bar, leaving Sheila to the interminable intricacies of her make-up.

Sitting at the empty bar was the Rt. Revd. Chantry Williams, Chaplain in Ordinary to HM Chapels Royal and Bishop of Bodmin and Exeter. A huge bugger, six foot three, at least. Forde inclined his head a stiff couple of inches in acknowledgement of the man's presence. According to the little bottle's label, the bishop was sipping a glass of Britomart Orange Crush, probably to fortify himself for the lecture he would be giving at six o'clock on Trajan's campaign against the Dacians, a lecture Forde would not be attending.

Forde thought the Bishop a bit of a berk.

For daily excursions he affected a sort of safari outfit, khaki shirt with epaulettes, cargo pants, combat boots, the ensemble topped by a silly Tilley-type hat sporting, on one side of it, a cockade of nylon feathers.

His last two lectures—*Feudal Monarchy in the Latin Kingdom of Jerusalem* and *Christendom and The Barbary Coast*—had ended with pleas for closer community with Islam. We must treat with respect and understanding, he had said, Islamic sacred law, *Shari'ah*. As ardent Christians, he had said, we must reach out to the *ummah,* the world-wide community of Islamic believers.

Just as within the Christian community the forces of eucumenicism . . . so in that larger community of People of the Book . . .

Forde was not an ardent Christian.

Embrace our fellow . . .

Forde had no desire whatever to reach out to unwashed wahabis and mad, hairy mullahs.

Embrace!

"Feh!" as Sheila would have said.

The Bishop of Bodmin could stuff the *ummah* up his jumper; Anglican clerics should confine themselves, thought Forde, to such essentially Anglican activities as the blessing of marrows.

He glared at the back of the bishop's head.

He began to feel the welcome bite of the Scotch.

From his table he could see directly down into the still water under the bow. Further out, sunlight sparkled on the water. He watched flocks of shearwaters, small groups of birds in brief flights before settling again to ride the waves, spirits, the stories went, of sailors drowned. He found himself thinking about the book he'd been looking at in the ship's library, with its reproductions of seventeenth-century woodcuts of fiendish Turks, ranked Janissaries, effete bejewelled pashas. Led by Sultan Mohammed II, the Turks took Istanbul in 1453. In 1461 Mohammed entered Trebizond in triumph and celebrated his victory by praying in the ransacked church of St. Eugenius, which he turned into the New Friday Mosque. Within two or three years, Mohammed had the deposed Emperor, David Comnenus, put to death together with all the males in the Comnenus line of succession. Forde thought of the ruins they'd visited that afternoon, rubble that once had been known as "The Golden Palace of the Comneni," home now to nettles, *capperis spinosa*, and the chill wind from the sea.

As he gazed down into the water, his thoughts washing over Sultan Mohammed and the Bishop of Bodmin and Exeter and Britomart Orange Crush, he became aware of something white, something white rising.

At first he thought it was probably garbage, a paper bag, perhaps, but as it rose up though the dark water he saw things trailing from it, strings . . .

He pressed closer to the glass.

He saw that the white thing as it rose was not flat like paper but domed like an inverted bowl. He saw that the strings were . . . trailing tentacles. A jellyfish. Another one rising up from the depths to touch the surface. And another. All along the side of the ship. He hurried the length of the room craning to look from every window. Suddenly dozen upon dozen of them rising through the dark water to hang for a few moments at the surface before sinking, sinking, and then gone from sight. The rise and fall was like a stately carousel, a slow-motion firework display, an underwater Swan Lake of jellyfish.

If he were writing, what words could describe this dance, this vision? They appeared larger as they rose higher, like flowers blossoming and opening. *Bloom.* He would use the word *bloom*. He had the sense somehow that the ship was being visited. He would use *visitant* and *visitation*, with their connotations of the supernatural, for there *was* something ghostly in the whiteness and the slow materialization of the jellyfish. He found himself in the odd position of not believing such chimerical nonsense but at the same time feeling it. He felt—embarrassedly—that he was being . . . there was no way round the feeling . . . blessed.

He caught the barman's eye and raised his empty glass, tapping it with his forefinger.

Or perhaps . . .

He shrugged.

Perhaps the feeling arose from the beneficent effects of *The Famous Grouse.*

He sat, his mind drifting.

Bar sounds.

Sheila's voice said, "Buy a girl a drink?"

He stood and pulled out a chair for her.

"We're very formal this evening, aren't we?"

"It's because of the suit."

The sparkle had left the waves. The light was fading. They sat in easy silence. Lights started to come on in some of the port buildings. He could just make out the shapes of the boys still fishing off the end of the dock. A tug, its bridge blazing with lights, its sides armoured with tires like a row of shields, thrashed past them out to sea.

"For God's sake take these peanuts away from me," said Sheila.

"Grand Comnenus and Emperor," he said.

"Pardon?"

"That's how the Comneni were referred to."

"Hmmm," said Sheila.

Forde sat in silence for long minutes.

"Sipping Britomart," he burst out, "while Rome burns."

"*What?*"

He sighed.

"Ah, well," said Sheila, always sensitive to his shifting moods, "cheer up! I expect the dining room'll be open now."

* * *

All was aglow and gleaming. Light from the recessed pot lights blazed down on glasses, cutlery, starched napery, mirrored walls. Banquettes down the room's sides were divided into booths by slabs of thick, minty glass etched with a design of Scottish thistles. Conversation rolled in waves, a surf of sound. As they waited for the steward, Forde watched the girls going round the tables with bottles of red and white wine, filling glasses. Waiters in bistro black and white. At their various stations, decorative silver wine coolers, massed flowers, elaborate ceramic cornucopias of fruit. Forde relaxed into the nightly theatre.

The steward led them up the length of the room to a table for two. They passed the little old lady with the make-up. She was wearing this evening, on her left hand, a gold ring with a bezel that clasped a green stone the size of a small frog.

At the next table over from them, the American couple who always introduced themselves with "We're Alan and Martin from Cincinnati." They were wearing identical Haspel seersucker suits, which put Forde in mind of ice cream. He noticed on the table between them a bottle of wine.

He nodded to them and said, "How did you end up with that?"

"We complained," said Alan.

"We lodged a complaint," said Martin.

"Well, really!" said Alan. "What we had last night."

"We made our views known," said Martin.

"We didn't pay all this money," said Alan, "to drink pooey old Merlot from Chile."

"We felt put upon," said Martin. "So Alan complained to that nice steward—you know, the comfy one? From Austria? Who wears pumps?—and he sent us this *Marqués de Cáceres*."

"Rioja," said Alan.

"Tempranillo," said Martin.

"Gran Reserva," said Alan.

"Two years in oak," said Martin.

"*Yum!*" said Alan.

Forde and Sheila busied themselves with menus and Apollonaris mineral water.

"In the hors-d'oeuvres," said Forde, "what does 'Goujonnette' mean?"

"Fish," said Sheila. "A small piece. It's fried usually."

... what with my knees and all that marble up-and-down ...

Forde sipped the wine the nice girl had poured.

He wondered why it was that some voices carried almost brutally through the general hive of sound. It didn't seem that they were speaking particularly loudly. Just a strange, penetrating timbre. Odd. This one was a small lady three tables away. He watched the girls filling wine glasses. Well-filled blouses, too.

"He noted, with approval," said Forde.

"Pardon?"

"No, nothing."

Indicating Alan and Martin with the slightest movement of his head, he said, "How old do you think they are?"

Sheila shrugged. "Difficult to say. Fifty? Fifty-five." He watched them covertly. Their lines were beginning to blur—the beginnings of plumpness, little tummy bulges, the suggestion of jowls. In their identical seersucker suits they might have been, thought Forde, a once-lauded vaudeville act from the Ed Sullivan era, about to glide from table to table on roller skates performing close-up with cards and coins.

All, all, it seemed to Forde, was stories or a play and the passengers character actors. It amused and pleased him to shape them and compose their pasts. Though his creation of Father Keogh's travelling companion as The Minder seemed not far off the mark. He had already decided that Woolly Bear had fought in the Korean War either as regular army or National Service conscript though he had more of a Sandhurst feel about him. Probably the knee socks and sun bonnet. Then there was the rude, loud man on the bus with his brass-bound walking stick. The Baden Powell man, Forde called him. Wore a lemon silk cravat with Viyella shirts and claimed to have been a second lieutenant in the Arab Legion under Glubb Pasha. The cravat did not completely hide the craters of old boils on the back of his neck.

Forde had heard him saying to a man on the bus that he sorely missed "my lovely brave young Bedouin"; *hmmm*. But at the same time, he roared words and phrases in Hindi and the dates seemed possibly dodgy. Though Jordan had not thrown Glubb Pasha out until 1954 and so if the Baden Powell man had joined the Legion after the 1948 war at the age of, say, twenty-one, then . . . but the mental arithmetic was hurting

Forde's head and he fell back into watching people and drifting reverie.

... and then I dropped the soap and those shower stalls are like upended coffins so I couldn't bend down ...

"Look!" he said suddenly. "*Look!*"

"What?"

"On your right. That woman!"

"Where? Oh."

"Fanning herself," said Forde with delight, "with a side plate!"

* * *

Forde sat glaring at the line cook—Filipino, Malaysian, or some other mixture—who stood with folded arms at the near end of the steam table. What could be seen of Sochi was not appealing. The ship had docked just after dawn. Concrete, a few tired palm trees, tall wire mesh fences, a flag drooping in the still heat. The day's promised excursion was to Dagomys in the mountains to see the most northerly tea plantation in Europe, a prospect that was not causing him palpitations.

Sheila was making her way through the breakfast throng towards the table for two he had secured them. She had been to the laundry room while it wasn't busy.

"I met Alan down there—he'd been drying two, well I don't quite know *what* you'd call them—'blousons,' perhaps. And do you know what he said?"

"No," said Forde.

"He said they were sixty percent cotton and forty percent 'the P-word, but strictly, *but strictly,* for travel.'"

"Hmmm."

"'The P-word,'" said Sheila. "And I asked him where Martin was and do you know what he said?"

"Of *course* I don't know what he said."

"He said, 'Oh, he's still tucked up in bed like a great big Gummi Bear.'"

"*Christ!*" said Forde.

"A touch homophobic this morning, are we?"

"No. Homicidal."

"*Now* what's the matter?"

"Nothing."

"But the main thing he told me was that a woman was attacked in the laundry. That nice woman who's a hospital administrator in Sheffield."

"What sort of attacked?"

"Well, sexually."

"Probably a lascar," said Forde.

"A what?"

"Like that one over there who makes himself awkward about fried eggs. I *know* he's got them. I know *where* they are. In that little oven under the counter. But every time I ask, the scrawny little sod goes into his 'No flied egg' routine."

"What *is* a lascar?"

"They run amok, rushing about in a frenzy and committing violent acts. They're noted for it. Conrad's full of them. You have to do something Conrad-ish to them when they're amok, lash them to the mast, hose them into the scuppers, conk them with a coal shovel."

"Is this because of the fried eggs?"

"I once read something Conrad said about the expression 'going great guns.' 'Going' implies movement and guns don't 'go' unless you mean 'go off' so the expression becomes somewhat unclear. It now seems generally and vaguely to mean *successful*. But there's a ghost of meaning in 'going' that we've lost. Now *Conrad* said it referred to a ship under full sail and the wind booming the canvas like great cannons firing. So you see what we've *lost* . . ."

"Forde!"

"What?"

"Alan said the man was *hissing*. He grabbed her from behind and put his hand over her mouth and while he was rubbing his thing against her bum he was *hissing* and *hissing* like those men do to horses."

"Ostlers."

"Yes. But he was hurting her too, squeezing, twisting flesh, crushing her breasts. And whoever it was had planned it. He'd somehow got most of the lights off so all she really saw was a shape."

Sheila fell silent.

"I wonder," she said, "if it *was* a crew member."

She set down her coffee cup.

She stared at him.

"Or was it a passenger?"

Then she said hesitantly, "It's . . . it's that hissing. That's what frightens me."

"Sorry about the fried eggs," said Forde.

She nodded.

"Something about it," she said, "that noise, that's insane."

* * *

"First Prize," said Forde, "one week in Sochi. Second Prize, three weeks in Sochi."

The utilitarian bus throbbed and shuddered as it waited for stragglers from the Botanical Gardens making their way back from gawking at the Tree of Friendship.

The wood-slat seats gave little ease. Someone had pasted a festive frill of scissored gold foil round the inside top two inches of the windows obscuring the view. Glued to every fourth or so strip of fringe, a cotton-wool bobble. The long gear shift was dressed in a knitted sheath. The punctilious guide kept testing his mike, peering into papers in his brief-case, counting and re-counting the passengers, fingers questioning the knot of his tie. The Baden Powell man began his daily bellowing and pounding the floor with his walking stick.

"You! Bloody driver! You! The tout with the microphone! Music *off!* Music *off!*"

The bus juddered on its way. The guide resumed his litany. There wasn't much to see. One after another, large white buildings, gardens surrounding. High hedges of dark yew. Sanitaria for apparatchiks.

... what you call in your countries not—hospitals? No. Spa. Just so mmmmm. There are many baths 50 metres by 25 metres that is mmm in the measurements of your countries 164.042 feet by 82.02 feet and these baths are full of water from the hot springs. The water is full of health but the smell is very rude.

The State Winter Theatre. Riviera Park with an opportunity to buy local handicrafts. In the grounds of the Zelyonaya Roscha Sanitorium, Stalin's Dacha.

... and a big surprise are the baths full of mud which is heated to mmmm 41 degrees centigrade or in the measurements of your countries 105.8 Fahrenheit which is 4 degrees higher than your blood ...

Forde squirmed on the unforgiving seat.

... and there are also mud mmm cabinets with just heads ...

"The Cabinets of Doctor Caligari," said Forde.

... and the mud sucks out the poison from the body ... not mmm suck ...

He riffled through some notes.

... leaches mmm leaches poison. ...

"Leeches?" said Sheila making a sucking face.

"Well, Mother," said Forde in a stage Yorkshire accent, "exfoliation they may call it but I've always said you've a long way to go to beat an old-fashioned scourging."

"And what would *you* know, you old stick-in-the-mud!"

And this got them launched into riffs on soviets spas, gleaming white resorts from the outside but inside crumbling Gormenghasts with lavatory-tiled rooms staffed by smelly crones and doctors with steel teeth. The Beria Room full of people wrapped in wet sheets and stacked. Skink-Extract Treatment in the Molotov Maceration Room. The Gherkin Diet. The Dry Cupping Room. Korean massage administered by Oddjob aided by his sinister henchman Blowjob. In the Malenkov Room, borscht enemas performed by Enigma Machines. On Thank God It's Fridays, the Siberian Plotz executed turn and turn about by the Smersh Sisters, three ex-KGB houris.

This giddiness possessed them until they reached Dagomys and the bus bumped over the gravel parking area and stopped parallel to rows of small green bushes.

"According to the daily bulletin," said Forde, "there's a lecture in Russian about tea, though excitingly with simultaneous translation into English, followed, the schedule promises, by tea grown *on this very plantation*. During the serving of which we will be further titillated by folkloric entertainment."

"Now don't start being difficult."

"Remember the wisdom," said Forde, "of Sir Arnold Bax."

"Who he?"

"A well-known composer I've never heard *but*, but smart enough to have said, 'you should make a point of trying every experience once, excepting incest and folk-dancing.'"

Alan was studying the writing on the back of the bus.

"Hey!" he said. "This bus is from Korea. *This is a Korean bus.*"

"Get a picture," said Martin.

Sheila was helping, along the aisle of the bus, the woman with the walker.

Forde returned to the bus's front steps and helped down the old lady with the make-up.

"*Dangerously* steep!" he said.

The make-up was so elaborate, so excessive, that the word "make-up" seemed inadequate to convey …

Maquillage, perhaps.

"What a lovely—would one call it a choker?"

She smiled.

"Victorian, isn't it?"

"Clever boy," she said.

"And not jet," said Forde. "Rather too matte for that."

She was watching his face.

"It wouldn't possibly be . . . coal, would it?"

"*Very* clever boy," she said. "How did you know that?"

"I've seen pieces in museums and at auctions."

"I *love* auctions," she said. "My name's Bronwyn."

"They still do it, you know," he said. "I've seen modern pieces for sale from a barrow on the seafront at Whitby in Yorkshire. Not with *that* refinement, of course. Robert Forde," he added, "though people usually just call me Forde. I don't really know why."

She took his arm.

"Nice sleepy auctions in country towns—*such* a pleasure," she said. "Like boxes of chocolates. Magical boxes, always full and waiting to be opened. I lead a lovely, selfish life going to antique shops and auctions, buying little things of beauty for myself. I *adore* Jermyn Street, don't you? Perfume from *Floris*. The Burlington Arcade for antique jewellery. *Paxton and Whitfield* for those special water biscuits. And then the bliss of afternoon tea at *Fortnum*. Of course," she went on, "I wasn't brought up here entirely . . ."

"Here?"

"England, I mean. Which rather explains it all. No. I spent my early years in Sarawak. My parents were missionaries, you see."

"Anglican?"

She batted her ancient lashes.

"Do I have a Baptist *look*?"

Forde smiled.

"And then I was shipped off to boarding school in England. Nine at the time. Plenty of love for the dusky indigenes but precious little for me. Anyway, that was the way I felt as a girl. Poor Bronwyn, less loved than a Dyak. So I've always comforted myself ever since with *objets d'art* and positively ruinous *delectabilia* and . . ."

"Wait for us!" called Sheila.

". . . and remain," continued Bronwyn, "with lingering hostility towards Dyaks."

They paused outside the listing wooden swayback shed, which served as a lavatory. Sheila joined the line. Seconds after entering she shot out again.

"Christ!" she said.

"It's easy to see," said Bronwyn, "*you've* never been to China."

The four of them made their way along the uneven path through the woods towards the shed where the lecture and tea-drinking and folkloric entertainment were to take place.

"No," said Forde at the door, after glancing inside, "I'll go for a stroll in the woods. At least they're not wearing clogs."

"Clogs?"

"Mmm."

"Why should they be? They're not Dutch."

"No, but the hulking bulk of them, and the jolliness and headscarves, and *accordions*. I don't know. Perhaps I was thinking of Lancashire."

It was warm, cloudless, the slow-wheeling shapes of hawks sliding down the sky. The rows of tea bushes were planted on hillsides that looked as though the trees had been bulldozed into wreckage. The soil was black and acidic. Rank bracken had grown back in between the rows.

A flicker of movement on the fringe of dappling oak leaves caught Forde's eye. Familiar brown wings laced by demarcating black lines and dots. Two fritillaries. He was excited and intensely pleased.

When he had first seen Monarch butterflies on coming to Canada he had been reminded of fritillaries, the colouration, the black lines of demarcation like niello jewellery, but Monarchs had seemed burly and muscle-bound in comparison,

NCOs of the butterfly world, while fritillaries were officers and aristocrats, the browns and ochres, umbers, burnt siennas of their wings like exquisite marquetry.

He used to wander in the New Forest when he was a child catching butterflies and hunting for grass snakes and adders. The boy he wandered with was four years older, and Forde had existed in a haze of love and hero-worship. The butterflies had been shaken from the net into a killing jar, glass and wide-mouthed with a large cork bung. Onto a pad of folded cotton at the bottom of the jar, a rag of an old shirt perhaps—not cotton wool as insect legs snagged in its wisps—he'd pour a few drops from a bottle of *Thawpit*, a commercial solvent used in dry cleaning and then freely available. It was only years later that he'd learned that *Thawpit* was actually carbon tetrachloride and considered to have near-fatal effects on the liver. He and David used to like the sweetness of its smell.

He could see them now, nosing the air for the faint smell of grass snakes, an unmistakable smell, musk and marsh. He could see the two of them now standing beside the silver glint of small streams, breathing open-mouthed so that their hearts would not pound in their ears and mask the faint slither of sound they were straining for, the pause as the head lifted and the black tongue flicked the air, then again the long whisper of sound resumed.

And into an old pillow case went adders, which they handled with dangerous familiarity. They carried an old tobacco tin containing a razor blade and purple crystals of potassium permanganate as first aid. They had sworn to each other that they'd cut a cross over the two fang marks and suck and spit and let blood flow and then force in the purple crystals. He'd had terrible dreams about the thought of cutting. Doing the cutting. He'd been—what? Twelve?

They'd sold the grass snakes and adders to the Ferndown Zoo for a shilling a foot, money that kept them in cigarettes. They'd smoked a brand called *Park Drive.*

Even then, nearly sixty years ago, fritillaries were seldom seen, very local in their distribution. He'd known only three rides in the New Forest near Ringwood, where they might reliably have been found. On St. Catherine's Hill outside Christchurch he remembered catching a Smooth snake, a species considered locally extinct. Remembered the wonder of it, David's jealousy.

He'd read just a couple of years ago a doom-laden list in the *Daily Telegraph* of creatures now extinct or nearing extinction, creatures common in his childhood, adders themselves, slow worms, cinnabar moths, Smooth snakes, green-throated sand lizards, palmated newts, fritillaries . . .

But here in the sunlight, in all their remembered grace and beauty . . .

There welled into his mind, along with that special Anglican smell of damp and dust and stone, a line from the psalms.

We bring our years to an end, as it were a tale that is told.

He stood staring, transported.

* * *

"Sir Charles," said Bronwyn, taking his arm again, "was a nasty old man. Very fierce and rude."

"But to think," said Forde, "that you . . . I mean The White Rajah of Sarawak! It seems somehow . . ."

"He didn't die until quite recently, you know—well, the sixties I think it was. In Cheltenham. Or Cirencester." She waved a dismissive hand. "He had a horrible glass eye he got from a taxidermist to cover a socket. Hunting fall. Eye on a twig. He got an assortment of eyes—rabbits, sheep, deer, and so forth and he used to wear different ones everyday. But yes, he was there—in Sarawak, I mean—well, until the Japanese soldiers came."

"And when you were a child, you remember . . ."

"Oh, but it was the Ranee all the stories were about! Sylvia, her name was. Oh, she *was* a baggage! Of course, I never saw any of the goings-on but all the children heard the stories from the servants and the agency men and *their* servants . . . Not that she was in Sarawak all that often. She much preferred Paris and London. 'Frivolous' was the word my father used—such a *weight* of disapproval. She was Lord Esher's daughter, you know. Sylvia Brett, she used to be. And a merry dance she led him, by all accounts. Do people use the word 'trollop' nowadays?"

Through the trees the buses in the parking lot came into sight.

"It was the drink," said Bronwyn. "Gin for breakfast rarely ends well. She was a living scandal. She even made the Dyaks nervous, and some of *those* johnnies weren't exactly strait-laced."

"Shrunken heads and such?"

She waved her free hand dismissively again.

"Nasty, smelly things," she said.

She paused to pat his arm.

"She refused, just *refused* to leave the table, and stayed on after dinner for port or brandy. Smoked the cigars and drank the brandy. Utterly foxed. And by then she'd be quite *raucous*. Not, apparently, that the esteemed Sir Charles Vyner Brooke appeared to care! He'd be as fuddled as she was and fumbling in some creature's placket."

Forde tutted.

"Too sordid, my dear," said Bronwyn.

She shook her head.

"It is *said*," said Bronwyn, "it is *said*, that after dinner the men repaired to the billiard room and she used to hoist up her skirt and clamber up onto the table . . . I'm not embarrassing you am I, dear?"

"No, no. Fascinating."

"And work herself against a corner pocket and open her legs wide . . . and shout . . . you're sure I'm not . . ."

"Please."

"By this time, of course, she'd be hectic with drink."

"And shout what?" he said.

"And she used to shout . . ."

Bronwyn paused and drew herself up.

"Come on, boys!" she cried. "Pot the red!"

* * *

The pork medallions, please.

Sir?

Blanquette de veau.

"Well, as I was saying, the pottery finds from any given site will be divided into *groups*, do you see, on the basis of different *fabrics*. Now what does *fabrics* mean? Well, pottery fabrics depend on the degree to which the clay was worked before the vessel was formed and the kind of temper that was used.

Certainly, Madam. Gazeuse or still?

Oh, um, fizzy.

Temper? The material used to reinforce and strengthen the clay. Clay is tempered—mixed with, do you see, shell, sand, straw, and ground-up, previously fired pottery—shards—which substance is referred to as *grog*. Haven't the faintest idea *why*.

Anyway, the archaeologists would define the groups, do you see, as handmade or wheel-made wares. As fine, medium, or coarse wares. As wares poorly fired or well-fired. And as wares tempered with . . ."

"Dear frantic God! DO SHUT UP, ROGER, and have another drink."

* * *

The Alupka Palace was designed, read Sheila, *by the Scottish architects Edward Blore and Henry Hunt and was built for Prince Michael Vorontsov between 1828 and 1846 . . .* "Are you listening?"

"No," said Forde, "I'm watching this snail."

He thought the Palace vulgar and ridiculous, a pot-pourri of clashing styles, less a house than a folly. Sheila went into the Palace to see the bedroom where Sir Winston Churchill slept during the 1945 Yalta Conference; he wandered further into the gardens. They funnelled out to the drive, which led down to what was now a parking lot at the entrance to the estate. The Palace had been set into a ledge cut in the mountainside. The drive up to it was walled on both sides. On the mountain side of the drive was a retaining wall well above head height. The other wall was lower, providing a waist-high barrier against the mountain's fall to the sea, where the sun sparked on water and Raoul Dufy sails stood white on blue.

The mountain was thinly wooded and he noticed an ochre scar carving down through the trees, a shallow gully of erosion. He probably wouldn't have seen them if not for the movement. They seemed to blend into the tumbled stone. A file of dogs.

The leading dog was tall and wiry-haired, greyish with something about it of an Irish wolfhound. The dogs following were mongrels, brown mostly, here and there a flash of white. Where the gully widened into grass and weeds, the dogs stopped and looked about. Then they sank almost out of sight as they worked forward to the coping on the top of the wall. Then nothing.

They gave a strong impression of tenseness, wariness. Forde waited until no one was near and gave a sharp whistle. A greyish ear flicked above the grass.

"What are you doing?" said Sheila. "Watching snails?"

He sensed covert movement along the coping and out of the corner of his eye caught the grey dog appearing at the foot of a flight of steps some twenty yards away. The dog sat.

It waited until the drive was clear then led the pack across the drive into deep shadow on the seawall side. They trotted down towards the car park seeming almost to flow.

As Forde and Sheila approached the buses, they saw the last two dogs, back legs splayed, squirming and scrunching themselves under the edge of their bus.

"Why are they getting under there?"

He shrugged.

"What if they get run over?"

"I expect they've done it before."

Sheila bent and banged the side of the bus with her umbrella handle.

A ferocious snarl ripped back.

"Perhaps," said Forde, "he's taken up a *querencia*."

"A what?"

"It's when a bull decides . . ."

"I'm not having Hemingway," she said, "before lunch."

She reversed her umbrella again.

"If something of that size has taken a fancy to the underneath of the bus, I personally would be somewhat circumspect about challenging it."

"I'm *not* challenging him. I just don't want him to . . ."

"It's not important whether you're challenging him or not," said Forde. "It's what he *thinks* you're doing."

"This is a ridiculous conversation," said Sheila.

"And especially," added Forde, "if you are armed only with a collapsible umbrella."

"WHY," said Woolly Bear, "IS THAT WOMAN HITTING THE BUS?"

"Snails!" said Sheila.

On the bus once again and driving along the coast road, Forde started reading the daily bulletin. "We're promised 'unique Crimean wines,'" he said. "Followed by lunch on the Naberezhnaya Lenina featuring 'wholesome Ukrainian cuisine.' Want to take bets?"

In the yard surrounding the winery building stood rusting, industrial-looking container tanks. The building itself was surrounded by straggling lilac bushes, under one of which lay two unconscious drunks.

Each visitor was given a tray holding twelve numbered glasses of wine, glasses about twice the size of a shot glass, the glass itself thick. A man in a suit expatiated at great volume through a sort of loud-hailer contraption on the qualities peculiar to each wine. They were all utterly undrinkable, each vilely sweeter than the last.

Forde pushed his tray away and shook his head at Sheila.

Tilting his head back, Father Keogh swilled each glass. Then his head came down again, his tongue searching into the glass, filling it, magnified, raw.

With a small movement of his head and a glance, Forde directed Sheila's attention to the sight of the fat tongue pushing in.

* * *

"You know," said Forde when they were yet again on the bus and waiting for lavatory-stragglers and wine-purchasers," I think the only wine I can remember being as foul as those came from Bulgaria. It was called *Boyar's Domain*. Unforgettable."

... *thirteen, fourteen, fifteen* ... counted the guide.

"Poor man," said Sheila. "He's so anxious."

Lunch was leisurely and awful.

Everyone was given an entire fish. Grey mullet, said the guide.

They seemed to be deep-fried.

Father Keogh spent the entire lunchtime drinking a brown liquid and gazing with obsessive intensity into Mrs. Cleary's cleavage.

* * *

The Romanov Apartments in Livadia Palace left them both feeling sad. The walls were hung with framed snapshots of Nicholas II, Tsar of All the Russias, the Tsarina Alexandra, the Grand Duchesses Olga, Tatiana, Maria, and Anastasia and Tsarevich Alexei.

The girls in summer white and wide, flowered hats.

On country walks.

Picking wild flowers.

Sitting at elaborate picnics in the woods, white linen tablecloths.

Paddling at the seaside.

Alexei on his tricycle.

Lessons on the terrace with their tutor.

Anastasia, feet swinging under the piano bench, doggedly working on her baggy knitting.

All murdered on the night of July 16, 1918 in Ekaterinburg in "The House of Special Purpose." And, over the years, to be followed by millions more.

Forde felt both moved and oppressed by the family snapshots, and leaving Sheila reading plaques and notices, wandered out into the gardens hoping the sunshine would lift his spirits.

"*Schwibzik*," they'd all called Anastasia—"*Little One.*"

* * *

The guide was approaching along the bus's aisle.

... sixteen, seventeen, eighteen, nineteen ...

Forde drew breath sharply as Father Keogh's knees, one after the other, slammed into the back of his seat.

"I could definitely use what Baden Powell would call a *chota* peg," said Forde. "No, no, I mean a BURRA peg."

"Well," said Sheila, "you've been looking forward to Chekhov's house all week."

"What's so special about this Chekhov fellah?"

Forde turned towards the voice and saw an eye and nose and part of the mouth of Father Keogh, who seemed to be bent double as he peered up through the armrest gap between the seats.

"I said what's so special."

"Well a lot of people consider him the world's greatest short-story writer."

"And you're one of those, are you?"

"Mmm-mmm, yes."

"I've not encountered him," said Father Keogh.

"Not had the pleasure of his acquaintance," said The Minder's voice.

"And, of course, he's also a great playwright."

"Plays, is it?"

"Yes, like *The Three Sisters* and *The Cherry Orchard*."

The partial face disappeared.

Forde raised an eyebrow at Sheila.

A knee slammed into his right kidney.

"And what is it about? This *Cherry Orchard*?"

"Well, it's about upper-class life in pre-revolutionary Russia and . . ."

"Upper class, is it."

To the armrest gap Forde said, "But it's more about class paralysis and stagnation. It gives a sense . . ."

"Sense, is it?"

Again a knee.

Forde rolled his eyes at Sheila.

"How do you do, Mr. Chekhov?" said Father Keogh.

"Well, well, I thank you, Father," said the minder. "In the pink."

"And how is your cherry orchard?"

"Laden, Father, absolutely. Yes, it is," said The Minder. "The branches all bent and weeping with fruit."

The partial face reappeared.

"'And the land shall yield her fruit, and ye shall eat your fill, and dwell therein in safety.'"

"Will you *please* stop banging your knees into my seat!"

"And a blessing it is," said The Minder. "A blessing it is."

* * *

Chekhov had lived in the White Dacha with his mother, Eugenia, and his sister, Maria, called Masha, and his wife, the actress Olga Knipper. Chekhov had lesions on both lungs and coughed out his life in these rooms while summoning the heroic energy to write the three great final plays.

For years he had suffered from colitis, diarrhoea, and haemorrhoids. For the haemorrhaging from his lungs he took creosote, which destroyed his stomach. To stave off pleurisy he endured compresses of cantharides. To sleep he drank chloral hydrate. As the pain and weakness bit in, he was given injections of camphor, arsenic, morphine, opium, and heroin. As his heart deteriorated, he was treated with digitalis. And through all this horror, he wrote.

But to Forde's disappointment the house gave up nothing of this. It remained resolutely ordinary. The feel was very Victorian and respectable, much more Masha than Anton. Chairs covered in loose slipcovers, every table covered with fringed tablecloths, along the top of the piano, with its brass swing-out candle brackets, a long runner crotcheted like a doily. Pelmets and flouncy valances. Massy, unattractive furniture. Iron bedsteads. Heavily framed photographs.

Forde prowled the house on his own, photographing the rooms hoping for some emanation of the spirit who'd written *Uncle Vanya*, who'd delighted in catching crayfish and picking mushrooms and wild berries, who'd loved a pet mongoose called Sod, which roamed the house at night extracting corks from bottles.

Each room was closed off to visitors by a furry rope across the open doorway. Taking pictures was difficult because of the ropes and because of the reflections off the glass framing the photographs on the walls. Forde leaned into the sitting room trying to take a photograph of a portrait of Chekhov, which stood on top of the piano. The glare of the glass was defeating him. He leaned in further over the rope. There was some sort of bustle and to-do in the hall behind him, shuffling, a sudden uprush of conversation, someone calling out. He glanced round and saw the museum guide rounding up stragglers and ushering people towards the front door.

"We must go now," he called back, "and the door be locked."

"Forde!" called Sheila.

"Coming!" he called back, his eye still at the viewfinder.

He turned to see Sheila alone in the hall. She was laughing.

The guide took Forde by the arm.

"Sorry," said Forde.

"You must be quick!" said the guide.

Unhooked the furry rope, which blocked entrance to Chekhov's study. Gestured Forde in.

"Get in front of the couch," said Sheila unzipping her camera.

Forde stood just to one side of the Isaak Levitan painting of the Istra River.

"Hurry!" said the guide. "Hurry, hurry."

The guide was shifting his agitated weight from foot to foot.

Took Forde's arm again, snapped the furry rope into place, hurried them to the front door and out into the small forecourt where the bus people were milling about.

"Well!" Forde said to Sheila. "What in hell was *that* all about!"

"I told him you were also a writer and how much it would mean to you."

"Good God!" said Forde.

"Very un-British, I know," said Sheila.

"Oh, that was so kind of you, Sheila, really . . . *And* of him. I mean just to up and chuck everyone out."

"And after I told him how much it would mean to you," said Sheila, "I gave him a bribe."

* * *

As they waited in a little crowd for the steward to show them to tables, Roger was patiently explaining to his wife and another couple that Bronze Age palaces were bureaucratic centres of economic redistribution, that clay tablets, both cuneiform and Cretan Linear B, were essentially *bookkeeping*, lists of stocks, of oil, wine, arrows, slaves, spokes of wagon wheels, shields, sheep . . .

"Roger. . . ." said his wife

Forde watched the girls circulating with the wine bottles.

There was something *about* girls wearing ties.

Bronwyn was sitting in solitary and bedizened state at a table for two. Forde smiled at her and gave a mock bow as they walked past. Their waiter presented them with the evening's menu.

Forde looked up from reading it to see Father Keogh approaching with The Minder. His hand and arm rested on The Minder's arm as if he were a woman being escorted at some formal function. His face was rubicund and sweaty. As they passed Bronwyn's table, he pulled free of The Minder and veered towards her almost with a lurch, seeming then to crouch over her tiny figure. Forde could see only his back.

Bronwyn's voice rang out.

"How dare you! How *dare* you!"

Father Keogh straightened up and turned.

"*The inhabitants of the earth,*" he pronounced in prophetic condemnation, "*have been made drunk with the wine of her fornication.*"

"Sot!"

Her voice followed after him through the generally subsiding conversation and rising tension.

"Hibernian *sot*!"

His face puce with drink and fury, Father Keogh passed their table, grinding out to The Minder, to the air, "'THE MOTHER OF HARLOTS.'"

He turned back and, arm outstretched, pointed at Bronwyn.

"'AND ABOMINATIONS OF THE EARTH.'"

"Oh, *dear*, oh, dear," said Forde. "*Revelation*. Always a bad sign."

* * *

Forde and Sheila climbed the Potemkin Steps towards the Primorskiy bulvar, described in the bulletin as Odessa's most graceful boulevard. They were free until ten a.m., when they were to meet at the Archeological Museum for a guided tour of the city. The influences were mainly classical, the buildings three-storey and based on the idea of the interior courtyard, the boulevards themselves tree-shaded. The town, they agreed, was rather like a miniature Paris or Madrid. They strolled to the end of Primorskiy bulvar and then all the way back again, past the Steps, to the Vorontsov Palace. Classical in style, still beautiful, but shabby now and run down, some doors and windows nailed up with sheets of plywood, and sadly still called Palace of the Pioneers.

The Pioneers was a Party organization with compulsory membership to indoctrinate elementary school children in communist thought. Upon completing the curriculum of the Pioneers, the children moved into the organization for teenagers, the Komsomol, before graduating into the full-blown embrace of Soviet life.

"Oh, fortunate Prince Vorontsov," said Forde, "that he died in—what was it?—1854."

Forde had had no great expectations of the Archeological Museum and was pleasantly surprised by the Black Sea Greek finds, some vessel-shapes he'd never seen before. He suddenly wished he had hours to spend. But the highlight turned out to be the Gold Room, coins and jewellery of Black Sea civilizations. And the highlight of all for Forde was a hoard of Scythian silver tetradrachmas.

There must have been about fifty of them spilling out of a broken pot of greyish ware. The heaping coins and the smashed pot were dramatically displayed on rumpled black velvet. The coins were slightly smaller than quarters, but thicker. They were displayed, for some odd reason, just above floor level. Forde knelt the better to see them.

He was gripped by the iconography, fascinated by the way the style had perfected itself. The images were various, Zeus with an upright sceptre, Poseidon, Pallas, a bull, a lone elephant, Nike, a caduceus, but more common than any other image a horseman with a spear.

"Sheila!" he called. "Come and see how *alive* these horses are."

* * *

In the precinct of the Ilinsky Cathedral, Alan and Martin pounced on two stalls, rough tables draped with old bits of carpet, the one displaying icons, the other naval memorabilia of the Russian Black Sea Fleet, badges, medals, epaulettes, oddments of uniform.

They bought an icon each, the wood distressed and pitted with precision worm-holes, but were even more overjoyed by the Russian high-peaked officers' caps, the badges worked in gold wire against an oval ground of white felt. They rummaged through the caps until they found snug fits and then fussed around each other tugging and tilting. Martin also bought epaulettes to sew onto his bomber jacket. They begged tour members to take their photos on the cathedral steps.

Alan saluted.

Flash

They mugged.

Flash

Linked arms.

Soyuz Sovetskikh, intoned Martin, *Sotsialistichesskikh Respublik.*

He turned his head to one side, and with a rigid forefinger at the cap's rear edge, tipped it rakishly forward over one eye.

Flash

Forde feared that they might, in tandem, clack into slick dance steps.

* * *

Outside the Ilinsky Cathedral the lady guide brandished her purple umbrella and cried, "Towards the bus!"

Their destination was the Monument to the Unknown Sailor, a granite obelisk on the cliff edge overlooking Odessa's harbour and wharves. They watched the performance of the Honour Guard. The three boys in the front row carried assault rifles held across their chests, the three girls behind them marched with their arms rigidly at their sides. They were all in ceremonial sailor uniform, white belts with gold buckles, gold lanyards, white gloves. The girls in blue serge skirts. They marched down the ceremonial approach past the flanking red polished granite gravestones of resistance fighters killed in World War II, and took up positions of respect at the monument's cardinal points.

The guide said the ceremony was repeated every hour throughout the day, the cadets drawn in rotation from Odessa's high schools. The goose-step marching was obviously inherited from the Russians. Forde was rather chilled by it, having seen it displayed by the Nazis, the Soviets, Il Duce's Fascists, by the dementedly vigorous North Koreans, and by Hezbollah parading through Beirut. The very youth and attractiveness of the cadets added to his discomposure. Such marching, he thought, proclaimed the suppression of the individual and implied what Yeats had meant by "the blood-dimmed tide."

They made halting conversation with the cadets, the girls in white knee socks and improbable, strapped high heels. Was this, Forde wondered, sanctioned formal attire in the Ukraine? Or were the girls naughty and illicitly changed into such shoes after leaving the house? The girls were so pretty in the morning sun but probably doomed, thought Forde in a sudden descent of gloom, to grow to great bulk and play the accordion.

People dawdled back towards the bus, reminding Forde of a herd of heifers on a country road.

Then the driver switched on the engine, the Baden Powell man shouting about having the radio turned off . . . *eleven, twelve, thirteen* . . . the Honour Guard marching *stomp, stomp, stomp* back up the avenue and an old man stood suddenly to photograph them through the window and dropped with a cry, felled into his seat by the overhead storage rack.

"And now," cried the amplified guide lady, "away we go to the Lenin Monument!"

* * *

"I thought you *liked* churches."

"I tire," said Forde, "of the odour of sanctity."

Sheila glanced at him.

"Watch it, Forde," she said.

The church sat across the top end of the long rectangular park, which sloped downhill to the immense, black Lenin

Monument brooding over the harbour. He sat on a bench waiting for her and enjoying the sun on his face. He watched a toddler gathering leaves and filling her push-chair with them, enjoyed the scent of late-blooming roses in the flower beds behind him. Sheila waving to him.

"Let's see the Monument," she said.

"I'm not going to look at bad Soviet art. It only encourages them," said Forde. "And I particularly don't want to look at a statue of *that* venomous bastard! You go. I'll wait for you here."

He watched her as she traipsed off to look at the statue and doubtless to read whatever plaques and notices were on offer. Her dedication to plaques and notices had mildly irritated him all their married life. He sometimes suspected that she preferred reading maps to looking at the landscape they represented. Similarly with attributions in art galleries. He, on the other hand, always wanted urgent, unmediated contact with things. If they appealed, he always told her, he'd find out more.

As she trudged back up the hill, he got up and advanced upon her with both arms out in front of him, his hands clenched into fists.

"What? What?"

He grinned at her.

She backed away from him.

"What is it?"

"Come here."

"Is it alive? Is it something alive?"

"Fresh-firecoal chestnut falls."

"What!"

"Look!"

He turned each fist over and opened his fingers.

Glowing on his palms.

"Conkers!"

* * *

Stained concrete. Shabby storefronts stuffed with shoddy goods side by side with stores selling international brand names. SONY, NIKON, PANASONIC, TOSHIBA. Abandoned lots strewn with rubble and refuse. Decaying buildings. Broken bottle-glass. Doorways reeking of piss. A used-up place, an old rind, all the juice squeezed out of it. And a miasma over all of a scarcely ousted bureaucracy.

Romania's principal seaport, Constanza, depressed them. According to the daily bulletin, the city had been founded in the seventh century B.C. by Greek colonists from Miletus in Asia Minor. It had then been known as Tomis. In the first century B.C. the Romans annexed the region and in the fourth century A.D. Constantine the Great reconstructed Tomis and renamed it Constantiana.

Tapping the bulletin, Forde said, "Ovid was exiled here in 9 A.D." He waved his arm in an encompassing gesture. "Look at it! Look at this bloody place. *Ovid!*"

They looked down onto the mosaic floor, which was protected from the weather by an open-sided, tin-roofed shed. The mosaic was dirty and the colours dull. Bits were missing, the patches filled with raw concrete.

"What's it depicting?" said Forde.

"Well, flowers," said Sheila. "And there's a bird. Oh, and a wine jar. And isn't that a Double Axe?"

"Yes, it's a *labrys* all right but *why?* What *was* this place?"

She shrugged.

"It's not gripping, is it?" said Forde.

Lunch was served in an echoing cafeteria. Forde ordered *scrumbie la gratar* which turned out to be a herring. Sheila was less happy with *mititei*, which when they arrived, were small, skinless sausages. With coffee Forde drank a couple of shots of a drink called *tuica* that someone at their table had recommended. It was a potent plum brandy and it cheered him up. They were then shepherded onto buses for the hour's drive to the ruins of Histria, Romania's oldest city, also founded by colonists from Miletus in the seventh century B.C.

Forde watched the passing countryside. It was as sad and bleak as the city. His *tuica*-induced cheer ebbed. Single fields stretched seemingly for miles with no trees or hedges in sight. Tractors ploughed six abreast. He began to brood about the destruction wreaked upon these people. The farms and smallholdings must have been collectivized during the Soviet period after 1945. It saddened him to think of homesteads destroyed, families forced out, trees felled, footpaths ploughed up, hedges grubbed out, memories obliterated, history erased. Mile after mile of meaninglessness.

The two villages they passed through were in vibrant contrast to this agricultural Passchendaele. They were squalid, ramshackle, two- or three-room houses patched with corrugated tin, beaten-earth yards with hens, ducks, and geese pecking over the garbage, fly-twitched donkeys and ponies tethered to fruit trees. In the gardens, cabbages and beans and grapes. In some stood stooks of cut rushes drying for bedding.

Pony-drawn carts with motor-tire wheels bowled along, stacked perilously with reeds and rushes. The grimy men driving them and lying across the reeds to steady the loads looked villainous. Children in gardens waved at the bus. A woman in a drab brown apron stared from a kitchen doorway.

"It's a bit Fiddler-on-the-Roofy, isn't it?" said Sheila.

"But muckier," said Forde.

The sky was darkening as they neared Histria, and by the time the buses bumped up onto the museum's parking lot of broken brick mixed with asphalt the sky had become electric with gloom and tinged with yellow and unearthly green, the sort of sky that Forde always thought of as Old Testament sky.

Histria was set at the edge of a vast reed-fringed swamp. The museum was a glass box set on a raised, concrete platform. Mosquitoes whined. No rain had yet fallen. All was unnaturally still. On a tussock of reeds rising above the water some fifty yards out stood a large bird startlingly white in the weird light, a crane perhaps, or an ibis.

The museum was intensely boring. The contents, mainly red Roman-ware, had nearly all been broken, and the missing shards had been reconstituted in white plaster. The two big rooms, at a glance, were a leprosy of red and white. No effort at aesthetics or even selection had been attempted; if it had been uncovered at the site, in it had gone, the rumbled rubble of Greece, Rome, and Byzantium. Shapeless, rusted lumps of iron were identified as "anchors"; the profusion of broken pots was labelled variously as "storage vessels," "wine vessels," "conical vessels," and "vessels with spouts"; a row of pieces of corroded bronze was labelled "mirrors"; scraps and unidentifiable fragments were identified as "decorative elements."

Forde stood in front of a glass case that contained a curved piece of metal.

The card read: "Strigil" [?]

Here and there the accumulated clutter was adorned by a stele, but the inscriptions were so weathered as to leave legible only a few words, such as *est* and *hic*.

The custodian or curator or whatever he was wore a black suit and, curiously, over it, a long black cotton apron.

The books were stacked on a table near the front door. The three main periods of the site were recorded in three massive and profusely illustrated hardcover tomes, which gave off a strong whiff of State Publishing. They had been compiled in the 1920s. The authors all wore pince-nez spectacles and wing collars with loosely knotted silk ties. The books cost twenty-five new *leys* each. This seemed to work out at an impossibly cheap eleven dollars or so.

He groaned as he waited for Sheila to stop inspecting a broken amphora.

Outside the museum, a muddy path led to the site itself through a remaining arch in a tumbling brick wall. It had started to drizzle. Feral dogs scoured the parking lot for crumbs. The path ended. The baulk of turf Forde was negotiating crumbled and his right foot slipped deep into the cold mire. A mosquito *zizzizzed* in his ear.

"I hate this place."

"Oh, stop being childish."

"My foot's wet."

"Oh, look, these must have been houses."

He looked at the jumble of low walls, footprints of buildings. Nothing was recognizably anything. Some of the walls were stone, some brick. Some bits of wall contained pantile so were probably Byzantine.

He slapped at mosquitoes.

Stared down what might have been a street.

Inside the stone squares grew sedge and wind-stunted bushes.

In one such square and behind one such bush, stood the Bishop of Bodmin and Exeter. He was standing completely still and staring out over the swamp. Forde regarded his silly hat with its cockade of nylon feathers.

"What *is* he doing?"

"Having a pee," said Sheila.

Although he was perfectly aware that the salutation was reserved solely for *archbishops*, Forde called out "Good afternoon, Your Grace," which caused a gratifying galvanization of the Bishop culminating in his raised Tilley.

The drizzle turned to a steadier rain.

"And what was this big place over here?" called Sheila.

"Fuck!" said Forde.

"What?"

"Blood!"

"Oh!" she called. "Here's a plaque!"

"I'm going back to the bus!"

"But we haven't seen everything."

"I don't wish to discommode you," said Forde, "but I am swelling rapidly."

"So *this,*" she said, pointing to an expanse of ruin and sodden debris, "was the apse but the dome fell in. *So,*" she said, glancing down at the diagram, "over *here,* this must be . . ."

"I don't care," called Forde, "if it's the collapsed apse of a fucking Byzantine *whorehouse!* It is raining. My foot is wet. I am getting bitten to death. My body is covered in infected Romanian lumps."

He glared at her back as she bent again over the plaque and diagram.

"Goodbye!"

He negotiated the slippery baulks of mud and turf and regained the pathway to the museum beyond the arch.

Alan and Martin were standing on the top step of the entrance to the museum, a step which extended into a terrace. Behind them the yellow-lit expanse of the museum's first room. They were singing. They were wearing their officers' dress caps of the Russian Black Sea Fleet and holding hands. They were singing to the parking lot as to an audience in a night club. With their free hands they were making corny gestures of desire and longing. They were utterly absorbed.

You are the promised kiss of springtime
That makes the lonely winter seem long.
You are the breathless hush of evening
That trembles on the brink of a lovely song.
You are the angel glow that lights a star,
The dearest things I know are what you are.

The custodian in his long black apron appeared at the front door and stooped over a deformed puppy, which kept trying to get inside. Its belly was swollen huge and one eye was much larger than the other and bulged out from its face, reminding Forde of those grotesquely overbred goldfish, goggle-eyed and trailing white fungus-like growths round the sockets. The custodian kept making scooping-water gestures with his cupped hands and shouting what sounded like "Marsh! Marsh! and every time he shouted the puppy whiddled on the step.

Entirely oblivious, Alan and Martin sang on

Some day my happy arms will hold you,
And some day I'll know that moment divine,
When all the things you are, are mine!

Back on the bus and in the seat they'd sat in before, Forde dried his glasses on a paper napkin he'd saved from lunch. Some of the stragglers appearing through the gloom had umbrellas, others wore transparent plastic hoods. Mosquitoes whined on the windows. The crinkle of cellophane, somebody opening a packet. The smell of damp clothes.

Forde watched the feral dogs lying on the asphalt and crusted rubble chawing, chawing at the dulled fur of their flea-bitten flanks and haunches. One showed patches of raw skin the size of saucers and the colour of ham. A female was lying on her side with what could have been the right hind leg broken. There was blood on it and its angle odd. Whenever she tried to get up her two half-grown pups pounced in, biting the dragging leg and toppling her. When she snarled at them, one in particular chop-chopped her mask, his lips drawn back in a way that seemed to Forde not at all like play.

The bus swayed again as Father Keogh and The Minder climbed aboard. They made their way down the aisle and sat in the seats in front of him.

"And your hat, now. Have you lost your hat? Left it somewhere. Did you have it in the museum? Or did you lose it in that horrible old bog? Fall, did you? Slipped and fell. Wandering off like that while I was in the water closet. And these stains on your good jacket. Mud from that bog. That's what it'll be. On your lapel, look. And your shoulder. Tweed's a lovely cloth, so it is. A lovely cloth."

Father Keogh sat in remote silence, staring straight ahead.

The Minder stood and took a plastic bottle of water from his little backpack in the overhead rack. He wet his handkerchief and sat again to dab at the stains.

"Is it mud? Mud, is it?"

Through the gap between the seats, Forde saw The Minder looking at the stains on his handkerchief.

Saw The Minder looking at his fingertips.

Smelling them.

Heard his half-whisper ...

... *Holy Mother* ...

A breathy exhalation.

Heard the little gluggings as he dribbled more water onto his handkerchief.

"It *is* mud, Father."

Coming into view again as he leaned across the gap to dab.

"On the lovely tweed."

The bus swayed again as Sheila climbed up. She plumped down beside Forde and said, "How are your bites?"

He gave her a cold glance.

"You smell," he said, "like a cloakroom."

"Air conditioning ON!" shouted Baden Powell.

... *eighteen, nineteen, twenty* ...

"Not *another* museum," said the man in the seat behind.

"It's mosaics," said his wife.

"I'd rather an early dinner."

"They're *Roman,*" said his wife.

"Oh!" he said. "Why didn't you say? Roman! Well, if I'd known they were *Roman* ..."

"Now Harold!" she said.

... *nine, ten, eleven* ... re-counted the guide.

The custodian had retreated into the museum and closed the door. The pack had materialized behind the puppy and sat watching the lighted windows.

In the middle of the bus, the guide was saying, "One is missing. We are missing a passenger. Does anyone recognize who it is?"

People craned about. Some stood.

"Where's Bronwyn?" a woman said. "Is it Bronwyn?"

"Which one is Bronwyn?"

"... with the make-up ..."

"... from Borneo."

"... the lady in question," Baden Powell was saying to the guide, "will doubtless have got on one of the other buses—silly old trout."

The guide, now standing beside the driver, spread his hands in a gesture of resignation and helplessness.

"*Jaldi*!" roared Baden Powell. "*Jaldi jao*!"

The bus bumped across the parking lot and ground up onto the approach road. As it began to pick up speed and the museum receded, the custodian shrank smaller and smaller, a black speck within the lighted cube.

ACKNOWLEDGEMENTS

My thanks to Dan Wells for judiciously applying the lash, to Chris Andrechek for his almost saintly patience in typesetting and design, to Katherine Barber for *The Canadian Oxford Dictionary*, and to Gordon Robertson whose brilliant cover art bestows upon reSet books added distinction.